W9-AED-156

Plowing My Own Furrow

Howard W. Moore

"Plowing My Own Furrow"

W · W · NORTON & COMPANY

NEW YORK · LONDON

UB
342
U5
M66
1985

FIRST EDITION

The text of this book is composed in Caledonia, with display type set in Typositor Corvinus Medium. Composition and manufacturing are by The Maple-Vail Book Manufacturing Group.

BOOK DESIGN BY MARJORIE J. FLOCK

Library of Congress Cataloging in Publication Data
Moore, Howard W.
    Plowing my own furrow.

    1. Moore, Howard W.   2. Conscientious objectors—
United States—Biography.   3. World War, 1914–1918—
Conscientious objectors.   4. World War, 1914–1918—
Personal narratives, American.   I. Title.
UB342.U5M66   1985   355.2'24'0924 [B]   84–22610

ISBN 0-393-01977-2

W. W. Norton & Company, Inc., 500 Fifth Avenue, New York, N.Y. 10110
W. W. Norton & Company Ltd., 37 Great Russell Street, London WC1B 3NU

1 2 3 4 5 6 7 8 9 0

Contents

Illustrations appear following page 111

Foreword

As the son of one very tall pacifist and the namesake nephew of another (the latter a really "troublesome" CO who spent some time in Leavenworth solitary confinement during World War I), I was brought up admiring and loving two extraordinary men of conscience. Strangely, though, I never came to identify with the heart-stopping experience of a living conscientious objector until there was submitted to me, as a veteran book editor, Howard Moore's *Plowing My Own Furrow*.

As an editor I had worked with a number of writers ranging from a "Hound-Dog Man" to a U.S. commander-in-chief (and also the chief of staff of the U.S. Army), from a Marine combat veteran to a British pacifist, but it wasn't until I read Howard Moore's *Plowing My Own Furrow* that I experienced the unique waking-and-sleeping identification with another human that this ninety-five-year-old writer inspired in this sixty-three-year-old grandfather. The author brilliantly describes his youth as an upstate farmer, his dramatic decision to be ruled in time of war by the visions of a rebellious free man, and the challenges of a war-filled postwar world.

EVAN W. THOMAS II

Foreword

Introduction

HOWARD MOORE AND HIS WIFE LOUISE live on a farm his family cleared a century and a half ago, just north of Cherry Valley, New York, with a view over the Mohawk Valley and far into the Adirondacks. The trees he planted as a young man are tall and stately. The garden of vegetables and flowers the couple cultivate flourishes in bright colors and varied greens. They stand before their long, low, stone house, straight and trim. He is ninety-five and looks a sprightly sixty. In the house are the latest books on international affairs, economics, politics; these have been read and digested, approved or repudiated by a mind shrewdly critical and fundamentally detached. This is a man who has never joined any party—for always he has made up his own mind. The key to his life has lain in his unalterable belief that in any conflict between authority and one's own conscience, only the conscience must be listened to.

This is a tenet that has been a recurring theme in American life from its beginning, a tenet that has puzzled, alarmed, and angered the orthodox, whether in religion, politics, or patriotism. Anne Hutchinson, Thomas Paine, Henry Thoreau, Robert Ingersoll, and Howard Moore were all people who knew exactly what Ralph Waldo Emerson meant when he urged his reader, "Trust thyself," rely on that inner voice and be willing to pay whatever price is charged.

At its core this book is an account of the author's refusal to serve in the armed forces in World War I and the price he paid for that noncompliance. However, the book only makes sense when seen as a whole, for Howard Moore came to his position in a surrounding of conformity and orthodoxy. That statement needs some qualification because his Uncle Rance, with whom he lived much of his boyhood and whom he admired greatly, was an agnostic and philosophic liberal, but rural New York State has generally stood to the right of center and viewed those to the other side of the line with suspicion.

Moore's account of hop farming at the turn of the century, the careful details of animals, crops, and domestic life, a boy and youth's pleasure in the outdoors have seldom been so fully and sympathetically remembered. There follows his discovery of New York City and his own rare abilities as a leader and innovator working for the New York Telephone Company in its early years of growth. Each time he was given more responsibility, he proved himself of more value to the company, rising rung by rung in the structure.

In the meantime, his reading was taking characteristically independent directions: Henry George, Edward Bellamy, Hegel, Kant, Shelley, Shaw, Marx, Veblen, the intellectual makers of a different world—different from Otsego County, different from the New York Telephone Company. He sorted out from these writings the ideas that he found sympathetic to his own spirit and code, the balance he discarded.

As World War I approached this side of the Atlantic, Moore gave increasing thought to the whole question of war itself. It was more than a moral aversion to killing another man caught in the same trap he was; rather it came down to a "deep philosophical and political conviction that war was futile and its use as an instrument of national policy a confession of moral bankruptcy." The starting place for his revolt was conscription and a refusal to obey any military order. The price Moore paid over the next three years, until Thanksgiving 1920, was paid in guardhouses, isolated barracks, and prisons of varied horrors. His treatment and that of other conscientious objectors is a disgraceful chapter in our military and political history and one that needs to be understood.

The confusion, puzzlement, and frustration this man created in the military authorities, to whom obedience was unquestionable, can only be imagined. Neither violence nor sweet reasonings would move him from his obdurate refusal to recognize the right of the military principle to control the nation's life. Few could recognize that to take so unpopular a stand as his in the face of almost universal disapproval called for the same quality of courage as they admired and honored.

I turn again to Mr. Emerson: "The great man is he who in the midst of the crowd keeps with perfect sweetness the independence of solitude." This is Howard Moore's achievement.

LOUIS C. JONES
Director Emeritus, New York State Historical Association

Acknowledgments

I OWE THANKS TO the many friends who have urged me to write these reminiscences.

It is doubtful that the manuscript would ever have been presented for publication were it not for the patience of my wife, Louise Porter Moore, in editing and typing it.

To Hilda Wilcox I am especially grateful for research, suggestions, and encouragement. She and Ruth Yule and Wendell Tripp all read the manuscript and offered useful criticisms, for which I thank them.

Louis Salomon's expert help with the proofs is also greatly appreciated.

HOWARD W. MOORE

1

THE TIME WAS 1884, a bright spring day in upstate New York, the air laced with bird song and fragrant with arbutus and apple blossoms. From the village of Cherry Valley two young girls walked north on the Fort Plain Road toward Judd's Falls to see the springtime flood water plunge over the limestone precipice and hear its roar as it fell a hundred feet into the gorge.

One of the girls, Gertrude Wilber, noticed a young man plowing a field near the road. She knew his name—Frank Moore—and when he looked up she waved her handkerchief to him. That evening Frank ran the two miles to Cherry Valley to call at her home; thus began the courtship of my parents.

The young couple were soon engaged, and after their marriage in 1885 Gertrude became a member of her father-in-law's family in his farmhouse overlooking Judd's Falls. Grandfather Philip P. Moore was a prosperous hops farmer of German stock, descended from one of several Mohrs among the Palatinate folk whom the British had recruited, long ago, to settle in the New World. Between 1710 and 1717, shipload after shipload of these immigrants had disembarked on the wooded banks of the Hudson River to work out their contract with the Crown by furnishing the Royal Navy with pitch, turpentine, and tall pine masts. As the king's people, they escaped the rent serfdom of nearby settlers on the estates of the New York patroons. Their land was their own for raising big crops and families.

For a century they kept their native tongue in use. The War of Independence disturbed them little; they identified neither with their American neighbors nor with the German-speaking Hessian soldiers of the invading British. But the German enclaves in Columbia and Dutchess counties finally broke open with their own numbers. Families began to move out; with a nose for good limestone soil they followed along the Mohawk and Schoharie rivers and into the highlands of Otsego County. The Mohrs had already Anglicized their name by 1828, when my grandfather's uncle Philip I. Moore purchased the Cherry Valley farm. Among their new neighbors they now had to speak English, but perhaps within the several families who came from down the Hudson at about this time German could still have been heard. There was a vague tradition in my family about the "old-timers" speaking "Dutch."

These old-timers included my great-granduncle Philip I. Moore and his brother William I., to whom he turned over the farm in 1831. William worked the land until he died in 1864 and was succeeded by his son Philip P. Moore, who already had five sons of his own.

Hops were the cash crop that enabled Grandfather Moore to buy farms for three of his sons when they married. But to Frank and the girl who waved her handkerchief he offered the inheritance of the home farm, if they would stay there and help him.

Perhaps it was Gertrude who did not want to do it. She was a town girl, pretty and popular, with Yankee ancestors on both sides. Her mother's Howe forebears had an aura of New England gentility, and the Wilbers were descended from early settlers of Rhode Island. A rumor of French and Indian blood clung to her middle name, Bervee; it was remote enough to be prized. Gertrude had stayed in school longer than had Frank, and she was expert at needlework. Farm life offered little scope for her young ambitions. She was no complainer, but years later she told me how grandpa used to get the family up before dawn to do chores and cultivate the precious hops; the days were spent in labor and after supper everyone went right to bed.

Frank too was restless and willing to try his strength against the world. But three years passed, bringing two little girls, Leila and Jane, while the relentless farm work went on. Frank's brother George was the only other one of the boys left at home. When he too brought a wife to the farm, Frank and Gertrude decided to leave and seek their fortune in New York City.

2

GERTRUDE'S BROTHER, Nash Wilber, was an officer in the New York City Police Department, and he encouraged Frank to apply for a job in the force. But the examinations proved too stiff for a young man who had spent his life with tools and animals and only a few years in a one-room district school. While he looked for other employment, the family sojourned with Gertrude's Aunt Cora on West 106th Street. Cora was a dressmaker, widowed and with a young daughter, Daisy, who could help care for Gertrude's babies. So Gertrude herself went job hunting and became a seamstress at Lord and Taylor's store.

There were other Cherry Valley people in the big city. Two of Gertrude's cousins, Merritt and Frank Dutcher, had found work with the New York Railway Company, which ran horsecars in the streets—predecessors of the trolleys, elevated trains, and still undreamed-of subways. Merritt and Frank were driver and conductor of a horsecar on the Fourteenth Street route, but they did not have many passengers. They figured Broadway would be more profitable, so at the intersection they switched to the Broadway track and made their way uptown, taking in lots of fares in competition with the appointed drivers on that route. The brash country boys lost their jobs, but their escapade was applauded back home in Cherry Valley.

Other friends of the Moores, Beekman and Frank Walton, had gone from Cherry Valley to the site of the new Croton Reservoir, answering an advertisement for men who could drive four-horse teams in the work of excavation. This was a job Frank could do well, and he joined his friends there, moving his little family out of New York City to the Hudson River town of Sing Sing (later renamed Ossining). There I was born, prematurely, at seven months. I had a heart defect and was what the doctors called a blue baby. The date was February 9, 1889, during the hard times of the Harrison administration.

After the reservoir job was finished, my father went to work at the Monitor Iron Works in Sing Sing, and Frank Walton became his assistant. One of my very early memories is of watching them build up sand cores on long steel rods. I can still see and smell the molten iron that was poured around these cores by half-naked, sweating men to form cast iron pipes to carry the Croton water to New York City.

Another memory of those days is the spring run of shad in the Hudson, so thick that my father could catch them in his bare hands to bring home for dinner.

And I recall seeing inmates of the penitentiary, in leg irons, cleaning the city streets. A few years later, in Cherry Valley, I recognized the chain gang shuffle in the gait of a stranger who worked by the day for my uncle. When asked, he admitted to having been in prison.

I was not yet four years old during the second Cleveland–Harrison presidential contest, but I remember my mother holding me up to the window to see a torchlight parade in which my father marched for the Democratic candidate Cleveland. The sight did not please me; I couldn't understand why the men were walking along behind the flaring torches. To this day I have never liked parades. One time while we were in Ossining, my mother took me with friends to see the West Point cadets drilling. This I really disliked. I had some tin soldiers at home, and it disturbed me to see real men dressed up and stiffly standing, or moving as though not of their own volition, like my toys.

My father became an expert molder at the iron works and was made foreman of the molding department. But during the depression of the 1890s the men in the foundry struck for better pay, and father walked out with them. The strike was lost and the men returned to work, but father was blackballed and never got his job back.

I was aware that something had happened that caused my parents to be worried and fearful. They did not know how they were going to pay the rent or the grocery bills. We were a family of six: besides Leila and Jane and me there was now a little brother, Frank. Jane fell ill with spinal meningitis. She survived, but it was years before she could talk again. I contracted diphtheria and was given up by the doctor, who told my mother it was doubtful I would survive the night. I remember my mother saying, "Well, if you're through, I'll take over." When the doctor left, she rolled a piece of paper into a tube, put some powdered sulphur into it, and blew it down my throat. I coughed violently and expelled a large lump of mucous that had been choking me. The doctor was amazed when he found me recovering the next day.

Our apartment was in a hillside house overlooking the Hudson, and while recuperating from my illness I watched the river traffic from the window: little tugs hauling big freighters and canal boats, sidewheel steamers on the passenger run from New York to Albany, sailboats; and sometimes there were warships at anchor in midstream, their heavy bulks gray and ominous.

During this convalescence I took apart an old clock and used parts of it to make a little engine that actually ran, on a track of wooden matchsticks, with grooved checkers for wheels. Father, who was working on an invention himself, was very proud of me.

His invention was a machine for picking cotton and hops. He patented it and gave a sixth interest to a carpenter named Chester Weller, who helped construct a working model, and another sixth to a doctor, John Gibney, who financed the project. After a successful demonstration of the machine in some Carolina cotton fields, the Deering Company, manufacturers of farm equipment, offered my father a hundred thousand dollars for the patent. When father rejected this, Dr. Gibney declined to advance any more money. His faith undaunted, father shipped the machine to Cherry Valley, where he thought a successful demonstration of hop picking would lead to fortune. But the machine failed to pick successfully; it tore the hops so that they lost much of the aromatic pollen that was essential to their use in making beer. As a cotton picker, the machine's only defect seems to have been its lack of mobility, for the principles it embodied are used in present-day picking machinery. All that was needed was self-propulsion and some additional promotion and financing.

But father was not a promoter or financier. Discouraged and broke, he had to turn his energies to the survival of his family. Years later I saw his invention still stored in my uncle's barn, covered with dust and chaff, a reminder of his bitter disappointment.

3

MY PARENTS DECIDED THAT they would move back to Cherry Valley as soon as possible, but meanwhile my father took me there, in the early spring of the year I was six, to live with my uncle, Van Rensselaer Moore.

This great adventure began with the train trip to Palatine Bridge, where we arrived sometime after midnight. We sat in the station, dozing between the commotions of long clattering freight trains, until the first light of morning showed in the sky. Father then led me across the bridge that spanned the Mohawk River, and we began a four-mile hike along the West Shore Railroad track, he carrying me on his shoulders. As we went along we passed mules on the nearby towpath pulling heavy barges on the Erie Canal.

Our destination was Fort Plain and the home of Henry Crane and his wife Mary, who was the daughter of Aunt Git, my grandfather's sister. Here Uncle Rance had come to meet us. At breakfast I was introduced to one relative after another and finally came to rest on Uncle Rance's lap, fascinated by the heavy gold chain that spanned his vest, one end of it attached to a large watch, which he held against my ear. Thus I first met an uncle who became something of an idol to me. He was shorter than my father and less strongly built, a quiet man with a smile and a good-humored glint in his eye.

Father caught an afternoon train back to Sing Sing, and I was not to see him again until late summer, when the whole family came back to Cherry Valley. Uncle Rance took me to the Grant Hotel, where his bay mare Daisy was hitched up to a buckboard wagon, and we set out on the twelve-mile ride to Cherry Valley. There was little conversation on that ride.

My eyes and mind were absorbed in things I loved at first
sight: rolling hills, trees, open fields, cattle grazing near farm-
houses and barns, dogs running after us, wagging their tails
and barking. Only once was I diverted from these sights. Daisy,
straining up a steep hill, raised her tail and farted; Uncle Rance
smiled and said, "Better an empty house than a bad ten-
ant!"—whatever that meant.

At about noon we came down Main Street in Cherry Valley, and on the southern edge of the village, opposite the
cemetery, we turned off Alden Street into a driveway, passed
a two-story white clapboard house, and drew up in front of a
large barn. Out came a big black mastiff to jump happily about
my uncle. He sniffed at me cautiously, but before we had
finished unhitching the horse he was my friend. My uncle and
I led the mare to her stall and gave her and each of the other
three horses a peck of oats. We climbed the steps to the loft
and pushed down hay into all four racks. Then we backed the
wagon into the barn and went to the house. In the large kitchen
Aunt Nell and her mother, Nanny Walrad, were preparing
dinner. What a fuss they made over me! I was hugged and
kissed and held on their laps. It was all quite wonderful.

In the late afternoon my cousin Daisy came home from
school. She was almost fifteen, with red cheeks, blue eyes,
and brown hair. I loved her at once.

After dinner Uncle Rance had taken me on a tour of
inspection: to the woodhouse, where there were axes and saws,
a chopping block and sawbuck, and many cords of wood piled
up; to the cowbarn with its stanchions for twelve cows and
pens for calves; to the hop house, a hundred-foot-long building that had once been a cheese factory. This stood near a
stream which flowed through the farm and was spanned by
two bridges giving access to the 125 acres of meadows, pastures, fields, and woods.

Back at the horse barn, I learned the names of the horses:
Daisy, the bay who had brought us from Fort Plain; her sister
Kit; Rex; and Nellie, who was to become my favorite. In the

wagon house I was shown the surrey with its fringed top; the Democrat, the buckboard in which I had already ridden; a handsome cutter; and a two-horse sleigh. Shiny harnesses and strings of sleighbells hung against the walls. My uncle also pointed out to me the two-hole privy, and I saw the pig pen and the poultry house with its population of chickens, turkeys, guinea fowl, and ducks.

The tool shed, a very important building, held plows and harrows (both peg and spring-tooth), a mowing machine, hay rake, reaper and binder, cultivators, pitch forks and dung forks, a fanning mill, a corn sheller, shovels of all sorts, grain cradles, scythes, saws, hammers and other tools, nails, and rolls of barbed wire. There was a work bench with a vise and an anvil on a huge block of wood. I was to become familiar with all this equipment through play and work. None of the women folk ever came to the barns, which were considered the men's world.

The house was the largest I had ever been in. There were four big bedrooms upstairs and an enormous attic above them. I was to have my own bedroom! In it there was a closet for clothes and a washstand with a large white china bowl and a pitcher of water. A commode held a china chamber pot. Baths were taken in a wooden washtub in the kitchen, on Saturday nights.

Besides the kitchen, the downstairs had a spacious company dining room, a family parlor, and Nanny's own living room, with one end curtained off for her bed. The large cellar supplied the kitchen from its crocks of corned beef and sauerkraut and pickles, its bins and barrels of potatoes, carrots, onions, and apples. Smoked hams and sausage hung from the joists. One section was partitioned off for making butter and cheese. A dog treadmill powered by the mastiff Bruno turned a barrel churn until the butter could be seen through a little glass window; this was removed and worked with a heavy wooden bar and with paddles on a tilted table until it was free of all milk and water, ready to be salted and packed into five-

and ten-pound pails. Some of the fresh buttermilk we drank, some was used in baking, and the rest went into the swill barrel for the pigs. Near the butter churn was kept the hand-cranked freezer in which we made ice cream by the gallon for Sunday dessert.

Buckwheat pancake batter in a gallon crock stood at the back of the kitchen stove, for we always had pancakes and maple syrup for breakfast, with bacon and eggs, huge molasses cookies, coffee, and milk.

While breakfast was being prepared, we men were doing chores: milking the cows and feeding all the livestock. After breakfast the stables were cleaned, horses and cows watered, and horses curried, brushed, and harnessed for the day's work. Then I would follow my uncle to the fields, closely observing everything he did, as I walked behind the plow or cultivator.

Those first years at Uncle Rance's were full of the joy of learning. By the time I was ten I could handle most farm operations except those requiring the stature of a grown man. I could milk the cows and drive the horses. Sometimes I drove for my uncle when he delivered milk from house to house in the village. When hay and grain were harvested, I raked and loaded in the fields.

Often Uncle Rance left me to cultivate corn or potatoes while he went to the barbershop to discuss politics and religion. He was a great admirer of Thomas Paine, Ingersoll, Rousseau, and Jefferson. Of my grandfather's five sons, he was the only one who had been sent away for "higher education"—he told me he had attended Rensselaer Polytechnic Institute. From him I got my first inkling of abstract thought and speculation.

Cousin Daisy enjoyed having a little "brother." She played the piano and sang and read wonderful stories to me: *Black Beauty* and Andersen's and Grimms' fairy tales. I remember one night when she was terrified by a thunderstorm she came into my room and took me back to bed with her. She was soon asleep, but I waited, raised on one elbow, for the lightning flashes to show me her lovely face on the pillow.

On rainy days I explored the attic. Among other things I found was a sheaf of arrows, a short Plains Indian bow, a pair of beaded moccasins, and a red sandstone peace pipe. They had been sent to Nanny by her brother Andrew, who was a scout with Buffalo Bill on the great Western plains. The peace pipe had been given to him by Sitting Bull, the famous Sioux chief who defeated General Custer. The moccasins and bow were from the Cheyennes. Nanny gave me these treasures, and I thoughtlessly shot away and lost most of the arrows, not realizing that they and the other articles were irreplaceable relics of the frontier.

The Indian tribes were being relentlessly pushed westward and herded into reservations to secure the rich plains for white settlement. One strategy of the federal govenment was to starve the Indians by exterminating the vast buffalo herds on which their livelihood was based. The slaughter of buffaloes was the principal occupation of the "scouts" employed by the army. Buffalo robes sold for a dollar apiece in the East in those days. Uncle Rance had one for his cutter.

4

FARMING was a way of life based on nature. The long rhythms of seasonal work controlled my growing years. The first food production, long before spring thawed the soil, was sap boiling. On a sunny day in late February or early March, when the temperature had finally gone above freezing, Uncle Rance would bore holes in the trunks of the maples along his driveway, insert short, spigotlike spiles, and hang a bucket on each one. Immediately a cheerful "ping . . . ping" announced that sap was dripping into the buckets. As they filled, they were emptied into a big iron kettle hung on a tripod in the yard. With great expenditure of firewood, the kettle was kept boiling until most of the water was evaporated and a light syrup remained. This we took into the house to be "finished off" on the kitchen stove, into maple sugar or heavy syrup, while a new batch began to boil outside. To make a gallon of syrup took at least forty times as much sap. This beginning of the year's farm cycle was often celebrated with a "sugaring-off" party at which thick hot syrup was poured on the snow, to congeal into a delicious chewy candy called jack-wax. Sour pickles would be passed around to give relief from the overpowering sweetness of the maple sugar.

Every farm had a large vegetable garden and an assortment of fruit trees and perhaps a berry patch. These were attended to as needed but were sidelines to the main work of the farmer.

Hops were at this time the chief source of cash income. Otsego County had the right soil for them and had once led the nation in hops production. Their cultivation was specialized, requiring much hand labor. A hop yard usually covered ten acres or more, with "hills" six or eight feet apart. They were perennial plants that died down to the root each winter. During the summer they would multiply, so an early spring job was to "grub the yard" with a tined hoe, roguing out all but three plants to each hill. The extra plants were discarded if they could not be sold.

The next step was to set poles. These were red cedar trees, three or four inches at the base and about twelve feet tall, stripped of branches and bark. Hundreds of them were needed, each to be set at least fifteen inches deep in a hole in the center of a hill. The holes were made by pounding into the ground an iron "hop bar" about four and a half feet long with a pointed end that swelled into a reverse bulb shape for enlarging the hole.

As soon as the hop vines began to send out runners, one plant on each hill would be tied to the pole to assist its natural twining, while the others were trained on strings stretched from the top of each pole to the bottom of the next. Stringing the poles was another specialized procedure, done with a ball of hop twine threaded through hook eyes to the end of a very long bamboo fishing rod. With this instrument a man could string a hop yard almost as fast as he could walk. Then the yard had to be cultivated and hoed all summer to keep weeds down.

In May, oats were sowed, sometimes mixed with peas. When the ground was warm enough, about the first of June, corn was planted. After it showed a few inches of growth it had to be hoed and cultivated and kept weed-free all summer.

By the end of June it was time to begin haying. Hay in those days meant timothy grass, perhaps mixed with alsike or large clover. Alfalfa didn't come in until thirty years later. In Uncle Rance's fields the mowed hay fell in five- or six-foot swathes, the width of the cutting bar on the two-horse mower. Along fences and around boulders, a man would trim by hand with a scythe. When the hay had partly dried in the sun and air, it was raked into windrows with a one-horse dump rake, then it was piled into cocks to cure. To build a haycock that would withstand rain required not only a pitchfork but a lot of skill and judgment. First a base of hay was laid, some five feet in diameter, then more was placed carefully to build a cone five feet high, which was capped with hay laid so as to shed water. Although apparently dry when raked, the hay inside the cocks would sweat and heat up a little and dry further. If this process were postponed until the hay was in the barn, it could result in spontaneous combustion and a disastrous fire.

The cocks might be opened and hauled away the next day in favorable weather, or they could be left even for weeks if necessary in a rainy spell. Meteorology was in its infancy, and even if there had been weather forecasts there were no radios or local daily papers to bring them to the farmers. Every hay maker had to rely on his own forecasting. If the hay did not dry fast enough in the cocks, it might be given the final treatment, tedding: the cocks were opened and flattened out and a machine was driven over them with revolving forks that tossed the hay into the air.

At last it was time to pitch the cured hay onto a wagon and take it to the barn. Again, skill was required. The wagon carried a hayrack, which multiplied its capacity. To load it with a ton or more of loose hay was an art that some men never learned. It took teamwork, with one man pitching up great forkfuls of hay and another "loading," placing the forkfuls solidly and uniformly to build a load that wouldn't slide off on the jolting ride to the barn. Robert Frost wrote about this in his "The Death of the Hired Man":

> He bundles every forkful in its place,
> And tags and numbers it for future reference,
> So he can find and easily dislodge it
> In the unloading.

The hay rig was driven into the barn, and again two or more men worked together, unloading and mowing away. Or the unloading might be done with a two-tined hay fork on a rope and pulleys, using horsepower. The loader drove the fork deep into the hay, and at his signal the horses were urged forward. Up went a quarter of the load to travel along under the barn peak until at the pull of a trip rope it fell into the bay, to be spread out and trodden down by the men who were mowing away (the hottest and dustiest job of the whole farm year). My uncle had one of the more advanced, straight-tined hay fork mechanisms.

Although hops were the moneymaker on Otsego County farms, hay was the absolutely essential crop. Without it one could not have cows, beef animals, sheep, or, most important, horses, the source of power and means of transportation. On some farms, surplus hay was raised to bring in cash. In winter, when snow made the going easier, teams of men with a baling machine would make the rounds of the farms and bale the loose hay in the barns. The bales were sledded to the railroad terminal in Cherry Valley for shipment to the livery stables of the cities.

After haying came the grain harvests: oats, wheat, rye, buckwheat, and then corn. The small grains had to be cut with a reaper and binder, which instead of leaving the stalks loose on the ground gathered them into bundles, tied them, and dropped them off behind as it went along.

Trimming beside fences was done with a scythe which had a cradle on it—four long, curved, wooden prongs as long as the scythe blade, attached to the snath, or handle. This was a heavy instrument that tested the skill and endurance of the user, but with it he could deposit, at each sweep, a neat sheaf of grain much like that of the reaping machine. Before the reaper was invented, all grain was cut by cradling, which had in turn displaced the ancient stoop labor of the sickle.

The sheafs of grain were stood upright, leaning on each other, and later hauled to the barn for storage or carried directly to a threshing machine in the field. In those days most of the custom threshing around Cherry Valley was done by John

Johnson, a tall, robust, jovial man with a white beard and
ruddy cheeks, rather like Santa Claus. He owned a farm
adjoining Grandfather Moore's but also went around helping
everyone with the harvest. His thresher was powered by a
fine team of white horses on a treadmill. As sheaves were
forked to him on the platform of the machine, he fed them
into the revolving, spike-toothed cylinder, which knocked the
grain from the straw. A man tended the spout where the grain
shot out, filling bags and tying them, while the straw was blown
into a stack which might later be baled and sold or taken to
the barn for bedding.

There might be a second cutting of hay in August,
depending on the weather. If it had been dry and the pastures
were getting thin, hay was cut and fed green to the animals,
without the long process of curing and storage.

The hop harvest was the high point of the farm year. On
misty September mornings I was up before daylight to drive
my uncle's wagon around the village collecting the pickers.
They were mostly local women bent on earning some pin
money. (Many of the larger hopgrowers had to bring in pickers from the cities.) The hop yard had grown all summer into
a green jungle festooned with heavy garlands of hops that were
sticky and fragrant with resinous yellow pollen. The riot of
vines was attacked by pulling out one pole at a time and cutting the strings on which the vines were trained. The poles
with their green load were laid against wooden boxes where
the pickers worked. I remember that most of them wore black
cotton gloves with the fingertips cut off, to protect their hands
as they stripped the hops from the stems. They earned fifty
cents for filling a box and could hardly make more than a dollar a day.

Several men, called box tenders, kept the women supplied with more vines and emptied the filled boxes into sacks.
This was one of the few farm occasions when men and women
worked together, and they made the most of it, with much
good-natured raillery and crude humor and horseplay. It was

a common joke to throw a good-looking girl into her box on top of the hops. She would climb out laughing, for it was proof of her popularity. On Saturday nights there would be hop dances, notoriously lively affairs.

Every grower had his own hop house, a square, two-story building with a cupola for ventilation. The sacked hops were emptied out and spread a foot or more deep on cheesecloth over a latticed floor, to be bleached and dried by sulphur fumes from a furnace underneath. The process took about twenty-four hours for each batch. I took part in all the operations, including the most arduous one of watching and turning the hops during the night, in the choking atmosphere of sulphur dioxide gas.

When the hops were dry and just the right golden color, they were baled to await a buyer. After all his work and expense the grower still did not know what he would be paid for his crop, or when, or by whom. Buyers representing the New York hops merchants or the large brewers such as Anheuser-Busch would visit the area sometime during the winter and call at the farms. They had an instrument to poke into the bales and bring out some hops to examine for quality. Then they would offer a price, and there was little use in holding out for a better one. The buyers knew the market better than the growers could.

Still, hops had been a generally profitable crop for three generations. Fine homes in the Italianate style, like my grandfather's, were their legacy to Otsego County, and the hop farmer was a man with status. No one anticipated that within twenty-five years the hops economy would end.

Corn was the final crop of the year to be harvested. Each stalk had to be slashed off with a special knife and stood up with others in a shock. The cornfield full of shocks looked like a camp of Indian tepees, a pleasant autumnal sight, especially if big yellow pumpkins lay among the shocks. The upright stalks shed water and kept the ears in good condition until they were taken later on to the barn for husking, then to be stored in a corn crib, and finally fed to the pigs and chickens. The husking bees in winter were social occasions in which both men and women participated, with much hilarity when one of the men found the occasional red-kerneled ear of corn that entitled him to kiss the girl of his choice. Usually someone had a fiddle, and when the work was done there was dancing on the barn floor, with plenty of cider, sandwiches, and pumpkin pie.

In winter there were sawing bees. The farmer brought in from his woodlot, by sled, thirty or forty logs, which were piled near the woodhouse. On an appointed day, friends came with their crosscut saws and sawed the logs into chunks of firewood length. It was the hired man's work on rainy days to split the chunks with axe, wedge, and maul and stack them in the woodhouse. Top wood and limb wood might be sawed up with a bucksaw at the bee or simply stood up on end in stacks until it was needed. The wood had to season before it was fit for the stove, so all the work of one winter was done in preparation for the next.

Soon after Christmas, Uncle Rance would join other farmers in cutting a supply of ice from the Cherry Valley reservoir. A horse pulling a marker scored the frozen surface in right angles; men with ice saws cut the blocks apart, and they were floated to a ramp and pulled out of the water with tongs. I used to drive my uncle's team back to the village and down the steep Lancaster Street hill, pulling two sleighs in tandem with more than a ton of ice. Most farms had icehouses, where the thick cakes were packed in sawdust for next summer's lemonade and ice cream, or for selling to the townspeople.

5

CHERRY VALLEY was a village of about eight hundred people, the business and social center for a larger rural population, which used its stores, bank, and post office, its feed mills, blacksmiths, and railway depot, consulted its doctors and lawyers, attended its churches and festivities, and patronized the saloons in its hotels. The streets were tree-shaded and lined with well-kept homes, mostly clapboarded and painted white. New porches and other Victorian improvements embellished some that dated back to the Federal period. Oil lamps over the sidewalks were lighted each evening by a village employee. The business section consisted of a few stone and brick buildings abutting the sidewalks, with stores on the first floor and apartments on the two floors above. At the main intersection, a fancy iron fence surrounded a Civil War monument inscribed with a surprisingly long list of local men who had died on Southern battlefields.

The village, dating from 1740, was the oldest above the Mohawk Valley and had seen more history and produced more distinguished men than towns far larger. Other settlements grew up where the roads were, but Cherry Valley was founded in the wilderness and roads came to it. The Great Western Turnpike, of which it had once been the terminus, still brought through the village travelers from Albany en route to the far end of the state. Another main road came in at the north end of town from the Mohawk Valley, after passing Judd's Falls and my grandfather's farm. Leaving Cherry Valley as Alden Street, it went by Uncle Rance's place and south toward the Susquehanna country. For the first four miles, one side of it was a "plank road," literally paved with wide, close-fitting planks, which made driving a treat. Often, in fine weather, Uncle Rance took the family for a Sunday afternoon drive down the plank road to Roseboom, paying the ten-cent toll for the enjoyment of scenery, a look at neighbors' farms, and a salute to friends passing by on a similar outing. The return trip, of course, had to be made on the unpaved side of the road.

The churches were Presbyterian, Episcopal, and Methodist. In the large cemetery across from Uncle Rance's house lay past generations of village families. Even some of the Moores were there, brought from the burial plot on the farm. A large monument near the street commemorated the victims of a massacre in 1778, when Tories and Indians burned the frontier village.

Now in the closing years of the nineteenth century, Cherry Valley had lost its preeminence. No longer did it boast an academy, a law school, citizens who were judges and state legislators, doctors known far and wide, a gunsmith whose rifles helped win Texas, a foundry producing plows for the Ohio settlements, an organ factory, and the string of taverns that sheltered travelers on the turnpike. A residue of wealth and culture survived in a few families who saw themselves as social leaders in the community but had little part in its intimate life.

The local economy was almost wholly based on farming. People could not commute, in those days, to earn wages elsewhere, so outside income reached the village mostly by way of the feed mill, the creamery, and Armstrong's chair factory. All three depended on the surrounding farms: the feed mill for the grain it processed; the creamery for the milk it shipped or converted into cheese; and Armstrong for the hard maple his crew of woodcutters harvested (at six cents a board foot) from the farm woodlots.

The elder William Armstrong was an enterprising Yankee who knew how to make money. He built an efficient factory that burned its own sawdust to provide the steam that ran some equipment directly and generated electricity for the rest.

His product was specialized—not chairs but chair rungs, which he sold by the thousands to furniture dealers elsewhere. He employed about twenty-five men, and his business sufficed for his son after him.

My father got a job at the chair factory when he brought the family back to Cherry Valley, after I had been there a few months. Armstrong took him on as night watchman at six dollars a week. My father supplemented this by picking up daytime work, usually at a dollar a day. The family moved into a house near Judd's Falls, rented from Ode Gilday, who had built it. On the other side of the gorge was Grandfather Moore's place, where my father could be of some help and in return get milk and other food. Uncle George and his family were still there, farming under the old man's rule.

I stayed on at Uncle Rance's but visited my family often. We were all together in the Gilday house on Christmas Eve 1895 when we four children—Leila, Jane, Frank, and I—crept out of bed to huddle at the top of the stairway and watch our parents trim the tree and set out presents. Not only was the Santa Claus myth shattered, but in the effort to see better we all came unbalanced and fell down stairs screaming.

Every year on Christmas Day we joined the uncles, aunts, and cousins for a feast at Grandpa Moore's. It was very much the home farm, having been in the family for seventy years, yet I have few memories of it. I do recall grandfather's dappled black Hambletonian trotter, which he kept at stud. George Wilkes, as he was named, had been clocked at a mile in two minutes, and it was said that the financier Jay Gould had wanted him put on the race track. Grandfather would not do it; he was content that when he drove the beautiful horse his carriage passed everything else on the road.

I remember a summer day's visit at the farm when Uncle George's son Phil and I started a fire in the barnyard, an extremely hazardous place for it, with straw around and clapboards near by. Some of the grown-ups saw us, and as my father was chasing me to administer punishment I heard

grandpa shouting, "Run, boy, run!" He probably didn't know
what we had been up to.

Another time, Phil and I rigged up a Fourth of July cannon from a short piece of pipe stapled to a block of wood. We
plugged the rear end, made a hole in the top for a fuse, and
loaded the barrel with a tablespoon of gunpowder, an old bolt
for a missile, and newspaper wadding. All was fine until we
lit the fuse and the pipe flew backwards off its mounting at
bullet speed to embed itself in the sill of the house. In terms
of celebration it succeeded very well by making a splendid
bang.

After a year the family moved to a rented house on Elm
Street in Cherry Valley, where they remained for several years.
Now I saw them often. Dad did not have the two-mile walk
to work, the children could attend the large village school
instead of a one-room district school, and my mother was happy
to be near her parents and girlhood neighbors again.

She even resumed going to the Episcopal church in which
she had grown up. But the rector, Mr. Hall, discovered that
I had not been baptized and told her that she had better let
him repair the omission or I would surely burn in Hell. That
was too much for my gentle mother; she gave up going to
church and I never did get baptized.

I noticed that the men of my family didn't have much use
for organized religion. Uncle Rance called himself an agnostic
and never went to church. But I had to go with Aunt Nell and
Daisy to the Presbyterian church and also, for a while, to the
Sunday school. I resisted both, but when I got older I was
pressed into the job of pumping the church organ because the
organist was my cousin Bertha, daughter of Uncle Gus Moore,
whose farm adjoined Rance's. I listened to the Reverend
Swinnerton's sermons and thought of Uncle Rance's quotation
from Voltaire. "If he believes what he says, I have no respect
for his intelligence; and if he doesn't, I have no respect for his
integrity."

There was a sort of traveling preacher who came to the

house at long intervals, perhaps encouraged by my aunt. We referred to him as the Circuit Rider, and he would have dinner with us and be asked to say grace, an observance that never occurred at our table otherwise. While the women bowed their heads, I would look at my uncle, who was smiling sardonically. The Circuit Rider had a beard exactly the color of the tail of his sorrel horse, which made Uncle Rance say something about his coming pretty close to a horse's ass.

6

ON MY EIGHTH BIRTHDAY Miles Butts, the hired man, presented me with an old English fowling piece, a muzzle-loading musket that was longer than I was tall. With it came molds for making shot from odd pieces of lead, a powder horn, and firing caps that fitted over the firing pin. With the further acquisition of some steel traps I became a hunter and trapper along Cherry Valley Creek. Muskrats were plentiful, and their hides brought ten cents apiece. Sometimes I caught a raccoon or a mink, which were worth more. Thus I began to make money and could buy presents for the family and an ice cream soda for myself.

Miles also taught me how to make snares for catching fish. Lying on the warm boards of a bridge, it was easy to slip the looped wire over the head of a sucker, a soft-fleshed whitefish common in the creek.

One day my uncle came home and asked me to guess what he had in his pocket. When I couldn't guess, he said, "Feel!" I put my hand in his pocket and brought out a very small, furry, blond puppy—a collie. She looked like a baby woodchuck, so I called her Chuck, and we became inseparable. I considered her the smartest of dogs when she discovered how to take an egg out of a hen's nest and drop it to break the shell before eating it.

I attended the public school on Lancaster Street but really learned more from my uncle and his books, along with the practical farm work, than I did in the classes. Farm kids learn by observing and doing. The use of an axe, a saw and hammer, a square and ruler in making birdhouses, a dog kennel, or a shack in the woods develops skill and judgment that are not to be had in a classroom.

Reading came easily for me. An English teacher whom I liked very much encouraged my fascination with books and said that I should go to college—an exalted goal in those days. By the time I was nine, I was reading Ingersoll's *Oration at a Child's Grave* and Tom Paine's *Age of Reason, Common Sense,* and *The Rights of Man.* But to the boys who joined me in our living room on rainy days after school I read aloud stories of Buffalo Bill and *The Liberty Boys of '76.* The only periodicals around the house were the *Saturday Evening Post* and the *Cherry Valley Gazette,* a typical small-town weekly.

In Uncle Rance's bookcase was a large tome dealing with animal diseases, which fired my interest. Its emphasis was on cows, and there was a picture showing the inside of the animal with all the organs and other parts movable. From this book and my experience skinning and dressing the animals I trapped or shot, I learned a great deal about anatomy and physiology.

Despite this interest, the fall butchering was a hard time for me. The animals had been my pets, and to see them slaughtered made me ill. The pig was caught by a long, sharp steel hook plunged into his lower jaw, and while he was held high off his front feet, squealing with pain, his throat was cut with a double-edged sticking knife. Then the animal had to be bled out by letting it walk around in the snow with blood gushing from its throat until it wobbled and fell. The carcass was plunged into a big iron kettle of boiling water and scalded for a few minutes to loosen the bristles, which were then scraped off with an instrument called a candle stick. Then a piece of wood sharpened at both ends, called a spreader, was forced through the hocks of the hind legs, and the animal was hoisted by a block and tackle to have its belly slit, entrails removed, and carcass sawed in two lengthwise.

One time, when I was older but still at my uncle's farm, a bull was to be butchered, an animal that I had fed since it was a calf. The ring in its nose was fastened by a rope to another ring in the barn floor, and its head was pulled down. In this position it was to be struck between the eyes and knocked senseless. My father was there helping, and boastful of my prowess, he ordered me to strike this blow with the back of an axe. Sick at heart, I swung the axe and the bull dropped to its knees, but I had only knocked off one of its horns, from which a stream of blood spouted. I dropped the axe and fled to a haymow, where my father found me vomiting. He grabbed me up with one hand and dragged me back before the other men and beat me with the buckle end of a hame strap until my uncle and others intervened.

I felt sorry for him. I had humiliated him by falling short of his proud expectations, but the real reason for his anger was his burden of frustration and insecurity. I condemned myself for not striking more accurately, but I knew that a shot from a gun would have been more effective and humane in dispatching both the bull and the pigs.

When I was eight or nine I had a teacher, Miss Edith Harriott, whom I really liked but who would send me to the principal on the slightest provocation. If anyone upset the good deportment of the class she generally blamed me, perhaps not always without reason. The principal finally warned me that on the next such occasion I would be expelled. But I was told once more by Miss Harriott to go to his office. While I dawdled in the hall he appeared and asked why I was there. I replied that I was on my way to see him. Looking at me sternly, he said, "Get your books and go home. You are not to return until you are ready to apologize to Miss Harriott."

I was hurt and angry for I had done nothing for which I thought an apology was due. I decided to leave school for good. I went home, and after making sure no one was around I helped myself to molasses cookies and other provisions from the cellar, found a partial roll of tar paper, a hammer and saw, and a pocketful of roofing nails, got my gun and a supply of matches, called Chuck, and headed for the woods.

It did not take long to build a shack out of saplings and

tarpaper. There Chuck and I settled down to await events. I had left a note at the house saying that I was going away and wouldn't be back for a while. I knew we could exist for a while on what I had brought, plus some potatoes and overripe corn from the field. And I could get milk from any of the cows in the nearby pasture, which were used to being milked standing in the barnyard.

All went well until about the third night. It was moonless and pitch dark when at what I thought to be shortly after midnight I was awakened by a thump that rattled the shack. Chuck crept close to me, and I could feel the hair bristle along her back. She was shivering but did not bark. We waited in silence. Again it struck! We crouched wide-eyed but could hear no movement outside. At long last daybreak came. I quietly poked a hole through the tar paper and looked through but I could see nothing unusual. When I finally ventured out I discovered the tracks of a cow that had stood beside the shack swinging her tail against the tar paper.

Toward the end of a week Uncle Rance discovered my hideout. He paid a visit and said that my mother, who was very worried about me, had been told by the principal that if I would return to school I would not have to apologize after all. My uncle thought it would be a good idea to come home. I agreed and was back in school the next day, and thereafter Miss Harriott and I got along well. A few minutes of terror in the night had convinced me that I was no hero.

A colt was born on the farm, sired by Grandfather Moore's famous stud George Wilkes out of the mare Kit. Uncle Rance indicated that he would be mine, and from the time of his birth I practically lived in the box stall with him. Prince, as I named him, was dappled black like his father and had a white star on his forehead. By the time he was a year old he knew the feel of harness and headstall and had learned to be guided by a bit. When he was in the pasture I only had to whistle and he would come racing to the barn to take oats or sugar from my hand.

One day when Prince was about two and a half years old I came home from school and whistled for him, but there was no response. After a while I saw him standing under an elm tree near the barn. His head was down, and it looked as though he had a red handkerchief hanging from his neck. Coming close, I discovered that he was standing in a pool of blood and his breast was a mass of lacerated flesh. He had been entangled in a barbed wire fence.

My uncle was not around, so in a panic I mounted one of the other horses and galloped four miles to the home of the veterinarian who occasionally treated our cows. He was at supper and did not want to come, but his wife joined in my plea and he finally hitched up his horse and wagon and followed me back. After a quick examination he told Uncle Rance that the colt's chest muscles were so damaged that he would never be able to work; he was worthless now and might as well be killed. Tearfully I asserted my rights as owner, pleading with the veterinary to help in some way. Uncle Rance said, "Go ahead, Doc. Do what you can."

But Prince reared and pawed the air when the vet approached him to try to repair his wounds. He quieted down when I spoke to him. "It's no use," said the vet. "He won't let me near him."

"I can do it," I pleaded, "if you just stand where you are and tell me what to do." And much to the men's surprise, Prince stood still and let me fit the shreds of flesh back into place and sew them fast. Then I improvised a bandage from a large towel. I stayed with Prince while the men went in to supper. Afterward my uncle brought a halter and a pail of oats, which the colt nibbled out of my hand. He didn't want to move, but we gently urged him toward the barn and his stall. The next morning I was out early with food and water and was rewarded by a recognizing whinny.

The wounds healed rapidly, and in less than a month I was leading Prince out for exercise. We were always accompanied by Chuck and a brown and white pigeon I called Chocolate that would fly from the barn roof to my shoulder when I fed the chickens. I spent much time training Prince, getting him used to saddle and harness, anxious to disprove the vet's prediction that he would never be able to stand pressure on his breast and shoulders. By the summer following the accident he was pulling both a cart and a light wagon.

I was proud of the beautiful and spirited animal and wanted to show him off. The following winter I had an English teacher, Miss Thompson, who came from East Springfield but boarded in Cherry Valley. I was fond of her, and on hearing that she wanted to spend a Sunday with her family, I offered to drive her home. When the day came, I had everything in readiness: the sleigh washed and waxed, the bells polished. Although Prince had never been hitched to a cutter before or had traveled in snow, I was sure he would respond to my voice.

When I opened the barn door and got into the cutter, Prince was off with a leap. The bells and the scrape of runners on the floor made music he had never heard, but as soon as the cutter slid into snow he quieted down. In a few minutes we pulled up at the house where Miss Thompson was waiting for me on the porch, her landlady beside her to see her off. But in turning the cutter around too quickly I upset it. I had trouble righting it and controlling Prince, and I heard the landlady say, "I wouldn't get in that sleigh with that boy for the world!" That didn't help my faltering confidence, but Miss Thompson restored my courage and earned my gratitude by getting in beside me.

Chafing at the bit, his head held high and picking up his feet like the thoroughbred he was, Prince trotted at a good clip through the village. We passed Uncle Rance standing with his hands in his pockets by the curb, and I could see his head turn as he followed us with his eyes.

It didn't take long to go the four miles to Miss Thompson's home, where we enjoyed a good Sunday dinner with her family. In the afternoon it began to snow. Great flakes fell slowly at first, but soon the storm was increasing—and along with it my nervousness about the trip home. We started out and were about halfway to Cherry Valley before the snow obliterated all tracks. Rounding the steep side of Cape Wycoff, I made the mistake of pulling Prince off the road. He had been following the invisible track perfectly, but now he sank to his belly in snow, began to flounder about, and upset the sleigh, spilling us down the bank. Fortunately, I held onto the reins. Prince had jumped back into the track and stood trembling. When I spoke to him he became calmer, and we got ourselves and the sleigh right side up and cautiously made our way home.

After unhitching Prince I found that he had cut himself when he got off the road and was bleeding from his left front foot. I cauterized the wound and bandaged the foot, using materials from the barn medicine cabinet, and it soon healed. But my uncle noticed the bandage and said, "When you asked me if you could take a horse yesterday, I didn't think you intended to take that colt." I felt ashamed, for I was conscious of having been devious, if not dishonest, in asking for a horse when I intended to drive Prince. And although Uncle Rance said no more, I heard for the first time a note of rebuke in his voice. I remember weeping a bit before I went to sleep that night, for I felt that there was a change in our relationship. I had done something that was irreparable.

This feeling never quite left me, but everything went on as usual. Spring came, and planting time, summer with the haying, fall with hop picking, then cold weather again, and there was the butchering of pigs and the sawing bee to fill the woodshed with the winter's supply of fuel.

That year Uncle Rance installed a furnace in the cellar. He also equipped the house with a real bathroom with a metal tub and a basin and toilet so that it was no longer necessary to bathe in a washtub in the kitchen or to break the ice in the pitcher on the commode, and the outhouse and chamber pots became obsolete.

7

IN THE SPRING OF 1901 my father decided to get back on the land by working a farm on shares. This was the occasion for my leaving Uncle Rance and rejoining my parents, who, I was aware, now needed me more than my uncle did. Sister Leila, however, joined Uncle Rance's household so that she could stay in the village to attend high school.

The rest of us moved to the three-hundred-acre Sutliff farm a mile north of grandfather's place, on the road to Sprout Brook and Fort Plain. There were several houses near ours: the Alonzo Bowman family across the road, with daughters Charlotte and Minnie, and on our side the Elwoods, who lived in a fine big house that even had a ballroom. This house much later became the Ramble Inn and eventually burned down. Then there was Harvey Wright with his wife and son Harry, and Chancey Clause with two sons. Frank and Jane and I went with the other children to the one-room school a mile south and uphill, near Judd's Falls. At school I contracted a case of mumps. How my swollen glands hurt when mother made pickles and the sharp smell of vinegar reached my room!

Father had bought a team of horses for a hundred dollars. They were old, and one of them had difficulty breathing, so when I was sent to harrow a field with them I let them rest in the shade of the woods each time across while I read a book I carried in my hip pocket, Goldsmith's "The Deserted Village." The lines:

> Ill fares the land, to hastening ills a prey,
> Where wealth accumulates and men decay

impressed me even then as good social philosophy. Of course, I took too long to finish the field and got a severe rebuke from my father. But I enjoyed the work; anyone who has never followed a spring-toothed harrow across a stony field has missed some great symphonies.

We left that farm after less than a year. Under the share-cropping agreement my father received only half of what he produced. Then in the fall Mr. Sutliff came without warning and picked all the plums and most of the apples on the place for himself. My father began looking around, and before spring he had rented a farm in Dutchtown, three miles west of Fort Plain. Uncle Rance and others helped us move to the new home.

Mother and father always were well liked wherever they went, and in this new neighborhood they were warmly received by the Failing families on two adjoining farms. The Failings and the Moores helped each other and were very congenial. With twenty-five milk cows my father could provide well for the family, and for the first time in years my parents were happy.

With the several Failing boys I attended eighth grade in a one-room district school nearby. This turned out to be my last year in school. During the summer, our former neighbor Charlotte Bowman visited us, and she suggested that I might get a job in Fort Plain, at Shearer's Department Store. I knew that my father needed me on the farm but also that I might be of more help to him by having a paying job in town. Without any objection on his part or mother's, I went to Fort Plain and made application for work at the store. I was interviewed by R. H. Shearer himself, a tall, bearded, white-haired man with a kindly expression. He hired me at six dollars a week and assigned me to the domestic goods department—sheets, towels, ginghams, etc.

The store occupied all three floors of a building on Main Street at the east end of Canal. Bears' Men's Furnishings Store adjoined it on the north, and Steward and Bergen's Hardware on the south. There were several clerks, all of whom were very nice to me; they taught me whatever I needed to know.

I remember two of them by name: Andrew Roorbach, in charge of dress goods; and Menzo Snyder, a short, bowlegged man, who ran the carpet department. All the other clerks towered above me; at thirteen I wasn't much taller than the counters, and with considerable stretching and standing on tiptoe I could just reach the little round box on an overhead wire that carried money and sales slips to the cashier on a mezzanine floor in the rear of the store. There the bookkeeping was done and Mr. Shearer worked in his office when he wasn't at his other duties as president of the bank on Canal Street.

Among the items on my shelves was women's cotton underwear. It was a difficult moment for me the first time I had to display these garments to a lady customer and ask her if she wanted them "open or closed." But I satisfied Mr. Shearer, and when manufacturers' salesmen came he insisted that I do the buying for my department. He said, "I'll tell you if you go too far" and sat on a counter nearby while I ordered goods to replenish the shelves. He seemed happy with my performance and patted me on the back as he returned to his office.

Part of that summer I bicycled the three miles to and from the farm in Dutchtown, helping to milk the cows before starting to work. One morning, going too fast down Sand Hill on the way, I tried to brake my bike by putting my foot on the front wheel and was thrown over the handlebars onto the road, scratching my face and hands badly. After that I rented a room with my father's cousin "Mate" Crane and her husband Henry, for two dollars a week. This was the house where my father had delivered me to Uncle Rance, years before. Staying nights in Fort Plain made sense, for the store opened at 9 A.M. and did not close until 9 P.M., and on Saturdays between 10 and 11 P.M. And my salary had gone up to ten dollars a week.

Another clerk was hired, John McShane, He later attended Albany Medical College and practiced as a physician in East Springfield. While John was with us, a young Jewish man came in the store, introducing himself as Phil Allen, a nephew of

Mr. Bears, who had the men's furnishings store next door. He was visiting his uncle and did not know how to pass the time and wondered if we would like to learn boxing. He had done exhibition sparring, he said, with Terry McGovern, a well-known fighter in New York. John and I were interested, and we got permission to practice boxing in the carpet department for ten minutes or so before the store closed at night. Phil provided the gloves. I think we had about six lessons before he had to return to his job as a sporting goods buyer for Hearn's Department Store in New York.

But Phil Allen had planted in my mind the idea of going to the city and had told me to look him up when I came. I had many friends in Fort Plain, went to many parties, and enjoyed skating in winter on the frozen Erie Canal from Fort Plain to Canajoharie and back. But I couldn't imagine spending the rest of my life in this fashion. One day I mentioned my dream to Mr. Shearer. He didn't think much of the idea and suggested that if I didn't want to remain in the store he could find a place for me in his bank.

Thoughts of a career in the city wouldn't go away, however, and in July 1903, the year I was fourteen, I told my family that I was going to New York.

8

_____

MY DEPARTURE from Fort Plain was no more spectacular than my arrival there with my father eight years earlier. I carried my suitcase from the Cranes' house through the village and across the bridge to the other side of the Mohawk River and boarded a New York Central train. After buying my ticket I had $11.72 in my pocket.

It was Saturday, and the train, a local, arrived late in the evening at the 125th Street station. Why I got off there I don't recall; perhaps I thought the train didn't go any further.

I had no special plan of action except to find work and be on my own. I thought I would look up Phil Allen when I got settled and sometime later call on my Uncle Nash and my mother's cousins—but certainly not to ask for hospitality. Seeing the Hotel Naomi across from the station on the south side of 125th Street, I walked over there, paid two dollars for a room, and went to bed.

After breakfast on Sunday morning I strolled west on 125th Street and to my surprise found a store open, the Davega Sporting Goods Store. I went in and asked for a job and got it, to start Monday morning, at six dollars a week, hours 8:30 A.M. to 9 P.M. and Saturdays until 11 P.M. I reported promptly next morning and met the rest of the staff. There was the manager, a very tall and corpulent man named Becker who smelled of perfume, a man named Jacobs in charge of cameras and musical instruments, Joseph Schweitzer, who sold Edison and Victor phonographs, and Albert Jusk in the bicycle department. I was to clean the store and make myself generally useful.

During the day the other men asked me questions, and I

happened to mention Phil Allen. To my astonishment, it turned out that Albert Jusk was his brother! The two were sons of Hungarian immigrants named Juskowitz. Phil, like many first-generation Americans, had adopted a name he thought more likely to advance him in business, while his brother had simply shortened the family name to Jusk.

Albert insisted that I go home with him that night and see Phil and the rest of his family. They lived on the second floor of a three-story tenement at 110 East 112th Street. Leaky open gas jets lighted the halls and flickered on the stairs. Albert opened a door, and we were in a small dining room with a round table in the middle. The room seemed to be full of girls who floated towards us. I was introduced to Ethel-le, Jennie-le, Rosie-le, and finally Mamma-le. Mamma-le was Mrs. Juskowitz, the mother of the family. I never did learn her first name. She was the widow of a junk dealer, whose crayon portrait stood on an easel in the middle of her parlor bedroom.

When Phil arrived home a little later he was delighted to see me and insisted that I plan to stay there. It was all a bit strange, but interesting, and I liked this family. So the following day I checked out of the Naomi and moved in with the Juskowitzes.

We three boys slept in the first bedroom of the "railroad flat." The three girls occupied the second room, and Mamma-le used the parlor bedroom. All had to pass through ours to get to theirs. Our bed had a sheet-covered mattress and a featherbed, which was pulled over us instead of blankets and was aired on the fire escape during the day. Mamma-le was the last to retire at night, after she had thoroughly cleaned the dining room and kitchen.

I was asked to pay only two dollars a week for my lodging with the Juskowitzes, and this included breakfast of coffee—mostly milk—and a poppyseed roll and frequently Sunday dinner of soup and matzo balls. I became one of the family, which Mamma-le ruled with quiet, gentle patience and love.

Ethel-le and Jennie-le worked in department stores. Rosie-le was very young, about six, and seemed to be crying most of the time. The oldest sister was married and lived elsewhere but visited the family often. She was an actress with the stage name of Frances Cameron, a beautiful girl with a lovely singing voice, who appeared in light opera and played the title role in *The Merry Widow*. Her husband, Julian Rose, was well known as a comedian on the Keith and Proctor circuit. His monologue *Cohen on the Telephone* always brought down the house and was reproduced on a Victor record. Both Frances and Julian were much loved in theater circles.

After only two weeks or so my employers transferred me to Davega's Hardware Store at Forty-ninth Street and Third Avenue. While "clerking" there I struck up a friendship with the manager, Joseph Boozer, who was a Southerner and a vegetarian. I temporarily became a vegetarian, too, living on fruits, nuts, and roasted sweet potatoes, which I bought from pushcarts along the avenue.

It was bad enough to be disturbed at night by the New York Central trains on the tracks over Park Avenue, but now I heard the racket of the Third Avenue elevated all day at work. I was glad to be transferred back to the 125th Street store, where I now became a full-fledged clerk.

Albert and I walked to work each day through Mount Morris Park. On Sundays the girls would join us for a picnic in Central Park, where we hired a boat for a ride on the lake and took pictures with a Brownie camera. Or we might take the elevated down to the Battery and the ferry to Staten Island. On this ride I saw the Statue of Liberty for the first time. Another recreation was the nickelodeon, where you put a nickel in the slot and turned a crank to see the "movies." The first real movie I saw was *The Great Train Robbery,* in a theater on Fourteenth Street that had vibrating seats to make the spectator feel that he was really on a train.

On my six dollars a week I could enjoy such treats, pay for my lodging and whatever food I bought on weekdays, and still, at Mamma-le's insistence, deposit two dollars in the

Immigrant Savings Bank on the Bowery. The cost of meals
was little, thanks to the generosity of saloons that provided,
with a five-cent glass of beer, a free lunch of pretzels, cheese,
cold cuts, olives, and pickles. Transportation anywhere in the
city was a nickel by elevated or trolley car. The subways were
yet to be built, and autos were barely coming in. Hansom
cabs were the taxis of that day, for those who could afford
them.

When winter came I caught a terrible cold. It was in my
head and throat and chest all at once. I could neither work
nor sleep, in my misery. Mamma-le nursed me like one of her
own and sent for her doctor, perhaps fearing pneumonia. The
doctor told me to hold my head, covered with a towel, over a
basin of steaming water in which some tincture of benzoin was
dissolved. The soothing heat and aroma opened my sinuses
and set me on the way to recovery.

A man who looked like a street bum came into Davega's
one day peddling another sort of cold cure. He had little glass
vials which he stuck under our noses, saying "Smell!" Sure
enough, a powerful whiff cleared the stuffiest head. I recognized it as horseradish, in which strips of old socks had been
soaked. Several of us bought these effective inhalers at ten
cents each.

Albert listened to my stories of hunting and trapping and
regarded me as something of a frontiersman. He borrowed a
revolver from the Davega Store and suggested that we practice marksmanship in the tenement courtyard, where there
was a telephone pole on which to put our target. We were
happily shooting away on a Sunday afternoon when Albert
suddenly cried, "Cheese it, the cops!" and scrambled up the
fire escape. I followed him, and we were soon on the roof and
down another fire escape to the street. Since I had been used
to handling firearms freely at home it hadn't occurred to me
that it might be illegal in the city. We were lucky not to land
in jail.

The streets were the children's playground, and in sum-

mer they seethed with them and with adult life, which flowed
out of the hot tenements. It was a bustling, colorful world.
Almost every day one could count on seeing an organ grinder
with his monkey on a chain doffing its little red cap for pen-
nies. The umbrella man was certain to appear, with a rack on
his back, ringing his bell and shouting, "Umbrellas to mend?
Umbrellas to mend?" A small German band would go about
playing in the tenement yards for coins thrown from windows.
The ice man, with a burlap bag over his shoulder, carried
huge cakes of ice up the long flights of stairs; one cake filled
four iceboxes and brought him forty cents. The greatest thrill
was when, almost daily, fire engines rushed by, bouncing over
the cobbles behind three galloping white horses and belching
sparks and smoke.

Under the elevated tracks and along Park Avenue for a
couple of blocks north and south of 112th Street was the uptown
ghetto pushcart market where Mamma-le went shopping with
her large mesh bag. Some of the pushcarts were heaped with
bananas or with citrus fruits. Some had hot baked potatoes,
sweet or white; others offered hot roasted chestnuts or pea-
nuts. There were all kinds of vegetables and fruits in season.
Barrels of dill pickles stood on the sidewalk in front of stores,
and inside the stores were delicacies like the huge rye bread
and sliced sturgeon sandwiches that I bought for ten cents for
my lunch.

In the fall of 1905 Phil Allen proposed that we go into
business by opening a five and ten cent store somewhere outside of New York City. After holding a routine job for more
than two years, I was challenged and excited by his idea. If
Woolworth could do it, why couldn't we? I had no money to
invest, but Phil thought my knowledge of dry goods would be
useful, coupled with his experience as a buyer. He had a friend,
George Balsam, whose father owned a shoe store, who wanted
to start out on his own. George supplied most of the needed
funds and was taken in as the third partner. After a few Sundays spent in surveying likely nearby towns, we found a vacant

store on Main Street in Peekskill that suited us. Phil and George signed the lease; I at sixteen was too young to do so.

The next step in my adventure into the free enterprise system was to quit my job at Davega's and join Phil and George in Peekskill, where they had rented a room for the three of us. They slept in one bed and I had one to myself. We ate our meals, such as they were, in a curtained-off area at the back of our store. Any cooking that was done I did on a Coleman camp stove.

Phil went back to New York to make purchases, while George and I painted the front of our store red and gold in imitation of Woolworth. It looked splendid, and the partners accepted my suggestion that we name it the Whirlwind Five and Ten Cent Store. I dreamed up an advertising campaign. We had large posters printed that said, "Watch for the Whirlwind!!" and "Warning! The Whirlwind Is Coming!" Then we hired a horse, covered it with a blanket on which large gold letters were sewn reading, "The Whirlwind," and I, dressed as an Indian, rode furiously through the streets of Peekskill and the countryside beyond.

The day of our grand opening approached and some merchandise was arriving, but because of the severe winter there was a huge backlog of freight in New York, which tied up shipments. Bills were already due for goods Phil had ordered but we hadn't yet received. When we opened our doors on the much-advertised date there was very little in the store to sell: some enamel wash basins, hosiery, Easter greeting cards, and other knick-knacks. People flocked in, took a look around the almost empty shelves, and flocked out. If it was disappointing for them, it was disastrous for us.

Finally, shipments began to arrive from New York, but no one was coming in the store anymore. So while Phil stayed there, George and I hired a horse and a covered wagon, loaded up an assortment of merchandise, and drove around the countryside trying to peddle it from house to house. At day's end our cash receipts just about paid for the horse and wagon.

It was a time of disappointment and frustration. What could be salvaged from the failure? Certainly our integrity, though our self-confidence and high hopes had been shattered. In May we decided to advertise the store for sale.

Before the month was over a man and his wife responded to our ad; they were interested in buying us out. After examining the inventory and accounts they settled with us for a figure slightly more than what was due on our bills. George had received some extra money from his mother, and so had Phil, from his. I was really broke, having used up all my small savings from the Immigrants' Bank. When we settled accounts among us I had enough to pay my fare back to the city, plus sixty-five cents.

9

MY SECOND ARRIVAL in New York was less promising than the first, three years earlier. Phil had invited me to come home with him, but without money or a job I could not impose on Mamma-le Juskowitz, and I didn't want to go back to Davega's, even if there were an opening. My injured pride demanded something new. I had not yet tried to locate my Uncle Nash nor my mother's Aunt Cornelia, who also lived in the city, but I was not going to do so now. As night fell I headed for Central Park.

The day, which had been balmy, became cool in the evening, and the park bench was hard. My suitcase was not a comfortable pillow, but under my head was the safest place for it. I needed to sleep, but couldn't. With a stray *New York Times* over my face I lay there thinking of the next day. Perhaps in the morning I would go back to Davega's after all and ask for my old job.

As soon as it was light I sat up and started looking at the help wanted ads in the *Times*. One of them announced that the New York Telephone Company wanted young men to operate hotel switchboards at night. The only trouble was that they specified young *college* men. But if the work was at night I might be able to study, perhaps go to school, in the daytime. So I hastened to Cortlandt Street and to the Public Telephone Department of the New York Telephone Company and was interviewed by the personnel manager, Mr. Nixon. After learning my age and experience he asked the unwelcome question, "Are you a college graduate?" I had to confess that I was not. He looked at me a moment in silence, then said, "We are organizing an interdepartmental baseball league. Do

you play baseball?" To this I could answer yes with enthusiasm, for I had been pitcher on a team in Cherry Valley. I was
hired forthwith and told to report for work the next night to
Chief Operator Mr. Conrad Printzlein at the Holland House
Hotel at Thirtieth Street and Fifth Avenue. My salary would
be ten dollars a week.

Since I had given my address as 110 East 112th Street, I
now went back to Mamma-le Juskowitz. The whole family
welcomed me and asked why I hadn't returned with Phil. I
told them frankly that I didn't want to sponge on them, but
now that I had a job I would be able to pay as before. It was
good to be with them again. And how soft the mattress and
featherbed felt after a night on a park bench!

The following evening I reported to Mr. Printzlein at the
Holland House and was shown how to operate the switchboard. Coin boxes had not yet been invented, so each public
telephone pay station had a separate switchboard with an
operator who put through the customer's call, took his money,
and directed him into one of several booths for his telephone
conversation. Every large hotel had such a facility in addition
to its own switchboard serving the room phones. In the Holland House, Mr. Printzlein supervised four operators at the
hotel switchboard back of the desk and one for the public telephone switchboard; this last was my station. It was in the lobby
outside the entrance to the main dining room, where genteel
society wined and dined to the music of Franco's orchestra.

My most frequent customer was the house detective, a
handsome man whose chief function, I soon learned, was that
of pimp, providing high-class ladies of the evening for gentle-
men who could afford to pay one hundred dollars a night. This
involved much telephoning. At odd moments he would chat
with me and point out some of the glamorous patrons of the
dining room. One, I recall, was the beautiful Consuelo Vanderbilt.

Another customer was a man named Walker, a transient

guest of the hotel, who was reported to have cornered the wheat market in a week's time. He was a showoff who handed out five-dollar tips.to impress everyone with his importance, and of course to buy special privileges. I disliked the man and thought there must be something wrong with a system that permitted a gambler to speculate in commodities and determine how much people would have to pay for food.

My supervisor, Conrad Printzlein, was studying law in his spare time. During the years of our friendship I saw him become a practicing attorney and then a judge. He and a switchboard operator named McCawley introduced me to Henry George's *Progress and Poverty*, to Bellamy's *Looking Backward*, and to Hegel, Kant, Adam Smith, Ricardo, John Stuart Mill, and Karl Marx, as well as to some poets, of whom Shelley was my favorite. It was easy to get books at New York's fine public libraries, and with plenty of idle time at the switchboard, especially in the early morning hours, I became a voracious reader.

I soon got to know Paul Suerth, the harpist in Franco's orchestra. I think he made the first harp recording for the Victor Company. He was also an accomplished pianist. He and his gracious wife invited me to their home, where I listened to his music with such appreciation that he offered to give me free lessons in piano and composition. I gratefully accepted his offer, although it meant looking for new lodgings with access to a piano.

With regret I left the Juskowitzes and moved to a room with a family named Mulligan, in a brownstone house on Sixty-fifth Street just west of Columbus Avenue. Mrs. Mulligan was an aging widow with a daughter Letitia and a son Gene, both in their thirties. Letitia soon married but continued to live with her mother. I made good use of their piano, and Paul Suerth approved my progress in both playing and composition, until Letitia had a baby, which ended my practicing in the house.

I was present at the birth of this baby. I am not sure why, as I was not asked to help, but I did render one crucial service. The practical nurse who helped with the delivery told me to go to the drugstore and get some prussic acid to wash the eyes of the newborn. None of the family seemed to think this odd until I pointed out the difference between prussic and boric acid.

The move to the Mulligans' meant the end of my close association with the Juskowitz family, but I kept in touch with them until the interruption of my life by the world war and always remembered with deep affection their warm hospitality and friendliness. When I last visited them, the children had prospered and insisted on moving out of the railroad flat to a much more convenient apartment in the Bronx. But Mamma-le was very unhappy there with the new carpets and wicker furniture. She missed her old neighbors and the push-cart market and perhaps the struggle for survival through which she had guided the family.

After a year with the telephone company I was given a vacation and for the first time in four years could visit my family back home. Great changes had occurred there, including one which seemed to announce itself to me by telepathy. On May 23, 1906, one of the last days of the Whirlwind Five and Ten Cent Store in Peekskill, I was sweeping the store in the early morning when I suddenly had a feeling that something had happened to my family, and a clear vision of my grandfather came to me. It was so vivid that I told Phil and George, who tried to reassure me. Late that evening came a telegram from my sister Leila: "Grandpa Moore died last night." I wanted to go home then but didn't have the money to do so.

From my mother and Leila, with whom I corresponded regularly, I had learned of later developments. Grandfather's will left the home farm jointly to my father and Uncle George, so one of them had to sell out to the other. The upshot was that my father moved there from Dutchtown, while George moved his family to Cherry Valley and went into the business of hauling and trucking.

It was a bad time to take over what had been primarily a hop farm for the price of hops, which had been as high as $1.08 a pound, was declining and in the years ahead would go down to eight cents. In order to buy out his brother my father had mortgaged the farm, so there were yearly payments to be met; it was hard going. More than once I sent home money at harvest time to pay the hop pickers.

My vacation trips home have merged together in my mind, for they were all very similar. I would take the Hudson River night boat, the *Adirondack;* it left in early evening, and after dinner, music, and a good night's rest in a stateroom (all for five dollars), we arrived in Albany in the morning. There I caught a train to Cobleskill, connecting with the Delaware and Hudson branch to Cherry Valley. The railroad passed through the Moore farm, and some of the family would always be at the crossing to wave a welcome, while my father was at the depot in the village waiting for me with his horse and buggy.

I soon got used to Grandfather Moore's house being my family home, for the welcome I found there was warm and satisfying. My sisters embraced me, my brother Frank eagerly told me all the farm news, while mother set before us chicken and biscuits such as I never ate anywhere else. I would take out presents from my suitcase, deliver messages from New York relatives, and tell of the latest developments in city life— for there were always new and incredible advances being made in building and transportation. I helped my father and Frank with the chores and farm work and in spare hours rode the horses in the upper pasture lots. Sometime during my stay I would go to see Uncle Rance and his family in the house that had been my first Cherry Valley home.

Things were very primitive in the country compared with

the city. Mother still used tub and washboard to do the family laundry. The house had neither running water nor electricity; wash basins, the outhouse, and oil lamps and candles were in daily use. Yet everyone seemed happy, and it always was good to be back among my own people, enjoying the country quiet, feeling the fertile soil beneath my feet, breathing the fresh air, and thrilling to familiar sights.

10

My career developed fast, for after a few months at the Holland House switchboard I was made night supervisor of telephone facilities in the old Waldorf-Astoria: a ten-position switchboard on the mezzanine floor and a public pay station switchboard in the lobby. The latter was such a busy place that one operator there made enough money from tips to become a heavy investor and eventually a director in the New Waldorf.

The clientele of the Waldorf seemed to me less elite than that of the Holland House, but the Waldorf had a great reputation for its cuisine. Its two large dining rooms were under the direction of the famous chef Oscar Cherky, to whom everyone kowtowed.

One evening soon after my arrival at the Waldorf, a man rushed into the switchboard room shouting incoherently. I didn't know what he was saying in his heavy accent, and jumping from my desk I ordered him out. He grew livid, and exclaimed, "You don't know who I am!" I said, "I don't care who you are, you are interrupting the telephone service." As gently as possible I shoved him out the door. The intruder turned out to be Chef Oscar Cherky, a man completely unaccustomed to such treatment. I learned later that at a reception for Mayor Gaynor in the hotel, the mayor had been attacked in some way by a Hearst newspaper reporter and that Oscar, in trying to summon the house detective by telephone, had accidentally been connected with the kitchen instead.

The next morning the roof nearly flew off the Waldorf. High officials of the telephone company were summoned to meet with the hotel management, which was demanding my dismissal. Later I was called into conference with my superiors and had a chance to tell them what had happened. Asked if I would take the same action again in a similar situation, I said yes very positively. Instead of being fired, I was told to resume my duties as usual.

Not long after that episode, as I was on my way to the pay station in the lobby, Oscar came up to me very pleasantly and asked if I would do him a favor. He wanted to close the restaurant for the night, but there was a tipsy female socialite there who refused to leave. He thought, I suppose on the basis of his own experience, that I might be able to ease her out. With his arm over my shoulder we went to the dining room, where he introduced me to the troublesome lady. She was really quite drunk, but still in the silly stage, and responded to a bit of flattery so that after a few minutes' chitchat I offered her my arm and took her to the Fifth Avenue entrance, got in a hansom cab with her, and saw her to her home a few blocks away. After this, Oscar never failed to greet me when we met and once told me that I had his authority to fire anyone in the hotel I thought inefficient.

Oscar and the wealthy people he catered to always wanted to solve any problem by firing someone, but I never resorted to that method. Among the permanent residents at the Waldorf were Mr. and Mrs. August Belmont, prominent figures in "high society." (Mrs. Belmont, in her younger years as the wife of William Vanderbilt, had used his money and her own wit to successfully challenge Mrs. Astor's domination over New York's "Four Hundred." She was now a formidable leader in the woman's suffrage movement.) Once I was summoned to their suite to placate Mrs. Belmont for an instance of poor service on the telephone: the operator had broken her connection, or kept her waiting too long, or something of that sort. She wanted the girl fired. I recalled her interest in a well-known philanthropy that specialized in rescuing "wayward girls" from a life of sin. "What do you think she will do," I asked, "if I dismiss her? She won't be able to get another

job. Do you know how she will have to make a living?" Mrs.
Belmont saw the point, blushed, and retracted her demand.

After about three months at the Waldorf I was advanced
to the position of night inspector of the company's switchboard facilities from Fourteenth Street to Seventy-second
Street. I supervised all the hotel switchboards in this area as
well as the public pay station switchboards in the hotels, the
Times Building, and the two railroad stations. My beat included
the Astor, the Plaza, the McAlpin, the Ritz, the Victoria, the
Prince George, the Park Avenue, and the Vanderbilt, besides
the familiar Holland House and Waldorf, and a few others,
perhaps two dozen in all. I would cover all I could in one
night and the others the next.

It was inevitable that on my nighttime walks from one hotel
to another I would be approached by many of the prostitutes
who frequented this part of the city. With their rouged lips
and heavily painted faces, none of them looked healthy to me,
and I remembered the warning timidly given by my wise
mother, as well as by Miss Robinson, the day supervisor at
the Holland House, against "women of the street." But I looked
so young and innocent that they did not seriously solicit me.
Sometimes one would walk along with me and in a motherly
way warn me against the others. They told me sad stories of
their lives, and I began to pity rather than fear them.

The pay telephones in the Times Building were almost
monopolized at certain times of day by a notorious gambling
ring whose members sported such names as Gyp the Blood
and Lefty Louie. They hung around the area taking bets and
calling them in to headquarters, and other people could not
use the phones. The operators were in trouble about it. I had
to tell these tough characters that they were tying up the lines
and ought to stagger their calls and find some other telephone
facilities at busy hours. I managed to get their sympathy for
the poor operators and to persuade them to do some of their
business from the phones at the Pennsylvania Station, and
they caused us no more worry.

There were seldom any problems in the hotels, but I remember once being called to Theodore P. Shants's apartment at the Plaza to handle some complaint he had. At the other end of the social scale from Gyp the Blood, Shants was equally predatory. He had fought his way up to become owner and president of the new Third Avenue Elevated Railroad, and like most of the tycoons of that era he was a blusterer. "You have to force things down people's throats, young man," he assured me: "You can't afford to be nice." I told him that he was speaking from the authority of his position rather than the authority of his mind. This rejoinder pleased him, and as he and his mistress were about to go to the opera—both in full evening dress—he invited me to come along. His last word was, "Young man, any time you want a job with the railroad, come and see me."

New York had many resources for self-education, and in my free daytime hours I began taking a few courses—one in bookkeeping at the Pratt Institute, others at Cooper Union, and an art course at a school on Fifth Avenue. In the latter I found that I could draw still life subjects to the complete satisfaction of the instructor, but I never got beyond this to a more creative level. The student beside me demonstrated what I wanted to do: he never copied a model exactly; his drawings were always in some way original. My limitations so frustrated me that I dropped out of the course, while the other young man went on to become a successful illustrator.

11

SOON AFTER RETURNING from my visit to Cherry Valley in the summer of 1907 I received another promotion, to the position of daytime inspector in the same area I had been covering at night. The day operators of the switchboards were women, and I soon made the discovery that the operator of the busy pay station in the Times Building was Daisy Perry, daughter of my mother's Aunt Cora. It was a happy meeting. I called on Daisy and her mother and shortly joined them as a roomer in their apartment on 106th Street, between Columbus and Amsterdam avenues.

Around this time, my evenings were often spent with another family connection, Billy Dickinson. Billy was a cultured Englishman, impeccable in dress and manners, a knowing and congenial guide to the night life of the city. His wife had been my mother's cousin, Harriet Dutcher. The two of them had called on my parents when I was still a small boy in Cherry Valley, and I remembered their coming into the village on bicycles, wearing fashionable cycling costumes, from the Dutcher farm, where they were vacationing.

Billy, now a widower, was a commercial artist with a studio on the Lower West Side, where he lived with his two fox terriers. One of these little animals, named Grit, was the model for the Victor Records dog listening to "his master's voice."

In the 1908 presidential campaign Billy was commissioned to create the official poster-portrait of William Howard Taft, who was running against William Jennings Bryan. One day while I was watching him at work on this painting we got into a discussion of Taft's character as contrasted to that of the incumbent president, Teddy Roosevelt. Just then a fellow artist and friend of Billy's dropped in. He had been one of Roosevelt's "Rough Riders" in the Philippines, and he had no use for the Hero of San Juan Hill. For one thing, he had seen him shoot fleeing Filipinos in the back. For another, he considered T.R. politically naive, since he never criticized the system under which he and his class were able to maintain their privileges and that supported the very trusts that he denounced as "malefactors of great wealth." Billy's friend concluded that self-aggrandizement and thirst for power dominated Roosevelt's every action, and he wished that the president had realized the ambition he merely liked to talk about—a career in taxidermy.

Billy Dickinson was a successful artist, but I thought he should have been an actor, with his impressive appearance and perfect diction. He sang a fine clear baritone, and whenever a tenor friend joined him in practicing duets in his apartment the whole neighborhood listened and applauded from open windows.

One of the places to which Billy introduced me was a little French restaurant in the West Twenties. The Gigot family lived in the brownstone house and operated their restaurant on the street-level floor in a large room with no more than ten tables. Although the place was not advertised even by a sign, faithful patrons, for the most part in evening dress, filled the tables night after night. Eating at Madame Gigot's was a ritual. One spent upward of two hours in leisurely progress from the aperitif through hors d'oeuvres, consommé, fish, entree, salad, dessert, and demitasse. Included in the price of $1.75 was always a bottle of claret. After the meal, acquaintances might join each other from different tables for greetings and conversation over their cordials.

It was a privilege to accompany Billy while he indulged in the role of sophisticate and bon vivant. We were close friends until he died in 1909 of pneumonia. I had the greatest affection for this talented and gracious gentleman, in spite of the fact that our deeper values were quite different. He represented the best of bourgeois culture, while I was becoming radical in my outlook and pretty much of a dissenter.

My telephone company badge gave me access to any public building, including theaters, and I made good use of it to see Broadway productions with such actors as the Barrymores, George Arliss, Richard Mansfield, John Drew, and Joseph Jefferson. I listened to opera at the Metropolitan, admiring Scotti's voice above all others. But even when the music was most levitating I could never feel comfortable with actors singing at each other instead of talking. The librettos struck me as childish, and there was something ridiculous about the corpulent Caruso's cries of "Ma-ma, Ma-ma!" in Rigoletto. Tetrazinni, too, seemed overweight for her role of Princess in Lohengrin.

I enjoyed vaudeville, the Follies (first presented about this time), and light opera, but serious drama meant most to me. George Bernard Shaw was one of my favorite writers. I admired his plays and books so much that Shaw in person was a disappointment when I heard him speak at the Metropolitan on his first appearance in America. His voice was too low for the great auditorium, and his attempts at humor did not come across well.

The rate of "progress" during these years was rapid enough to match the aspirations of a young man. Typical of the fast pace of history was the fact that in 1903, when I arrived in the city, the Wrights made their first airplane flight at Kitty Hawk, the Curies in Paris announced the discovery of radium, and the Republic of Panama was set up by the United States as a prerequisite to building the Panama Canal. Year by year, in the city, I saw more automobiles and fewer horses, while elevated lines and trolleys extended their reach. "Tallest" buildings held their titles for a few years and were outdone by others. Many if not most of the hotels I frequented were new. The "old" Plaza, opened in 1890, was torn down in 1906 to be replaced by the eighteen-story Park Plaza, acknowledged as the world's most luxurious hotel. Construction of the Pennsylvania Railroad Station began in 1906, and the new Grand Central was completed in 1913. My own career happened to be in one of the most rapidly growing businesses of all, for telephone use nationwide doubled from 4 million in 1903 to 8 million in 1908.

A day in March 1911 left me with my most somber memory of the city. I was making my rounds of inspection on a Saturday afternoon when I heard fire engines, and then more and more apparatus, rushing south on the avenues toward the garment district around Washington Square. As I got nearer, I saw great clouds of smoke rising from a building at Greene Street and Washington Place. I got through the fire line by showing my telephone company badge and jostled my way through crowds of people to where I could see both smoke and flames belching from windows on the three upper stories of a ten-story loft building.

Then with horror I saw figures dropping from the fire and smoke: girls were jumping from ninth- and tenth-floor windows with nothing to break their fall to the pavement below. Bodies were piled up on the sidewalk. Some had gone right through it. Firemen had given up holding nets, which were torn out of their hands by the hurtling bodies. The tallest ladders they had reached only to the sixth floor. This was the fire in the factory of the Triangle Shirtwaist Company, which took 146 lives, mostly of young Jewish and Italian girls working under sweatshop conditions. It appeared in the subsequent investigation that the doors of the workrooms had been locked and the fire escapes were dismantled; the girls did not have a chance.

A great public outcry after this tragedy resulted in laws regulating the sweatshops that were exploiting cheap immigrant labor, paying sometimes as little as $2.50 a week. More importantly, the workers themselves redoubled their efforts to organize, and public sympathy was with them. The International Ladies Garment Workers Union got its start at this time.

12

In 1911 THE TELEPHONE COMPANY sent me to Buffalo to take charge of its public telephone department that extended from Rochester to Lockport. I was also to help three men from the advertising department who were assigned to conduct a propaganda campaign against the Rochester Telephone Company and its innovation, the Stroeger coin box telephone. The two companies competing in western New York made it necessary for every business to have two switchboards and every home two telephones, on different lines.

Our company used the entire sixth floor of its new nineteen-story building on Franklin Street as a public relations center. There, an operating section of the central office switchboard could be watched behind glass. Elaborate facilities for food and drink permitted the company to entertain the local board of trade and chamber of commerce and other civic groups and the general public, who incidentally were lectured on the economy and efficiency of having only one telephone system and the importance of manually operated switchboards.

I do not recall the details, but apparently one threat posed by the Rochester Telephone Company was that it held patents promising a higher degree of automation. Therefore the New York company went all out to condemn automation and play up the human element in switchboard operation. One of our weapons was a movie entitled *Weavers of Speech,* made for us by Pathé Frères. The scenario was as follows: .

A well-to-do young couple is celebrating their two-year-old daughter's birthday with cake and candles. They then depart for the theater, leaving the child in the care of a maid. But the maid has a date with her policeman friend in the park nearby. While they are spooning on a bench, the toddler is busy in the empty house, pulling the tablecloth off the party table. Lighted candles fall and ignite the cloth, and a tragedy is about to occur. Fortunately, the telephone also has been upset and the receiver is off the hook. We see the central switchboard of the telephone company and an operator responding to the signal. She hears the screams of the little girl on the open line and quickly calls the fire department. The Buffalo Fire Department was actually used to make the ensuing scene in which the child is rescued and the flames are extinguished.

The rivalry between the two companies was eventually settled, and duplication of service was eliminated by interconnecting lines. In a few years the New York Telephone Company was automating its service as though it had never preached anything else. One of the first steps was the introduction of coin boxes on public phones so that there no longer had to be a switchboard and operator for every pay station.

When my work took me to Lockport, I stayed overnight at the big Lockport Hotel, and I still remember the sumptuous country breakfasts there, which were included, along with supper, in the five-dollar charge for a room. I watched with amazement the platters of steak and potatoes, ham and eggs, and griddle cakes and sausage (a mere side dish) ordered by the wholesale vegetable buyers who were there from New York. Also I heard these men, in their suppertime conversations, agreeing on the prices they would offer the farmers for produce the next morning, instead of bidding against each other. The growers were helpless in this manipulation of the so-called free market.

On moving to Buffalo I had joined some of the other telephone company men in a boardinghouse on West Ferry Street, but I was not satisfied there. One Sunday morning while walking down Lynwood Avenue, a tree-shaded street of fine homes, I was attracted to an especially beautiful residence. On a hunch I went up to the front door, which bore the name Squires on a brass plate. I gave my telephone company card to the butler who answered the bell, inquiring whether the Squireses were at home. Shortly there appeared a gray-haired, patrician-looking woman, to whom I apologized for my intrusion and went on to say that I had recently arrived from New York City and was looking for a place to stay. Mrs. Squires was obviously shocked, but still courteous. She excused herself, telling me that her son was seriously ill with pneumonia, and that ended our conversation.

About a week later, Mrs. Squires called me at my office to say that her son had died and that she and her husband, with their daughter-in-law, were going on a trip and would like to talk with me about occupying their house during their absence. An appointment was made for that evening. Mr. Squires, who with his pointed white beard looked like Buffalo Bill, was president of the Craver-Dickinson Seed Company in East Buffalo. I welcomed his proposal that I stay in his home while the family was away, but I was hardly prepared to hear that they would not let me pay anything for the privilege. This embarrassed me, but they insisted that I move in the following week. I found myself living in luxury, attended by a butler.

When the Squires family returned in about a month, they wanted me to stay on. Each morning my host, in his chauffeur-driven limousine, dropped me off at the telephone company offices. On Sundays he liked to ride horseback in Delaware Park, and on learning that I could ride he took me to the stockyards and bought a bay mare that I admired. Thereafter I was his companion on the bridle paths. We met other riders there whom he knew, and I became acquainted with some of Buffalo's aristocracy, including A. J. Albright, who later gave the city its art gallery. Despite their social position the Squireses lived a quiet life into which I could fit unobtrusively. I seldom ate at their house, but during the summer they invited me several times for picnics with the Jacob Dole (of the pineapple company) at Point Breeze on Lake Ontario. This pleasant relationship lasted for almost a year, until my return to New York.

When the clubwomen of New York State held their convention at the Lafayette, one of the hotels where I supervised telephone service, I met two outstanding women. One was Helen Varick Boswell, who, back in 1895, had organized the first women's political clubs in New York City. Roosevelt, and also Taft, had sent her on fact-finding missions to the Panama Canal Zone, to report on the condition of women and children there.

Mrs. Boswell introduced me to another delegate at the convention, Mrs. Gardner Raymond, wife of the president of the Dime Savings Bank in Rochester. She had been honored by that city for her philanthropies. Although she was probably twice my age, a fellow feeling developed between us immediately, and I was invited to spend some weekends with the Raymonds in Rochester, where my hostess drove me around the city in her Baker Electric. It looked like a two-seated buggy and had a steering device that pushed from side to side. On New Year's Eve we went to a party at the home of George Eastman, the mansion that is now a museum.

Mary Raymond had an eager, inquiring mind. Her way of thinking appealed to me, and she welcomed my iconoclastic opinions. She introduced me to Veblen's *Theory of the Leisure Class*, currently a great subject of conversation among the "idle rich" whose mores it analyzed. Veblen gave me a springboard to express my radical views and get into arguments with the Raymonds' moneyed friends. Somehow my youth and enthusiasm made a certain degree of brashness acceptable.

However, my social life was creating comment among my

telephone company colleagues. I was twenty-three, the youngest of the group that had been sent from New York, and to outshine them in any respect was not wise. Rumors began to circulate about my association with Mrs. Raymond, and for this or other reasons I was recalled to New York after a year and a half in Buffalo.

13

NOW I FOUND MYSELF in the private branch exchange engineering department. My first big job there was to make a study of the McAlpin Hotel, owned by the DuPonts. The manager, Lucius Boomer, had appealed to the telephone company for help because the hotel's own telephone service was notoriously bad.

I learned that when the system was designed the DuPonts' efficiency engineer had insisted on installing TelAutograph machines on the switchboard equipment, so that any of the six operators could take an order from a guest and transmit it in writing to any department of the hotel. After making a time-and-motion study, I recommended that the switchboard operators be relieved of this extra duty. Four TelAutographs were installed separately with their own operators. The changes cost the McAlpin $25,000, but the telephone service improved to the satisfaction of the management.

After that I was assigned the job of laying out the telephone switchboard systems for three hotels: the new Biltmore, the new Waldorf, and the Pennsylvania. This last was being built by E. M. Statler. During a conference about the telephone facilities I happened to remark to him that there wasn't an efficiently designed hotel lobby in New York. Statler jumped at this and said, "Then, young man, you lay out my lobby for me!" This was my chance to express some ideas I had developed in years of observing hotel patrons waiting in line to register at the room clerk's desk, their baggage cluttering the lobby. I pointed out to Statler's architects some principles of traffic flow, and the Pennsylvania's lobby was redesigned incorporating my suggestions.

The first transcontinental telephone line was opened on January 25, 1915. While the connections were being tested, the chief engineer, J. J. Carty, invited some of the headquarters staff members of the New York Telephone Company to get on the line. We put on earphones and were treated to the sound of sea lions roaring on the rocks of San Francisco Bay. At the official ceremony a little later, the inventer Alexander Graham Bell spoke from New York to his former assistant, Thomas A. Watson, in San Francisco. Watson had been the first person ever to receive a telephone call when, in 1876, he heard Bell's voice from a room on the floor below his, saying, "Mr. Watson, come here, I want you." Now, thirty-nine years later, Bell repeated the words across 3,400 miles of copper wire, and Watson responded, "It would take me a week to get to you, this time."

The telephone network on that occasion was actually 4,750 miles long, for it branched off to Boston, extended down south to Jekyll Island where Theodore Vail, president of the AT&T, was vacationing (along with J. P. Morgan, who also got on the wire), and included Washington to pick up President Wilson's congratulations. Many other dignitaries had gathered in the terminal offices to take their turn in speaking and listening across the continent, and a long front-page article in the *Times* next morning described the important event. When the system opened for public use on March 1, the announced price of a transcontinental call was $20.70 for the first three minutes and $6.75 for each additional minute. It took at least ten minutes to make the connection, and nothing else could go through simultaneously, so two million dollars' worth of equipment was tied up for each call.

A minor incident in my work has always stayed in my mind as an example of how New York City was run by the politicians. It was early in 1918 (I am ahead of my story here), and Mayor Hyland, a former judge, had just taken office. He had been the candidate of Tammany Hall, the city's notorious Democratic machine. I was checking the service at the switchboard in the office of Charles Murphy, the Tammany boss, and overheard a call come in from the new mayor, rather diffidently telling Murphy that he would like to go to Miami for a few days' vacation. Murphy asked gruffly, "Have you made those police appointments I told you to?" The mayor replied that he had done so, whereupon the boss said, "Okay, take your family along and have a good time," and hung up while Hyland was thanking him.

After returning from Buffalo to New York City I had invited my sister Leila to join me, and we lived together in an apartment while she looked for a job. I helped her get a position in the Addressograph Company, but routine work under supervision did not suit her personality, and one day I came home to find her in tears after being fired. Meanwhile, the smoke and stress of the city had stirred up a latent tendency to lung trouble, and she was presently diagnosed as tubercular and had to go to Raybrook, the state sanatorium in the Adirondacks, for a year's treatment.

I gave up the apartment and returned to my room at Cousin Daisy's but did not stay there long. At a party somewhere I had met a very beautiful girl who, when she was not working as a model, helped her sister run a boardinghouse in Brooklyn. I must have been much smitten with her, for I moved into the boardinghouse forthwith. It was a well-run, comfortable place near Prospect Park, which offered recreation and shady walks and a change from the bustle of Manhattan.

The beautiful model lost some of her glamour on closer acquaintance, and anyway she soon married a doctor. But I met a family at the boarding house who were to be my friends for many years. They were Bill Reynolds, his wife Lillian, and their young daughter. They had a home in New Jersey but were sojourning in Brooklyn for business reasons. I do not recall what Bill's job was at the time; he seemed to prosper in various commercial undertakings as long as I knew him.

The Reynolds invited me to go with them for a weekend

at the Sound View House, on Bell Island, South Norwalk, Connecticut, and there, on July 18, 1915, I had an experience that later sent echoes back into my life.

We had been canoeing on the sound but came in because the water was too rough, and after dinner we were sitting on a second-floor balcony with a view of the water. We noticed a lone woman swimmer who seemed to be enjoying the waves. Suddenly, however, we heard her scream. I saw an arm disappear about a hundred feet from shore. Trying to fix the spot in my mind, I scrambled down the fire escape ladder from the balcony, ran into the water and as far out in it as I could, and then swam to where I thought the girl should be. Not until I swam under water could I see her, still trying to swim but gradually sinking. I grabbed her floating hair and brought her to the surface, making the mistake of pulling her close to me. At once her arms were around me like a vise, and we both began to sink. In desperation I raised my knee to her stomach and managed to knock her out; then, turning the limp body away from me, I grasped her shoulder and headed for shore. I saw someone wading out towards us. He seemed a long ways off, and I was not a strong swimmer and didn't think I would ever reach him. When he took hold of me I found that we were no longer in deep water, but I had been afraid to try to touch bottom. On shore, hardly able to stand in the weight of my wet clothes, I learned that the unconscious girl was one of the hotel waitresses, and my rescuer was the proprietor, who alone of all the people watching had waded out, fully clothed, to give me a hand.

A few days later in New York I received a letter on the stationery of the Sound View House:

Mr. Moore
Dear Sir,

I am writing you a little note of thanks for your kind act in saving my life on Sunday—Which I appreciate very much—Sorry I was unable to thank you before you left. So thank you from the bottom

of my heart and the only reward I can offer you is to remember you
in my prayers for your kindness to me.

Very respectfully yours,
May Hanney

The local press in South Norwalk gave the episode some
publicity, and my sister Leila, against my wishes, sent the
newspaper clipping to the Carnegie Hero Fund Commission,
from which there was no response at the time.

That same summer, the Reynolds went back to their home
in Elizabeth, New Jersey, and I lived with them there until
fall, commuting to work in the city. The Central Railroad of
New Jersey took its passengers to Hoboken and transferred
them to its own boat, which delivered them across the Hudson to Manhattan. One morning when the water was rough
and the boat rocked a bit, a girl tripped over my feet as I sat
in the lounge reading the paper. By the time I had helped her
up and apologized for causing the mishap, I realized that this
was an attractive and intelligent young woman whom I would
like to know better. Fiffi Wurtzweiller was German-born and
had not been in New York long, but she had a well-estab-
lished cousin in whose dress factory she was head designer.
She was talented and well educated, spoke English fluently,
and best of all in my eyes, she was an independent thinker.
We began a friendship that has lasted until this day and con-
siderably influenced my life.

14

WAR HAD BEEN RAGING IN EUROPE and on the seas since August 1914. Humane people were horrified by the carnage, but a billion dollars' worth of orders for war materials, pouring through the J. P. Morgan Company as purchasing agent for England, France, and Russia, could overcome many scruples. Ever since the financial panic of 1907 the American economy had been weak. Now, many businesses rejoiced in outrageous war-fed profits, and jobs became more plentiful. By and large, people welcomed the new prosperity, cheered for the Allies, but wanted to stay on the sidelines of this war.

England with her superior navy blockaded the Central Powers, and Germany retaliated with a counterblockade. Her advantage was in her submarines, which patrolled the Atlantic, sinking as many as they could of the cargo ships that carried American munitions to the Allies. It was inevitable that incidents would occur involving American lives. The most serious was the sinking of the *Lusitania* in May 1915.

This great passenger ship, in speed, size, and luxury the pride of the Cunard Line, was well known to me. A few years earlier I had watched her docking in New York and noticed the stampede of disembarking passengers to the nearest public telephones. Naturally the facilities on the dock were inadequate, and people were waiting in line with urgent need to make calls, for they had been completely out of touch with shore during the voyage. I went to Captain Turner and suggested that coin box telephones be installed that could be connected with the shore by a temporary cable even before the gangplanks were down so that passengers could make their calls while waiting to disembark. He liked the idea and I then cleared it with my superiors in the telephone company, and under my supervision the *Lusitania* and her sisters of the Cunard Line were soon equipped with ship-to-shore telephones. Captain Turner became friendly with me and invited me to make the Atlantic crossing as his guest, but I had no wish, or opportunity, to do so.

Before the last sailing of the *Lusitania* the Germans published in New York papers a warning against traveling on British ships. They stated that the waters around the British Isles were a war zone in which enemy shipping was fair prey. None of the passengers booked for the crossing took this warning seriously; they simply did not believe that the submarines would torpedo an unarmed passenger ship carrying, as they believed, no war materials. When the unthinkable happened, with 128 Americans among the nearly 1,200 lives lost, the shock could have swept America into the war if President Wilson had chosen to exploit it, but he stuck to his policy of nominal neutrality. Years later it became known that the *Lusitania* had indeed carried some munitions in her hold.

Private life goes on regardless of newspaper headlines, and in 1916, while making my rounds for the telephone company, riding in the subways and looking at the advertising in the cars, I had an idea that seemed promising. The hundreds of laundries in the city were using blank sheets of cardboard to keep men's shirts smooth and flat in their packages. Why couldn't these cards be printed with advertising? I discussed it with a lawyer friend who encouraged me and drew up a contract to offer to the laundries, binding them to use only the cardboards I would supply. I had no trouble getting them to agree, since they would get the cardboards free. Working only on my days off and in the early morning, I soon had enough orders to use a freight-car load of cardboards.

But securing the advertising, the source of income for the enterprise, was another matter. I first approached Cluett-Peabody, important manufactures of men's shirts. They were interested but said their advertising budget was made up for a year and couldn't be changed. And so it went with one company after another. Meanwhile, the laundries which had stopped their purchases of cardboards were clamoring for delivery of mine. I began to see the importance of working capital. Having an aversion to debt, and with the fiasco of the Whirlwind Five and Ten Cent Store still in my mind, I decided to drop the venture. Fortunately, none of the disappointed laundries gave me any trouble.

This fruitless episode led indirectly to a quite different interest. I had rented an office in the Metropolitan Building, and on my trips there, especially on Saturday afternoons, I often stopped in Madison Square Park to listen to the soapbox orators who were holding forth. There I heard Margaret Sanger advocate birth control, Elizabeth Gurley Flynn speak for organized labor, and Emma Goldman, with Alexander Berkman, preach anarchism. Down the walk, Marxism and Ethical Culture had their exponents, suffragettes demanded their rights, and a follower of Bernarr McFadden sold copies of *Physical Culture Magazine,* displaying his well-muscled torso to advertise vegetarianism. Some speakers tried to explain the thought of Spinoza, Spengler, Hegel, and Nietzsche, whose works they were selling. One could hear almost any sort of philosophy, economics, or religion expounded eloquently. I became an eager listener and a persistent questioner.

On the suggestion of some of these super-salespeople I visited the Rand School of Social Science, headquarters for the Socialist party. In the fall of 1917 the school was moving to a building at 7 East Fifteenth St. and I helped with that move and thereafter returned frequently to hear stimulating lecturers: Charles and Mary Beard, Scott Nearing, H.W.L. Dana among them, and of course Eugene Debs, who led the Socialist party in its rapid growth and was repeatedly its candidate for president. Another speaker was a Socialist lawyer, Morris Hillquit, who twice ran for mayor of New York and five times for Congress. Although foreign-born—a native of Latvia—he had a fine command of English and was the most effective debater I have ever heard.

Norman Thomas appeared there also, a young man destined to succeed Debs as Socialist leader and rival Hillquit as an orator. A graduate of Union Theological Seminary with a passion for social justice, he soon left church work for a long career in fighting the battles of the oppressed. I did not know when I first heard him speak at the Rand School that he would run six times for president and earn the title "Grand Old Man of Socialism," much less that he and I would become personal friends.

For a short time I taught one of the evening classes at the school: simple English for Russian immigrants who had escaped the pogroms in Kiev under Czar Nicholas II. I was impressed to see that their experiences had given them an awareness of social, political, and economic issues that was utterly lacking in the average American.

Stanley Adler, a writer for the Socialist paper *The Call*, frequented the school and became my longtime friend. He asked me to join him in organizing a group there called the People's Society for Music and Drama. We sponsored some concerts, the most distinguished musician being the violinist Fritz Kreisler. It was a scoop for us, because Kreisler at the time was refusing engagements in America. As an Austrian, he had been the target of anti-German hostility, at which he was justifiably offended. But he played at the Rand School and was moved to tears when the audience, mostly foreign-born, threw their caps in the air and shouted, "Come again, Fritz, and bring your fiddle!"

The Socialists had one thing in common with other political parties: they were always in need of funds. So the People's Society for Music and Drama decided to help out by presenting the trial scene from *The Merchant of Venice* in the various Socialist locals throughout the city, charging a small admission fee. We at once began casting and gave the part of Shylock to an Irishman named Frank Merlin. Two girls were chosen to alternate in Portia's role. Stan Adler played Gratiano and I was Bassanio. For the judge, I brought in my judicial-looking friend Printzlein, although he was not a habitué of the Rand School as the rest of us were. Our first performance, at a Socialist club in the Lower East Side, was a howling success. The Jewish "cluck and suiters" (as the garment trade workers called themselves) almost rolled in the aisle when Shylock, thirsting for blood and stropping his razor on the sole of his boot, spoke his lines with a broad Irish brogue and met defeat at the hands of a Jewish Portia. Undaunted, we repeated our show several times in different parts of the city.

The People's Society did more serious productions after bringing in Frank Short of Harvard as director. In *Song of Solomon*, the leading role was taken by Sam Jaffe, who later had a movie career and played the Lama in *Lost Horizon*. We produced much of Schnitzler's work. A play called *War Brides*, starring Alla Nazimova, went to Braodway but was closed because of its antiwar theme. I took the part of a German lieutenant in the one-act play *Barbarians,* which we thought was headed for Broadway, but some power behind the scenes blocked it. Finally the city authorities decided that the Rand School lacked proper fire escapes and could no longer have public performances. No such objections had ever been raised against the building in its earlier years when it had housed a YWCA unit.

My activities at the Rand School lasted less than two years before the draft interrupted my life in New York. Despite my sympathy with the Socialists' goals, I never joined their party, nor any other.

On Sundays, in this period, I often went to hear John Haynes Holmes preach in his church at Thirty-fourth Street and Park Avenue, or attended services at the Free Synagogue to hear Rabbi Stephen Wise, or joined Dr. Felix Adler's followers at the Ethical Culture Society meetings. All three of these men were eloquent and provocative and spoke to my condition. Wise preached like the ancient prophets, a burning message of social justice. He was the son of a rabbi from

Hungary. With a keen mind and the most resonant and powerful voice I have ever heard, he was in demand as a speaker and had turned down an invitation to lead the great Temple Emanuel on Fifth Avenue, preferring to start his own Free Synagogue, where he presided for many years.

Felix Adler was a German-born scholar of formidable intellect and organizational ability. After a few years as a professor at Cornell and Columbia, he freed himself from academic bonds to make a career of teaching his humanistic philosophy. In 1876 he founded the Ethical Culture Society which drew many adherents from among idealistic people, both Jews and Christians, who could not accept the dogmas of traditional religion. I found Adler's well-reasoned lectures as stimulating as Wise's fiery sermons.

John Haynes Holmes was still another kind of preacher, a great orator like Wise, or even superior to him, but with a Harvard and New England background. He was a young man, only ten years older than I. His Church of the Messiah was Unitarian. Although its members included leading figures in the business world, Holmes's preaching packed the church with visitors like myself who came for his radical message. He spoke without a manuscript, and usually for a full hour, holding the congregation spellbound with what always seemed to me less like a sermon than a gripping drama.

I remember one young man at the church whom I used to see also on a soapbox in Madison Square, speaking on socialism and trying to imitate Holmes's pulpit style.

I admired John Haynes Holmes, became friendly with him, and attended his services pretty regularly. His ideas, like mine, were influenced by Ingersoll, Paine, Henry George, and Bellamy's utopian *Looking Backward*. Especially regarding war we saw eye to eye. In 1916 he stirred up controversy with his book *New Wars for Old*, expressing a pacifist view. This may have been what first attracted me to hear him preach. He steadfastly opposed America's involvement in the European conflict, and when it was inevitable, on April 1, 1917, he stepped down from the high pulpit to deliver "A Statement to My People on the Eve of War," which left no doubt of his refusal to cooperate with the government, which was trying to use the churches as patriotic propaganda centers. It was a courageous act in which he risked his career, but the trustees of the church supported their minister's right to express views with which they disagreed. Some other dissenting ministers in those days did lose their pulpits.

Holmes continued to denounce war and to work tirelessly in every reform movement that came along. He helped found (among other organizations) the National Association for the Advancement of Colored People, the American branch of the Fellowship of Reconciliation, and the American Civil Liberties Union. All three exist today with a long record of accomplishments, but the third has special significance for me.

The ACLU began as the Civil Liberties Bureau of the American Union Against Militarism, under which name its pamphlet *Conscription and the Conscientious Objector Question* appeared in July 1917, dealing very clearly with the collision between authority and conscience under the new draft law. I did not see this pamphlet until later, but in the difficult times now ahead of me I was encouraged, like many other dissidents, by the energetic support of the bureau. It was directed at first and for many decades by the tireless Roger Baldwin, with wholehearted support from leaders of its parent organization, including Jane Addams and Lillian Wald (both founders of famous settlement houses), Max and Crystal Eastman, John Haynes Holmes, Rabbi Wise, Scott Nearing, Norman Thomas, David Starr Jordan, and the Quaker, L. Hollingsworth Wood.

15

WHEN WOODROW WILSON CAMPAIGNED for reelection in 1916, against the challenge of Charles Evans Hughes, the Democrats advertised: "If you want war, vote for Hughes. If you want peace, vote for Wilson." As usual, the people were hoodwinked. Even before his reelection, Wilson had conscription plans secretly in place. In his ambiguous rhetoric, the draft was "by no means a conscription of the unwilling" and was necessary only to fight the "war to end war."

The British were already openly recruiting in the city streets, in violation of our neutrality. I repeatedly watched one British agent, named Taylor, who would drive into the crowd in Madison Square with a huge double-decker bus filled with bums he had picked up in Union Square by paying them a dollar apiece. They would scatter among the crowd while he began a spiel about the European war, ending with a call for volunteers. "Is there an Irishman in this crowd who will enlist?" and one of the bums would come forward and get on the bus. "Now, is there an Englishman?" and so on, naming other nationalities until the bus was filled again with the passengers he had brought. Finally he would shout, "Is there an American who wants to volunteer?" When there was no reaction he would get angry and threaten, "Well, we'll get you if we have to take you by the neck!" Sometimes he would have a small band on top of the bus, playing "The Star-Spangled Banner." He evidently expected everyone to stand at attention. Getting no response, he would threaten and curse and finally drive away.

I had no claim to inside information, but from all I had

read I was convinced that the conflict was basically economic. Germany was demolishing European boundary lines to build herself a continental empire that would challenge England's control of overseas resources and markets. England was reacting to this threat. It was Woodrow Wilson himself who said later, "Is there a man, is there a woman, is there even a child, who does not know that this was an economic war?" But from 1914 to 1917 a steady campaign of lies and half-truths had convinced the public that the war was a crusade to save civilization from the barbarian Huns. Gallant France, motherland England, martyred Belgium, were struggling to hold aloft the torch of freedom, were calling on strong young America for help! The clinching argument from platform and pulpit and editorial page across the country was that this war would end all war—if the Western powers could win it.

So the original will to peace was subverted by government propaganda, and all pretense of neutrality disappeared as soon as Wilson was reelected. Anyone who didn't go along with the tide was now called pro-German or downright treasonable.

The Socialists didn't go along with the tide, and they were in trouble. In New York they had succeeded in electing six candidates to the legislature in 1916, but these new members were denied their seats when they arrived in Albany. The Anti-War Declaration issued by the party in April 1917 resulted in many Socialist headquarters offices over the country being vandalized by mobs in which soldiers and sailors were conspicuous. The directors of the Rand School were fined three thousand dollars for publishing Scott Nearing's *The Great Madness*, and the American Socialist newspaper was banned from the mails.

All these happenings made my antiwar feelings more intense. I had long regarded war as an ugly, bloody business, carried on in the name of patriotism and national security but actually for economic reasons and the profit of a few. I decided to take no part in it, whatever this might cost me. I joined the soapbox speakers in Madison Square who were denouncing the war and also made my views known to my associates in the telephone company.

The first test of my convictions had occurred in 1916, when the telephone company was called on to set up private branch exchanges in the various federal departments in Washington, a move which to me indicated that the government was gearing up for war. One morning I found on my desk a card informing me that I had been automatically assigned to the Army Signal Corps. Over the signature of J. J. Carty, chief engineer, it announced further that I had been chosen to take charge of the work in Washington.

Incensed, I took the card to the office of Mr. Haldane, head of my department, and told him that no one had any right to assign me to anything without my consent and that I had no intention of going to Washington on any assignment. Haldane, an Englishman, argued that I would be exempt from actual military service and would be privileged to hobnob with politicians and officials in Washington. I was amazed that he thought I would be diverted by such arguments. I tore the card in two and laid it on his desk and went about my work.

There were no repercussions from this episode. Mr. Haldane was a figurehead who seemed to spend the day in his office reading the *Times* and occasionally signing papers that were brought in to him. The Private Branch Exchange Department was actually run by his assistant, Mr. Jacobs, with whom I worked closely and harmoniously.

The Conscription Act was passed by Congress on May 18, 1917, shortly after the declaration of war. It provided for the draft of a million men between the ages of twenty-one and thirty-one, in two stages. I was twenty-eight at this time. The machinery of conscription consisted of local and district draft boards, the latter to receive appeals from decisions of the former.

The first step in the conscription process was registration of the nine and a half million men who were eligible for mili-

tary service. This was to take place on a single day, less than
three weeks after the draft became law.

Meanwhile, the state of New York had automatically
enrolled in its militia all young men of military age whose
names could be obtained. I was enrolled, along with other
employees of the telephone company, by Frank Jordan. a
payroll officer of the company. I protested this arbitrary action,
but in any case the federal draft soon took precedence over
that of the state.

The question of voluntary registration for conscription was
a hard one over which I pondered long. Draft evasion was
much in the news; it was later estimated that over 125,000
"slackers" had failed to register. I didn't want to evade anything; I wanted to oppose war openly and take the consequences.

I drew up a declaration of protest and handed it in to the
local draft board when I registered, bringing on myself a storm
of argument and abuse. I had first taken this statement to an
English teacher at the Rand School, asking her for criticism,
as I wanted it to be as strong as possible. To my surprise, she
and others at the school treated me rather coolly. Much later
I learned that they had suspected me of being a government
plant, trying to trick them into incriminating statements.

By the end of 1917 I knew that my turn in the draft would
come before long, so on December 28 I sent a formal deposi-
tion to Local Board No. 130, stating:

I am not a member of any religious sect or organization whose creed
forbids me to participate in war, but the convictions of my own conscience as an expression of my social principles forbid me from so
doing. I hold that all war is morally wrong and its prosecution a
crime. I hold life as a sacred thing and cannot bring myself to join
in the slaughter of my fellowmen. Moreover, I claim the same rights
and considerations as are accorded under the law to members of a
well-recognized religious sect or organization whose principles forbid their members to take part in war.*

*I copy these words in 1983 realizing with satisfaction that the Supreme Court years

The draft board classified me 1-A on January 22, 1918. On February 20 they notified me that I had passed the physical examination and was ready for induction when called. From this point on I would be subject to military rather than civil law. My protests had achieved nothing, except that government agents searched my room at Cousin Daisy's home and made several calls to the Rand School, as I learned from Shirley Ahrens, the switchboard operator, seeking information about me.

My associates at the telephone company knew about my stand, and some secretly agreed with me. Others were hostile. One day in the usual morning discussion of the news, a payroll clerk, after listening not for the first time to my opinions, blurted out, "The trouble with you, Moore, is that you're a coward." In weight he would have made two of me, but I said, "If you think your point of view can be proven by violence, I'm willing to challenge you. No matter who wins the fight, it will prove only that one of us is stronger and more brutal than the other. It would be irrelevant to the war, but just as stupid." He turned away without replying.

This man was a nephew of one of the company's attorneys, and I suspected that my job could not last much longer now. I was already cleaning out my desk when I was called to Haldane's office and told that the telephone company, as a public service corporation, could no longer countenance my antiwar attitude and had decided to dispense with my services.

It did not matter, for shortly afterward, on April 20, an order of induction brought me the president's greetings and a sternly practical letter from his servant, the local draft board:

Failure to report promptly at the hour and on the day named is a grave military offense for which you may be court-martialed. Willful failure to report with an intent to evade military service constitutes

ago confirmed the right I claimed, in its decisions in the cases of *U.S.* v. *Seeger* (1965) and *Welsh* v. *U.S.* (1970). However, I now feel that registration, as the first step in the draft process, is the point at which I should have refused to conform.

desertion from the Army of the United States, which, in time of war, is a capital offense.

Upon reporting to your local board, you will not need, and you should not bring with you, anything except hand baggage. You will not be permitted to take trunks or boxes with you on the train. You should take only the following articles: a pair of strong comfortable shoes to relieve your feet from your new regulation marching shoes; not to exceed four extra suits of underclothing; not to exceed six extra pairs of socks; four face and two bath towels; a comb, a brush, a toothbrush, soap, tooth powder, razor, and shaving soap. It will add to your comfort to bring one woolen blanket, perferably of dark or neutral color. This blanket should be tightly rolled, the ends of the roll should be securely bound together, and the loop of the blanket thus formed slung from your left shoulder to your right hip.

You should wear rough strong clothing and a flannel shirt, preferably an olive drab shirt of the kind issued to soldiers.

I made one more effort to put my convictions on record, by writing to the board:

Dear Sirs:

In acknowledgement of the receipt of your communication ordering me to appear for military service on April 29, I wish to advise you that I shall report in compliance with the law but again wish to emphasize the fact that as a conscientious objector, I shall refuse to accept either combatant or noncombatant service.

16

AT 9 A.M. ON APRIL 29, 1918, I arrived at the draft board office at 2741 Broadway to find hundreds of other men stolidly waiting. They were being harangued by a white-bearded patriarch who had appointed himself to raise their patriotic spirit with the gratifying assurance that the government had already shipped thousands of coffins to Europe so that "our boys" could have a decent Christian burial instead of being used for fertilizer as the Germans were (supposedly) doing with their dead. This poor old man, I am sure, would have been shocked to see babies thrown into a fire, yet he was undisturbed by the thought of engulfing in flames the towns that sheltered countless "enemy" babies and their mothers. He seemed to me symbolic of all the war-minded people who were eager to satisfy their vanities and hatreds and earn their own security from fear by sacrificing the youth of America.

A working-class mother pled pitifully for the exemption of her son as her only means of support and was bellowed into silence by a clerk who, pointing to me in apoplectic fury yelled, "You wouldn't want your son to be like that yellow-bellied coward over there who refuses to serve his country, would you?"

All of us were soon dispatched to Camp Upton, Long Island. All I remember of the trip is one of my companions saying, "I wouldn't be in your shoes for a million dollars!"

At the camp, I was assigned to the First Casualty Battalion as a private, and we were immediately issued uniforms. Up to this time I had stated my protests all along the line, trying to be very nice and gentlemanly about it, but this was as far as I intended to go. I refused to accept the uniform and received instead a storm of epithets and foul abuse.

Returning to the barracks, I sat on my bunk, ignoring the whistles and shouts to line up for reveille and retreat. These ceremonies over, an officer with two sergeants appeared in the barracks. The sergeants grabbed me and threw me out of the second-story window. I landed in the cinders of the company street with the window sash around my neck.

Aside from some bruises, I was unhurt and at once demanded to see the captain of the company. He was a former Episcopal minister who was teaching bomb throwing. We got into a great argument about that, and he finally shouted at me, "I won't have a man like you in my company!"

The company to which he had me transferred was composed of men with venereal diseases. Petty officers constantly threatened me with infection.

So far, I had encountered no other conscientious objectors, but here there were several, assigned in much the same way I had been and recognizable by their civilian clothes. A labor organizer named Harry Lee told me they had been going through nights of terror; soldiers on the floor below would "accidentally" discharge rifles, and the random bullets would come up through the floor near the men's bunks. We made a practice of moving our cots every night.

But at the end of a week or so all the COs in Upton were put in one barracks, about fifty of us. Some were religious objectors, and after a time many of them were discharged for "inadequate personality." The rest were radicals of one sort or another. They included a few who became my lifelong friends, Evan Thomas, Roderick Seidenberg, and Julius Eichel among them. We exchanged ideas and experiences and had lectures every night, largely autobiographical talks so that we would know each other's background and reasons for opposing the war.

On May 11 I had written to my family:

It has not been easy traveling, but of course I didn't expect that it would be. When I first came the boys with whom I was quartered were like pals. The officers . . . with the exception of one or two were very considerate. But like all good things, this didn't last long.

Last Monday I was transferred to the Twentieth Company among a pretty hard crowd. On Tuesday the whole company moved to new barracks about a mile distant. We tramped like a lot of immigrants with our bedding on our backs to our new quarters.

Wednesday we (the conscientious objectors) were ordered out with bedding, etc. packed again to move. So we sat huddled around our bundles, cold and dirty, in the face of a gale which drove the sand through our clothes. About six o'clock we got under motion, glad to move anywhere. We were being transferred to the Thirteenth Company, famed for its treatment of and reigns of terror for the COs. . . . One boy who is with us and was in the Thirteenth about a week ago was terrorized until he almost took his own life. In the middle of the night they poured pails of cold water through the window over his bunk until his clothes were soaked. Then they threw bricks and threatened to kill him, but his courage carried him through, and after three nights of such treatment he was transferred. I mention this merely to show that these men, standing firm for their ideals, are built of real stern qualities, and the war will produce no greater heroes. Insulting remarks, jostling, and open threats are the least that is required for all to stand.

Last night they called us out and marched us to a show with about a thousand soldiers. When we arrived and most everyone was seated, we left. It had begun to rain. . . . When we finally reached our quarters the lights were out. . . . we located our bunks only to find them wet and the water pouring in from a thousand crevices. . . .

We refused to turn out at reveille and were forced out—this was considered necessary to bring the matter to a head. Then we went to mess to again run the gauntlet of abusive and insulting remarks. The soldiers are all drilling now or are out on detail, so we are alone and free to walk where we please.

At first I used to speculate as to what was going to happen next. This is a phase of psychology which we pass through, then you no longer speculate and it doesn't worry us what happens next. Without any apparent reason you get an order to go with a guard or orderly to appear before this or that officer or colonel or General Bell and submit to cross-examination. According to the boys that came months ago, they used to get you in a room under a strong light before a half-circle of officers who shot one question after another—regular third-degree methods. These seem to have been discarded. I have had no such experience, but quite to the contrary have been treated by the higher officers with surprising courtesy and consideration.

Apparently this letter or another one upset my sister. On May 25 I wrote more reassuringly:

Dearest Leila,

From your letter—the one previous to the last—I should judge that my rather careless divulgence of certain little aspects of the life of a CO in camp made the fur fly. I can just imagine you, impulsive, blazing-eyed little sister, laying out the powers-that-be in no uncertain way, and I love you for it. Your letter just reflects all your spontaneity. It was as refreshing as a breeze from the hills—and encouraging too. *But,* one should be patient and not too ready to condemn. The things that have occurred are, after all, of little consequence and not at all due to any lack of desire on the part of the administration to ameliorate bad conditions. You must remember that we are surrounded by all types of men, and everyone is particularly fortunate that the people in the real high places have dealt with so aggravating a problem with such a degree of liberality, especially in view of the public clamor for our heads.

All of which is to say that you should be careful when you write to me not to be impulsive and make statements actuated by your sympathetic nature that might be construed by the censor as seditious.

I have a copy of the president's proclamation, and so far everything has been carried out. We have been segregated in separate barracks from the other men. Virtually prisoners, but not under *armed* guard. The greatest freedom is permitted. Each morning, always accompanied by an officer of course, we take long walks along the highways and byways of Long Island. There are many little beauty spots in the landscape, and the freshness of the spring and the fragrance of lilacs and apple blossoms add to the joys of our exercise. Being pretty tired after our walk, a shower refreshes us and then it is about dinnertime. At about two o'clock we go to the post office, and this is a time of pleasure or disappointment, depending upon whether or not a letter is waiting there for you.

There is always some discussion going on—political, economic, philosophic, or metaphysical, and these are a source of diversion and instruction. The boys are all radicals with the exception of a few who are extremely religious, and it is worthwhile to find such sterling characters willing to make any sacrifice for their ideas and ideals.

One of the men here is a very good organist, and he has a small portable organ on which he renders *real* music. The tension under which we lived before being segregated has been allayed, and we can relax and read to advantage. I have been reading *The Evolution of Property from Savagery to Civilization* by Paul LaFargue, a book of travel by de Maupassant, *The New Spirit* by Havelock Ellis, and have a number of others scheduled.

Despite the uncertainty as to how long we shall remain here, we have planned to make the most of our time. The boys have become quite enthusiastic over a suggestion of mine to start a course of study, a sort of CO university. We shall take up English and Spanish, mathematics, including arithmetic, algebra, geometry—plain, solid, and analytical—trigonometry and economics. I am to undertake the English course as instructor so will you send me my Bulick's *Business English*, also Read and Kellog and my Spanish book. I am sorry that these things were not thought of when I asked for my shoes and underwear and other books, all of which reached me okay.

What made you think I couldn't keep my clothes, dear? They are all on my back as I refuse to wear any uniform or accept anything from the government except sleeping blankets and food. It would probably help save the blue trousers I have on if you will send me the torn pair of oxford gray, when you send the books.

I don't know if I can tell you anything more except to add that I am getting as brown as an Indian and feel fine.

Mr. Printzlein was out to see me yesterday, and I expect Will Reynolds to come soon. He wrote me that he would.

Love to all,
Howard

No policy having been formulated for dealing with us, we roamed the encampment at will, neither soldiers nor prisoners. Uniformed men were forbidden to talk with us, under threat of court martial. Nevertheless we heard ugly rumors. One concerned Ernest Gellert, brother of a well-known artist on the *Masses* magazine.

For no obvious reason, he and another CO had been taken to the outskirts of the camp, where a squadron of soldiers ordered them to dig what they thought were to be their graves. They refused and were knocked unconscious. When they came to, they were made to stand in holes the soldiers had dug. If they leaned against the sides, they were prodded with bayonets. It was winter, and water collecting in the holes froze around their feet. At the end of the day the second man was returned to his barracks. The next morning, Gellert was found dead. According to the report, he had *borrowed a rifle* from his guard and shot himself, as a means of publicizing the CO problem.

Another CO, named Clody, was said to have had his jaw, nose, and frontal bone crushed by repeated blows from the butt of a rifle for refusing to clean the floor in a guardhouse cell. His face was restored to some semblence of the original by plastic surgery using a silver plate. I believe the records of the American Civil Liberties Union can verify the essential facts of these two cases.

A Russian, who was not a citizen and should not have been drafted, was taken to a latrine and beaten into unconsciousness with a two-by-four for having asked for an extra plate of beans in the mess hall. Months later I saw this man in the shower room in Leavenworth Prison; his body was a mass of brown-scarred welts. On the day of his discharge he couldn't say who he was.

Reports from Camp Upton reached the National Civil Liberties Bureau, as it was then called, and Fanny Witherspoon, an associate of Roger Baldwin, came to question the COs about their treatment. She also interviewed General Bell, commander of the camp, and suggested that he talk with me. One of the stock attitudes of the military was that all the conscientious objectors were foreigners. "Not an American in the bunch!" was a sneer we often heard. Some of the political objectors did have foreign names and accents, so Miss Witherspoon may have been looking for an unimpeachable native son to call to the attention of the general.

I had several conversations with General Bell in his office. On the first occasion, I told him that while I respected him as a person, I had no use for the artificial discipline that, for example, compelled Major Morsehauser, who had escorted me there, to remain at stiff attention until ordered to relax. Embarrassed by his oversight, the general snapped, "At ease!"

He tried to justify the treatment of the COs, for he knew that his methods had succeeded in breaking over four hundred men to the point where they took some form of service. Nevertheless, I had a feeling that while he did what he had to as a military man, it was not in the elderly general's character to be brutal. He may not have known of all the excesses that went on. When I condemned the ruthlessness of war, he listened sympathetically and once said that if he were not in uniform he could tell me many things.

Life at Upton was not without its humorous incidents. On one of those sultry June nights, with the air swarming with mosquitos, characteristic of that part of Long Island, a group of us decided to walk to the Sound, ten miles away, for a swim. Our guard, not knowing what else to do, followed at our heels pleading with us to come back. But we went on and found a refreshing breeze at the shore. The air grew chilly, so we made a fire of driftwood. Through the night we alternately swam and lay in the glow of the fire listening to the boom of the sea, disturbed by nothing but the uneasiness of the guard. At daybreak, as we were making ready to start back, we were surrounded by a company of soldiers who had been searching for us all night. From then on we were confined to the barracks under heavy guard. A story in the *New York Times*,

from a military source, claimed that we had escaped from camp
and lit fires on the beach as signals to German submarines.

A visit by the Special Board of Inquiry broke the monotony of our confinement. This board consisted of Major Richard C. Stoddard, Harlan Stone, dean of Columbia University
Law School, and Judge Julian W. Mack of the U.S. Circuit
Court. They had been appointed by the president to determine the sincerity of the conscientious objectors and make
recommendations.

General Bell sat in on the hearings, and when my case was
considered he told the board: "I regard this man as intelligent, and he knows what he is doing. He is gentlemanly and
has not given me any trouble." He then recommended that I
be sent out of the country for the duration of the war. How
different this old soldier's attitude was from that of Teddy
Roosevelt, who suggested that the COs be put on a mine
sweeper and dumped into the ocean!

After cross-questioning us on our beliefs, religious and
otherwise, the board found most of us to be sincere and offered
us farm furloughs or home parole, but with soldier status. Some
accepted, but our group of men, who were to call ourselves
the thirty absolutists, could not take this easy way out. It would
have been accepting a role in the war and under military command, and on this principle we would not compromise.

It was a crucial decision for us all, but especially for me
because of my family situation and farm background. I had
already written home: "I should like to be there to help work
the farm, because I know Dad is having more than his hands
full as usual trying to get along alone. Here I am doing nothing, an expense and nuisance to the government. Were I discharged I could do some constructive work."

Here was the opportunity I had wished for—but it came
with strings attached. Even on the farm I would not be a free
worker but a subject of the military rule that had taken over
America. Regretfully I refused furlough or parole.

17

─────

SHORTLY AFTER the board of inquiry hearings, all the remaining conscientious objectors, about fifty-six of us, were handcuffed in pairs, loaded into mule-drawn wagons, and taken to the nearest railway station to begin a journey to Fort Leavenworth, Kansas.

Our transfer at the Pennsylvania Station in New York gave the heavily armed military escort a chance to kick and shove us around for the benefit of spectators before we were finally shackled to the arms of our seats in a mainline coach. The officers had suddenly become tough and moved up and down the aisle of the car swinging their clubs.

The trip to Kansas took three days and two nights, during which we were never unchained from our seats except to go, still handcuffed in pairs, to the toilet at the end of the car. Our rations consisted of hardtack, a food resembling dog biscuits. The window curtains remained tightly drawn day and night. We never had a chance to lie down.

Arriving at Fort Leavenworth, we first saw the massive and forbidding walls of the prison known as Leavenworth Disciplinary Barracks, but we were kept outside it, in the post guardhouse. There we met our counterparts, COs from all over the country, and learned of the brutalities in their camps. The most common stories were of beatings into insensibility and of men being held head down in latrine pits until they nearly suffocated. But in other camps little violence had occurred.

Harold Gray reported an easy three months at Camp Custer, Michigan. He was the son of a wealthy Detroit family and had left college to do YMCA work in England, visiting wounded German prisoners. Evan Thomas was in the same work, and both men, outraged at what they saw, decided to come home and make a stand against the war. Now they were reunited in the custody of the army.

Another of the COs whom we now met was Erling Lunde. His father, a Chicago industrialist, was to prove a resourceful advocate for us all. Erling had been at Fort Leavenworth for some time and was trying to mediate between the COs there and the officers.

The morning after our arrival, we were led by armed officers to an open field in which a lot of army tents had been piled. When we had lined up, a major flipped open his holster and with one hand resting on his revolver and the other pointing to the tents said, "Now, I want you men to erect those tents which you are going to occupy. If there is anyone who refuses to do so, let him step forward." The line moved forward as one man. The major dropped his hand from his gun, emitted an oath, and declaring that we were the most goddam useless lot of men he had ever seen, marched us back to the guardhouse.

In a week or so we were moved to Fort Riley, about 138 miles west of Fort Leavenworth. I wrote to Leila on August 4:

We are in tents in an open field, about fifty-six of us in all. Temperature 104° in the shade—when there is shade.

The book, chocolates, and cigarettes reached me day before yesterday. *Thanks.* While I had given up smoking, Pall Malls looked good to me and I couldn't resist the temptation. I feel much better however when I don't smoke, so now that the cigarettes are gone I shall continue my abstinence.

Have you ever read *The Unsocial Socialist?* I think the principal character is stretched . . . but Shaw's inimitable style is always enjoyable. Shall send it home as soon as it is finished.

Mother says you are carrying on a correspondence with Fiffi. If so, I am glad, for I think you will find her both interesting and instructing.

Am feeling fine mentally and physically.

Love to all,
Howard

P.S. Read *Sanine* by Artzybashef if you ever get a chance. One of my friends has compared *Sanine* to me. I have never read it.

I did not want to give my family all the details about life at Fort Riley. The 120 COs had been told to build, under direction, a cantonment for themselves, and the fifty-six of us who refused to thus cooperate in our own imprisonment were turned loose in a field where tents were in place but no latrines or cooking facilities existed. At some distance was a single hydrant to provide water for all of us. Still further away—nearly half a mile—was the commissary, where we could, for each meal, receive raw food in our open mess kits. Wood for open fires had to be carried the same distance. The absence of latrines made flies a major problem. We were raided several times by squads of soldiers, who tipped us out of our cots and scattered our belongings. At night we endured a barrage of stones; several men were cut and bruised.

On the day after being put in the tent colony, I walked with Evan and Harold Gray the four miles to Junction City—the nearest place to mail a letter without censorship—and before returning we decided not to eat until the army either provided our meals or set us free. Some of the other COs joined in our protest.

Two days later the authorities gave us a field kitchen and permission to draw our rations in bulk rather than individually. This partial concession made a problem for the hunger strikers. About half the men in the encampment still refused to do the work of maintaining themselves in custody, but the others offered to cook for all of us, and word came from Washington that the situation at the camp was only temporary. So we began eating.

Naturally the new arrangement did not work for very long. The meals were irregular and inadequate, the cooks soon tired of a thankless job, and the rest of us felt more and more uncomfortable about eating without helping in the work. On August 19, some twenty men declared a new hunger strike, demanding prepared food. Evan, Gray, Lunde, and I broadened the issue for ourselves, sending the following letter to the secretary of war:

Company A, First Casualty Battalion
Fort Riley, Kansas
August 21, 1918

Hon. Newton D. Baker
Secretary of War
Washington, D.C.
Dear Sir:

We, the undersigned, have refused to obey the Selective Service Act under which we have been conscripted into the United States Army. Realizing the difficulties facing the Government in the question of conscientious objectors, we have heretofore endeavored to comply, so far as we were able, with the provisions made by the President for conscientious objectors.

After having met the Board of Inquiry appointed to decide as to our sincerity, and over a month having elapsed, we have now decided, as we are unalterably opposed to the principle of conscription and believe it to be un-American as well as the very backbone of militarism and war, hereafter to resist any restrictions on our liberty under the Selective Service Act.

We are ready and eager to work for society as private citizens, nor do we desire to engage in propaganda work against the State, but to live useful, constructive lives in society.

We have read the President's order of July 30, 1918, regarding conscientious objectors, and we understand that the Government is not prepared to exempt conscientious objectors from compulsory service. We have therefore determined to refuse to eat as long as we are kept from following the pursuits we feel called upon to follow in life. We fully realize the gravity of this stand, but we are determined to starve rather than passively submit to an Act which we believe to be opposed to the principles which we hold dearest in life.

> Respectfully yours,
> Evan W. Thomas
> Howard W. Moore
> Erling H. Lunde
> Harold S. Gray

Although I had drafted the above letter, I also wanted to say something on my own, so I sent the following to Secretary Baker on the same date:

Dear Sir:

Since my induction into the United States Army, on April 29, 1919, under the Selective Service Act, despite my protest and objections to war and the reactionary measures through which war is promoted, namely, conscription and compulsory service, I have consistently refused to enter into any branch of the Army, nor can I permit myself to be conscripted for farm work under the provisions of the President's order of June 1, 1918.

Under the Draft Act, the State has denied all my rights to personal liberty and freedom. While protesting against this denial of my rights, I have waited four months for the state to restore me to society as a useful member, during which time I have twice been denied prepared food on account of my refusal to do work which I could not conscientiously perform.

It has been a month since the Board of Inquiry reached a decision as to my sincerity, yet I am still held from civil employment for which I am fitted by training and experience.

Since 10 A.M., August 19, 1918, I have refused all food and shall continue to do so while I am held here, as I prefer to starve rather than passively submit to this enforced idleness while my mother and ill sister toil in the hay and harvest fields at home. This letter is written not as a complaint but merely as an explanation of my position and of my present refusal to eat.

> Respectfully yours,
> Howard W. Moore

We soon grew weak and dizzy in the hot winds that blew across the plains, drying the corn in an adjacent field to a yellow crisp. About the sixth day of our hunger strike, army doctors began coming to take our pulses. On the eighth day, Evan was taken to the post hospital.

The army's chief psychiatrist, Major Adler, arrived with his staff to investigate us. They decided we had a martyr complex, and since we weren't going to be permitted to die, they advised us to eat and save ourselves the inconvenience of forced feeding. But we were not seeking martyrdom; we were making a protest and were willing to suffer to get our point across.

As I recall it, I was the last of our group to be hospitalized. There were between ten and twenty hunger-striking COs scattered in different wards in the military hospital. I did not see many of them, but probably all were being fed, as I was, on milk and eggs poured down our throats through a rubber tube. The orderlies in charge of the feeding would pull the tube out of our stomachs so rapidly that it felt like hot iron; they expressed regret that they couldn't cover the tube with sandpaper. They were encouraged by the doctor in charge of the section, a hard-boiled captain named Henry.

Harold Gray and Erling Lunde had been sent to the hospital three days after Evan. About twenty-four hours and three tube feedings later, Gray decided to give up the strike; Lunde agreed with him. Gray, a religious objector who was constantly scrutinizing his own motives, reasoned that the logic of the hunger strike led to suicide, which was morally wrong. Also, he learned that Evan had just been confronted with a military command to eat, by disobeying which he became subject to court martial. Gray wanted to be court martialed on the issue of military service rather than that of eating. So he and Lunde addressed a telegram to Secretary Baker calling off their hunger strike.

Evan's brother, Norman Thomas, had arrived at Fort Riley with their mother, who pled with Evan to eat. She succeeded where the authority of the military could not, and he gave up the strike shortly after making his point by refusing the military order to eat.

OPPOSITE, ABOVE: Fort Riley, 1918. C.O.'s, *left to right*, Henry Monsky; Harold Gray, whose father, next to Henry Ford, was the largest stockholder in the Ford Motor Company and who "owned half of Detroit"; Roderick Seidenburg, artist, architect, and philosopher; Evan Thomas, brother of Norman Thomas, later a physician; William A. Dunham; Sam Solnitski; and Howard W. Moore.

OPPOSITE, BELOW: The conscientious objectors' tent encampment at Fort Riley, August 1918.

BELOW: At Fort Riley: 1) William A. Dunham; 2) Howard W. Moore; 3) Henry Monsky; 4) Sam Solnitski; 5) Evan W. Thomas; 6) Harold S. Gray; 7) Roderick Seidenburg.

Leavenworth disciplinary barracks, drawn by Howard Moore in 1918.

The solitary cells in the detention barracks at Fort Leavenworth, Kansas. Behind the wooden door are bars. The planks and blanket, at right, were for comfort while sleeping.

Fort Douglas, Utah, November 1918. Playing baseball, with the author at shortstop.

Howard Moore at Fort Douglas.

OPPOSITE, ABOVE: At Fort Douglas. Left to right: Bruno Grunzig, Howard Moore, Ben Breger, Erling Lunde.

OPPOSITE, BELOW: Sentenced to death for refusing military orders, these four civilians were H. Bernstein, T. Shotkin, Jacob Schneider, and Ben Salmon. A reviewing board later reduced their sentences to twenty-five years in prison.

Cartoons by Fred Jerger

—conscientious objector incarcerated at
Fort Douglas, Utah—1919 and 1920

My own mother wrote me a pitiful letter, but I believe I finally stopped fasting mainly because everyone else had done so and it was no longer a group action. My recollections of this period are hazy. I know I was fasting at least two weeks. Then we all were kept in the hospital for about ten days to restore our strength.

Both Evan and I had stated that we would fast again if conditions at the encampment were not improved. When we were sent back on September 12 we found everything the same. But a few days later the authorities began a strategy to get everyone out of the encampment, the troublemakers first. Colonel Waterman came down one day and read us a presidential proclamation assigning COs to noncombattant work under military direction. Then eight men were individually ordered to shovel a pile of rubbish into a wagon. Evan and I were in this group. We all refused and were taken to the guardhouse charged with violation of the Sixty-Fourth Article of War. This was repeated each day, until the encampment was emptied and the guardhouse was full.

The same board of inquiry that had interviewed many of us in Eastern camps arrived at Fort Riley for another round of hearings. During my interrogation, Harlan Stone argued that I was inconsistent because I bought postage stamps, which helped the government and hence the war effort. While I was smilingly assuring Stone that he was welcome to any satisfaction he could get out of such sophistry, Judge Mack turned to him and said sharply, "Why quibble? The fact is that if everyone believed as Moore does, there couldn't be any war. Our job is to determine what to do with him." There were no further questions. Mack had put his finger on the crux of the problem. Again the board offered farm furloughs, and again we all refused.

We had been taken before the board by Captain Price, who was in charge of the guardhouse. Seeking, perhaps, to impress the judges, he insisted on our marching in military formation and under heavy guard. When we failed to keep formation he ordered a guard to get us back in line. The guard rushed forward and plunged the muzzle of his gun into the spine of a man named Caplovitz, just in front of Erling Lunde and me. We heard bone crack as he fell to the ground. While we tried to help him up, Price grew livid with rage and, uttering obscenities, threw his Sam Browne belt and revolver on the ground and challenged any of us to fight him. Since there were no takers, he had to proceed with the straggling COs, a disgruntled and much deflated officer. We carried Caplovitz, who was in great pain and later had to be hospitalized.

When we got back to the guardhouse after the hearings, Captain Price ordered me to clean out a solitary cell. When I refused, he drew his revolver and holding the muzzle against my temple said, "I'll give you just one minute to change your mind." I told him he was going too far and he knew it, that I had no quarrel with him personally, but if he had orders to shoot me he should go ahead. Lacking such orders, he instead put me in ball and chain for about an hour.*

At this time I was already on a hunger strike which I had begun when I was put in the guardhouse. So I was soon in the hospital again, being tube-fed and this time with two armed soldiers following me around or sitting by my bed because I was technically a prisoner. When they thought I was asleep they would talk about me: "What's the matter with the son of a bitch? He ought to be hung." My weight was down to ninety pounds despite the forced feeding.

Captain Henry began to get a little chummy. He would come around and look me over. "How'd you sleep?" he asked me one time.

"How do you think you would sleep with guards coming and going all night?" I replied (for the guards were changed every two hours).

---

*This officer some time later shot a black bellboy in a Philadelphia hotel for refusing to bring him some whiskey. We read about it in the paper, and one of the COs in Leavenworth received a letter from him saying that we would probably be glad to know that he was in prison for killing a man.

He said, "You can eat anytime you want to."

And I said, "Well, I'm not eating."

Finally he said, "I wish you would eat. You can just go to my office and order food, whatever you want. Because if anything happens to you, I'm in trouble."

I answered, "That's up to the government. When it has installed a proper kitchen and latrines for the men in the encampment, I'll eat."

Mrs. Waterman, wife of the post commander, was helping the sick men—reading letters to them and that sort of thing— and she buttonholed me one day and said, "You know, wherever officers meet, you men are the subject of conversation." While we were standing there talking about the COs, the guard behind me got impatient, and he pricked me with his bayonet and motioned me back to bed. I turned to him and said, "If you have orders to run me through, go ahead." Mrs. Waterman slumped to the floor in a faint. While we were trying to revive her, Captain Henry came in and learned what had happened. He called the prison officer and assumed personal responsibility for me and wanted every guard taken out of his hospital section, and this was done.

Finally, one day he came to me and said, "Now you can eat. The men at the camp have a kitchen and latrines." He led me to his office and said, "Just eat slowly. Don't eat too fast." And he had them send chicken and biscuits. It was a fine meal.

When I had finished eating he told me that he was going to keep me in the hospital under observation. He didn't want me to go to prison. We had gotten rather fond of each other. He'd start an argument about the CO position, and I'd ask, "How many hospitals could you build for the cost of a battleship?" and we'd have a long discussion.

About this time the great influenza epidemic—according to Captain Henry a pneumonic plague—had reached Fort Riley, and the sick began to flow into our hospital section. In less than a week they were coming so fast that men lay in the corridors, on the stairs, even on the grounds outside. Some were able to walk, but a great many more were carried in on stretchers. The black patients always came on stretchers because no one would send them until they collapsed.

Captain Henry asked me if I would mind giving some of the patients a drink when I passed them. I assured him that I would be happy to help all I could if he would exempt me from any military routine and supply me with a coat and trousers instead of the bathrobe I was wearing.

He agreed, and I then suggested that we upset routine at once by putting the sick men in bed first and letting the paperwork flow backward. It was the practice to take a patient's record at the section office, although it had already been taken at the receiving-in station before assignment to a section. The patient was then sent to a ward, where a record was again taken before he could be put to bed. This went on while men were lying around with high fevers and in some cases already unconscious.

My suggestion was adopted, and when Colonel Bliss of the Medical Corps visited the section later he expressed surprise that no sick men were lying around the corridors as was the case elsewhere. Captain Henry pointed to me and said, "This conscientious objector has organized my section."

Some nurses and corpsmen were assigned to me, I was given a stethoscope, and I took charge of a ward in which most of the patients were delirious. Nobody there knew I wasn't a doctor. Although I did not wear a mask, which was required of everyone else, and slept in the ward with men dying all around me until space was made for my cot in the linen room, I was never ill. One day when I did have a slight fever Captain Henry suggested that I go to Junction City and get a haircut. After this outing my fever disappeared.

The Army Medical Corps was prescribing treatment for the flu consisting of two compound cathartic pills on admission and next morning thirty cc's of magnesium sulphate, aspirin every three hours, and in a crisis, digitalis. They would try to get the fever down with ice packs; I saw men killed that way. One man who had a high fever was wrapped in a sheet wrung out of ice water and an electric fan was played on him. He turned blue and died in twenty minutes. In my ward I threw out the ice packs and gave the men hot water bottles, and they were grateful. Statistically, our section had the fewest deaths, but in the whole hospital men were dying so fast they could not get corpsmen enough, or guards to station around the bodies that were piled up like cordwood on the parade grounds. One night when a storm came up there were twenty-eight patients on a verandah for lack of room inside. We carried them on our shoulders to an attic space, and I was covered with blood from their lungs. Only four of them survived.

After several weeks, the captain called me into his office and told me that he had been trying to stave off my court martial but that Colonel Waterman was insisting on it. He said that if I would agree to stay with him and study medicine, for which I seemed to have a special aptitude, everything could be arranged. I would not have to sign anything, only agree verbally. He believed that the war would be over in six months and was equally certain that I would not live six months if sent to Leavenworth. He was going to fight to keep me from prison.

A mutual respect had developed between us in the weeks we had worked together. I knew that Captain Henry was sincerely concerned about my future and that what I was going to say would hurt him. But I told him that even if it were certain that the war would be over in one minute and I had to make my decision first, there could be but one answer: prison. Seldom have I seen anyone more disappointed than he was at this reply.

Several days later, on October 21, I was again summoned to his office, where an armed guard was waiting to take me away. Captain Henry ordered the guard to wait outside. He then told me that he had been working for hours on my behalf but that his superiors were adamant for my court martial and there was nothing left to do but have a last cigarette together.

Strangely, I felt jubilant. At last there was no more uncertainty. The military knew what it was going to do with me.

As I carried my suitcase across the parade ground with the guard at my heels, I heard a shout behind me. I looked around and saw the hospital porches crowded with corpsmen and ambulatory patients, waving goodbye.

At the registering-out office of the hospital unit, the officer asked me if I had been through Wood's Mill yet. What his question implied I was soon to learn, for I was taken to nearby Camp Funston, which was in the charge of General Leonard Wood.

In the two-story wooden guardhouse behind a barbed-wire stockade I met nineteen conscientious objectors whom I had known at Fort Riley. They apparently had been singled out for Wood's Mill because they were political objectors and many had foreign names or were foreign-born. "Not an American in the crowd!" was the sneer of the officers. Those of us who could claim to be native sons did not feel like doing so.

Ever since their arrival at Funston, some six weeks ago, some three and a half, these men had been subject to prolonged, repeated torment by companies of soldiers who raided them every two hours, day and night, dragging them out to run around the parade grounds at the point of a bayonet, scrubbing them with brooms and latrine brushes under icy showers, beating, kicking, and manhandling them. They had been held incommunicado and much of the time on a bread and water diet. Some had been hunger-striking.

I also learned that while still in the Fort Riley guardhouse, some of these men had endured the "water cure," a form of torture used by Wood's soldiers in the Philippines during the Spanish-American War. As practiced at Fort Riley, it consisted of hanging a man with two ropes, one around the neck, the other on the arm. The victim, for refusing to put on a uniform, was suspended by each rope in turn until he was unconscious, then laid on the floor and water forced into his mouth from a hose while his stomach was pounded. One of the victims, Frank Burke, died later at Fort Douglas as a result of suffering this treatment at Fort Riley.

The COs at Funston had recorded their daily ordeals on the backs of labels from tin cans, which were smuggled out by sympathetic garrison prisoners on the floor above them in the guardhouse. The message reached the National Civil Liberties Bureau, which appealed to Washington. An investigation was going on by the time I arrived. Two majors, Taussig and White, were made scapegoats and dishonorably discharged, but everyone knew that General Wood himself was responsible for the abuses. Even one of the soldiers raiding the COs had said, "Sorry, but it's the king's orders."

One by one we were brought to trial in the military court. Without ever having accepted military status, we were court-martialed as recalcitrant soldiers who refused to obey orders: we were simply a problem of military discipline. Our appearance was merely perfunctory, as most of us were advised beforehand that we would receive twenty-five-year sentences.

Most of the COs made no defense but read prepared statements of their position for the record. Some stood mute, refusing to recognize the court. Lester Ott, a lawyer, who was tried in the same session as I, made a brilliant statement, concluding dramatically, "Rather than serve a term of years in America's medieval prisons, I urge the death sentence!" His words roused the members of the court from their bored indifference; newspapers were dropped and feet came off the desks. But like most of the others, he was given twenty-five years. A few got fifty-year terms, and four men, Mayer Bernstein, Thomas Shotkin, Jacob Schneider, and Benjamin Salman, did, without explanation, receive the death sentence, which was later commuted to twenty-five years.

In my own case, the adjutant failed to recommend any sentence but urged leniency because of my helpfulness at the hospital, which Captain Henry had personally brought to the court's attention. In fact, this officer was so unexpectedly nice that it was a bit embarrassing. Confident of my ability to speak extemporaneously, I had prepared no statement. I wanted to say that my refusal to obey military orders was based on deep philosophical and political convictions that war was futile and its use as an instrument of national policy was a confession of moral bankruptcy and that I preferred to die for something that I believed in rather than live for something I didn't.

But Lester Ott had so impressed me with his statement that my mind went blank. Afterward I had no idea of what I had said and was amazed at the version of my statement that appeared in the transcript of the trial. I do have a clear recollection that Lieutenant Donaldson, one of the witnesses, testified that I was an agnostic, and when asked by a member of the court if he knew what that was he replied, "It's one of those new kinds of religion." The court stenographer improved this to read, "One who is not sure of what he believes in." So I do not have much confidence in the transcript, but if I was incoherent it didn't matter. I was sentenced to five years, the shortest time given to any CO as far as I know. But as it turned out, I was, with one other man, the last to be released.

18

ON ARMISTICE DAY, November 11, 1918, I arrived with a number of other COs at the Fort Leavenworth Disciplinary Barracks. Many of us had seen this forbidding mass of steel and concrete when we first came west from Camp Upton; but now we entered the military prison for the first time, and immediately came to grips with its realities. For refusing to work in the prison I was placed in solitary confinement, shackled to the bars of my cell in a standing position for nine hours each day, on a bread and water diet.

"The hole," as solitary confinement is called in prison, meant a cell nine by five feet, with a barred door, and usually a heavy wooden door in addition so that the only light came through small ventilation slits at top and bottom.

All of the solitary cells were occupied by conscientious objectors. Six of them contained Molokans, members of a Russian religious sect opposed to war and also vegetarian in principle and practice. Evan Thomas, who had been court martialed at Fort Riley and sent to Leavenworth October 19 and at first worked in one of the administrative offices, was in solitary too for joining in the Molokans' protest against their treatment. He had seen these simple and devout young men, who could hardly speak English, dragged across the prison yard by their beards, forced to stand for hours, and clubbed whenever they slumped or leaned against the wall.

I had a cell without the wooden door, so at least I saw the light of day. There was no bed or blanket, nothing but a toilet at the back of the cell. Here I was to stay until I agreed to work and otherwise conform to regulations.

I soon learned that I was not alone. The cell was alive with bedbugs, which furnished an uneasy diversion as I watched them crawling up my manacled arms and dropping into my hair from the ceiling. By twisting and pressing my body against the bars I could crush some, but not all. Standing nine hours in one spot is exhausting; to sit or lie becomes a pressing need. At the end of the day when the shackles were unlocked, even the concrete floor seemed a haven of rest. But soon it felt cold and unbearably hard. At night the bedbugs were more numerous and more active and were joined by rats, which kept pouncing on my chest as they played around the cell. Since no attempt was ever made by prison authorities to rid the place of vermin, I had to conclude that they were part of my punishment.

When the officer of the day with his guards made rounds to count the prisoners, a guard would shout "Attention!" and all prisoners were expected to stand with folded arms near their cell doors. But he found me lying on the floor—such an affront to his dignity that he lost count and bellowed that I had better be standing when he came around again. Finding me in the same position on his second round, he became apoplectic and ordered the guards to lash me upright to the cell-door. This was done, but apparently their heart was not in their work, for I easily loosened the ropes and slipped to the floor again. On his third time around the officer turned livid with rage and ordered the guards to enter my cell and teach me a lesson. They proceeded to beat me with their clubs. When I regained consciousness my head was in the lap of the regular guard on the wing. He was soaking up the blood from my hair and face with a handkerchief and saying as though to himself, "Jesus, if he can stand that, he'll win."

I relate this incident not boastfully. I knew from past experience that once you conform in any way it will be used against you. It was hard to know just where to draw the line to avoid mere pettiness, but I had determined that I would never work in prison or willingly cooperate to keep myself there. I had to make sure there was no question as to where I stood in my absolute refusal to accept the status of soldier. After this episode I was not again singled out for extra punishment.

On my second day in solitary I heard someone in the adjoining cell trying to talk to me. There was a space between the barred door and the cell partition, through which I could see an eye peering. Through this channel of communication I learned that my neighbor was Jacob Wipf, a member of the religious sect known as Hutterites. Their Anabaptist faith originated in Austria in the early sixteenth century, but the Hutterites had fled to Russia to escape persecution and had lived there for many generations. Finally they were given twenty years to accept military service or leave Russia. They had come to the United States during Grant's administration and established successful farming communities in the prairie states.

In the wartime drive to sell Liberty Bonds, the Hutterites in their community near Alexandria, South Dakota, refused to buy the bonds but offered to contribute to the Red Cross instead. This did not satisfy their patriotic neighbors, who rounded up the Hutterites' cattle, sold them at auction, bought Liberty Bonds with the proceeds, and threw the bonds into the Hutterite church building.

Then the local draft board decided that since the Hutterites farmed communally, the women and old men could harvest the crops and the young men would be subject to the draft rather than having the usual farm exemption. Jacob Wipf, a blacksmith, and four brothers in the Hofer family were taken forcibly from their homes. Refusing to put on uniforms, they were sent to Alcatraz Prison, where they were forced to stand in the dungeon clothed only in their underwear. The dungeon hadn't been used since the Spanish-American War. Sea water seeped through its walls and stood on the floor.

An alert reporter for the Hearst papers discovered their plight, and the resulting publicity forced the government to do something; the men were transferred from Alcatraz to solitary confinement in Fort Leavenworth. The Hofer brothers contracted pneumonia, and two of them died at Leavenworth. One of the bodies was returned to the Hutterite community dressed in the uniform which the men had refused to wear.

All this I learned in whispered conversations with Jacob. Later, after handcuffing was discontinued and writing became possible, my account of the Hutterites was smuggled out and appeared in Norman Thomas's magazine, *The World Tomorrow*.

After two weeks in solitary I was taken to the prison basement for a shower bath. Some of the other absolutist COs were there, Evan and the Eichel brothers among them; the brief meeting was a delight and our spirits were strengthened. Then we were conducted to the prison office and asked if we were now willing to work. One by one we refused and were sentenced to two more weeks in solitary, shackled as before for nine hours daily. But this time we were to receive full diet. I looked forward to my first meal in two weeks. It consisted of a plate of soupy beans, which the guard shoved under the cell gate and then deliberately spit into. If this was intended to curb my appetite, it was successful. I continued to live on bread crusts, the *pièce de résistance* of the various garbage that was offered to us.

By this time the prison was filling up with soldiers from overseas, sentenced by courts martial for infractions there. It was so crowded that the corridors of the cell blocks were used to house them. These men, who worked in prison without question, could hardly be expected to see the significance of the thirty pairs of shackled hands sticking out between the bars of the solitary cells. But some kind of sympathy apparently stirred a black man, who concealed a raw onion in his shirt and, at the risk of being put in solitary himself, threw it into my cell as he passed. It was a kindness I would never forget. I hid the onion behind the broom near the toilet, and although it was shared by a couple of rats it lasted nearly two weeks. A little piece rubbed on the crust made the bread more palatable.

One day Jane Addams of Hull House in Chicago, accompanied by two other ladies, one of whom I think was Emily Green Balch, author of *Approaches to the Great Settlement*, visited our wing of the prison and talked with each of the thirty manacled COs about conditions there and especially about our health. As a result of this visit we were given wooden pallets to lie on and one army blanket apiece.

Shortly afterward, Colonel Rice, the commandant of the prison, made a tour of inspection with several other officers. It was an episode worthy of comic opera. The colonel entered a few cells and bent over from the waist stiffly to avoid any contact of his immaculate uniform with our blankets, which he examined carefully through his pince-nez. Of course he found nothing, for bedbugs hide their blood-swollen bodies in wall crevices during the day. Had he stayed inside any of the cells for an hour he would have carried away a few bugs in his clothes.

Occasionally Clark Getts, the CO son of a Chicago banker, who was working in the prison office gathering statistics, and so had some freedom to roam around, would appear with chocolate bars and brief us on the news of the outside world. He also took oral messages, which he wrote down and smuggled past the censors.

One day, standing chained to the bars, resting my head on my arms and lost in daydreams, I felt a sudden burning pain in my hand. A trusty was holding his lighted cigarette against my fingers. Trying to smile, I asked him if he enjoyed hurting me. Had I cursed him, I am sure he would have continued with sadistic delight to torture me. But some color appeared in his pasty face; I don't know whether he felt ashamed or was merely taken aback by my reaction, but he turned and sauntered down the corridor. Later I learned that this man, known as Red, was the terror of the prison. He had murdered a paymaster and was serving a life sentence. He seemed to enjoy his reputation, swaggering about, carrying a

stocky bullwhip, his arms covered with studded leather
gauntlets.

But Red came peaceably to my cell many times after this.
He would bring letters from his sweetheart to share with me.
Several times he came with pencil and paper and asked for
help in writing to the girl. I imagine that the letters I dictated
affected him more than her, for I always presented him as a
kind and understanding person. I hoped to influence Red in
this way if it were possible. It was a satisfaction when he told
me one day that he had never before known anyone whom he
could regard as a friend.

It is to men like Red that prison authorities turn to carry
out petty torments. He was just another link in the chain of
terror forged to reduce the inmates to meek obedience. Leavenworth radiated currents of fear that reached beyond its walls
to the whole army. But the military hierarchy still was ner-
vous; like every totalitarian regime, it dreaded heresy and saw
every dissenter as a threat.

From the utter monotony of the day, the nights offered
little relief. When the lights went out the bugs became more
ravenous and the rats more active. There was no way to shut
out the prison noises. Men talked in the corridors, their conversation mostly obscene and profane. Sharp cries came from
the wing that held the sexual deviants. And day and night I
heard a cry of "Fight ! Fight! Fight!" as regular as the ticking
of a clock—the litany of some demented soldier, perhaps a
once healthy but sensitive young man whose mind had cracked
under military pressures and like a broken phonograph record
continued to repeat the same note. Were the thousands of
other inmates conscious of any more purpose in their lives?

At last the morning light, like a gray mist, filtered through
the barred windows. Bugs disappeared into crevices; where
the rats hid by day I did not know. There was a clang of bells,
and the officer of the day made his rounds. The chains of the
handcuffs rasped against the bars as they were applied to our

wrists, and another day of standing in shackles began.

My thoughts, like shuttles on a loom, began to weave images. I could hear my father's steady tread crunching the cinders along the West Shore Railroad tracks as he carried me on his shoulder from Canajoharie to Fort Plain. The acrid smell of soft coal smoke and the oil and steam of a locomotive were in my nostrils again. I was counting the clicks of a freight train's wheels as it rumbled past the station where we had waited for daybreak. Then I was walking behind my uncle as he cultivated his cornfield. It was the time when after unhitching the horses to go to dinner he tossed me on Daisy's back, slapped her rump, and shouted, "Hang on, boy!" as she galloped to the barn with me desperately clutching the ball-knobbed hames. Uncle arrived on Kit shortly after I had slid off, pretty well shaken up. He was laughing, and said, "Boy, your shirttails were sticking straight out in the wind!" He always called me boy, as did Grandfather Moore.

Now, half dozing on my manacled arms, I heard the voice of Arthur Dunham, a religious objector who had shared our tent at Fort Riley during my hunger strike, asking, "If you don't believe in God, what sustains you?" and I answered him again, "My own sense of moral responsibility. To accept an authority outside oneself is to deny oneself the right to make an ultimate decision. Understanding that and the consequences likely to follow is to know freedom in the deepest sense."

Freedom! Can there be any freedom under military authoritarianism? Emphatically, yes. Though brutally confined, I can still fight for the ideals in which I believe.

Where is God? He hasn't prevented war or war's atrocities. God as usually conceived is beyond my comprehension, but I can understand and agree with the teachings of such prophets as Isaiah, Amos, Jeremiah, and Jesus, as well as other great moral teachers. How can the organized churches, except for a few minority sects like the Quakers, Mennonites, and Hutterites, always support one or another warring nation?

A shuffling of feet broke the thread of my thoughts as prisoners returned exhausted from their work and flopped onto
their bunks in the corridor outside my cell.

During my second two weeks in solitary, the guard told
the prisoner who swept the corridor to sweep toward the cells,
so that we were forced to breathe the dust. I developed a
severe cold and was taken to the prison hospital. While waiting there for laboratory tests I saw Evan Thomas, looking pale,
weary, and thinner than ever. When I rushed forward to greet
him the guard threatened to beat me with his club, but we
managed to shake hands before I was pushed into a corner.
Evan had been in one of the dark, solid-doored cells ever since
his protest on behalf of the Molikans. Like me, he was now in
the hospital for laboratory tests.

A sample of sputum was taken and I went back to the hole.
A few days later, coughing badly, I was again brought to the
hospital, where a technician told me the test for TB was pos-
itive. My weight was 90 pounds, down from 150 when I left
the hospital at Fort Riley. I was given some cough syrup and
an extra army blanket.

One day I was taken out of my cell and escorted to the
visiting room. Someone had come to see me! It turned out to
be my old friend Mary Raymond, from Rochester. Now a
widow, she was on her way to California, accompanied by a
young officer in an immaculate uniform, who looked me over
with amazed scorn. Mary was shocked to tears by my appearance. We hardly spoke the same language now, and the interview gave neither of us much satisfaction. That was the last
time we saw each other.

We received no mail in our cells, but on one of my visits
to the prison office to repeat my refusal to work, followed by
a return to the hole for another two weeks, I was handed a
letter. On the impressive stationery of the Carnegie Hero Fund
Commission, it referred to my rescue of May Hanney "from
death by drowning in Long Island Sound, at South Norwalk,
Connecticut." Mr. F. M. Wilmot, manager of the fund, said

he had much pleasure in informing me "that in recognition of your heroism on that occasion the commission has awarded you a bronze medal and the sum of five hundred dollars for a worthy purpose to be approved by the Executive Committee."

Mr. Wilmot, who had sent the letter in care of my sister Leila, obviously in ignorance of my situation, asked me to advise him whether I wished to accept the awards. I saw an opportunity to help my family in their struggle on the farm, so I replied affirmatively suggesting this "worthy purpose" for the five hundred dollar award.

Late in May 1919, after being prodded by Leila, Mr. Wilmot replied, vetoing my idea as not in accordance with the Carnegie Fund's guidelines. I don't know when he discovered that his commission had honored a conscientious objector in prison for defying the government, but the incongruity was noted by various newspapers, one picking it up from another, in garbled versions, across the country. Later, when sympathetic articles about the COs began to appear in a few magazines, my Carnegie award was repeatedly mentioned as proof that we were not, after all, cowards.

On my thirty-first day in solitary, the absolutists' endurance was rewarded. The guards removed our manacles and opened the cell doors in preparation for a visit from Colonel Rice, who read us a telegram he had received from Secretary of War Baker. It stated:

Fastening of prisoners to the bars of cells will no more be used as a mode of punishment. Willful or stubborn prisoners of the usual military type who would not submit to the work requirements of the disciplinary Barracks, instead of being allowed to lie in bunks while others work, have been compelled to choose between working and standing in discomfort during working hours.

Under usual conditions this has been more a threat than an actuality, and as such has been effective. But during recent months with the influx of political prisoners, extremity of attitude on the part of this new type of prisoner has at times led to extremity of discipline as provided by military regulations.

These clearly were not formulated with the political type of prisoner in mind, and their effectiveness has been questionable. Men have returned for repeated experiences of the severest form of discipline. The most extreme of these is now discarded and the order is comprehensive. It applies not merely to political prisoners but to those of every kind.

Colonel Rice remarked that, before our arrival, three days in solitary was the longest on record. Incidentally, this was the first time I heard the conscientious objectors called political prisoners.

After two more weeks locked in the solitary cells, we were given the freedom of the cell wing. A quantity of newspapers were provided, and the first thing we did was to make torches of them, which when held against walls and ceilings brought down such a rain of bedbugs that we slid around in their crunched remains on the floor. I shall never forget the smell of these vermin.

Next we were transferred out of the prison to the post guardhouse, and later to barracks inside a stockade. There we could have books and writing materials. We were allowed to exercise in the open air, and the food was not obviously contaminated. My coughing stopped, and I never developed the threatened tuberculosis.

Major Adler, the army psychiatrist, visited us and argued that we had been ineffective in stopping the war. He said that we were intelligent enough to realize that we were a thorn in the side of the War Department and that if we would agree to accept noncombatant service we could be released in a matter of days. No one in our group of absolutists rose to his bait, but after repeated visits and closer acquaintance with some of the men he concluded that prison was not the place for us. However, his recommendation to Washington that we be unconditionally released only resulted in his own discharge.

Meanwhile, many of the religious objectors, particularly those who had worked in prison, were released shortly after

Christmas. Evan Thomas also was freed, on the technicality that he had been court-martialed for disobeying an order (to eat, while on his hunger strike) that was not a proper military order. Evan felt unhappy about leaving the rest of us in prison, but now he could join his brother Norman in working for the freedom of all the COs. He immediately wrote an exposé: "Disciplinary Barracks: The Experience of a Military Prisoner at Fort Leavenworth," which appeared in *The Survey* magazine February 1, 1919. It told of his own experience, of the conditions and methods of the prison, the cruelties, the absurdities, the graft and misappropriation of goods produced by prison labor. It included the story of the Molokans, the bit about my Carnegie medal, and the punishment of Clark Getts, who when he was finally caught smuggling messages out was first manacled in the hole for two weeks and then, because he was "too cheerful" for the circumstances, was put in a prison hospital ward with the insane and feebleminded.

Others, especially Erling Lunde's father, were busy on our behalf. Theodore Lunde mounted a campaign of complaints to Washington, and through his efforts and those of the National Civil Liberties Bureau, reports were read into the *Congressional Record* by Representatives Charles H. Dillon in January and William E. Mason in March, detailing with names and dates the sufferings of the COs at Funston, Leavenworth, and elsewhere, and bringing to light also some atrocious injustices to ordinary soldiers. The material was shocking, and Lunde distributed it as widely as he could. But its effects, if any, were a long time in reaching us.

On Christmas Eve 1918, a near riot occurred in the prison mess hall. Eighteen hundred inmates threw food and tableware around, shouting and defying the orders of guards and officers, even of the commandant. A company of soldiers armed with rifles herded them back to their cell blocks after an hour of commotion in which no prisoner actually left his seat. Next day the COs in solitary, who had not even been on the scene, were lectured for causing unrest in the prison. We did have

among us Ben Salmon, who had worked in the commissary
and used his job to gather information that explained why the
men had cause to resent the prison food. Many of them worked
on the prison farms producing ample supplies of meat, poultry, dairy products, and vegetables. Under the designation
"surplus," much of this was being sold, to someone's benefit,
while the kitchen prepared what Roderick Seidenberg
described as "a steamed and slimy flow of garbage." For his
efforts, Ben Salmon had joined us in the hole.

But the prison was smoldering with greater complaints,
chief of which was the length and inequity of the sentences
the inmates were serving. Some men looked forward to twenty-
five years for infractions of army discipline that in peace time
would have cost them no more than a couple of years. There
were prisoners doing vastly different time for identical offenses.
Unexplained reductions of time in some cases left everyone
else dissatisfied. Smaller grievances, about the food and working conditions, the tyranny of the guards, censorship and delay
of mail, etc., were magnified by the overwhelming sense of
unfair and arbitrary punishment.

The crisis began in late January 1919 with a spontaneous
strike by one of the work crews. That night a warehouse on
the grounds was set afire. Next day, thanks to the fumbling
and indecision of the administration, the prisoners had time
to organize, and an almost complete strike of twenty-three
hundred prisoners took place, led by some of the working
COs. Carl Haessler, H. Austin Simmons, and Oral James were
three who served as spokesmen for the strikers. Committees
were formed in the several wings of the prison and a central
committee drew up demands. The COs kept warning against
any violence that would defeat their cause, for the administration had four thousand armed soldiers on the base to call on,
a thousand of them already waiting outside the prison gates.
They could make short and bloody work of the strikers.

But Colonel Rice did not want bloodshed. Realizing that
the men had just complaints, he received their representa-

tives, headed first by Simmons and at a second meeting by Haessler, and told them that he had already written to Washington asking for a reduction of all wartime sentences to a peacetime basis. Now he made a trip to Washington, and as a result many sentences were reduced and men were discharged, including some of the COs. The inmates were allowed to set up a permanent grievance committee, and other reforms were promised.

The following July, after most of the COs were gone, a tragic sequel took place: a "mutiny" which seemed to have been instigated by the authorities was put down brutally with the loss of six lives, and "iron rule" returned to Leavenworth with a vengeance.

We absolutists in our barracks heard about the January strike but could not participate: we were already strikers who had made our point. Time dragged along. On April 21, 1919, in a letter to my sisters, I wrote:

Despite my desire to come home and be with you all once more, I shall never come home on a "home parole" if one is offered. I go out of here *absolutely free* or not at all. I am not a low criminal that needs to be watched when I leave here. If I could take a home parole I would have worked here or even accepted the farm furlough. And if the government still refuses to come through on the issue we have raised then it can keep us, or at least me, and most of the fellows feel the same, until the expiration of our sentences.

My letter ended:

I am perfectly well, and feeling fine. Yesterday we were moved from the cantonment back to the Post Guard House where we were after we were taken out of solitary. Don't know where we are going from here. We may stay—it's hard to tell. We have become so used to changes that we are indifferent to the whole business. Don't worry.

This stoical state of mind was tested by an episode that occurred only two days later. My account of it, written on Red Cross stationery, is dated April 24, 1919:

Last evening a few of us in cell No. 4 were lying on each other's
bunks and conversing in low tones after lights were out. Others
were waiting their turn at the latrine before retiring. Most of the
twenty-six men who occupy this cell were already in bed. Garrison
prisoners above us were talking and singing.

Sometime between ten and eleven o'clock as near as I can judge,
the officer of the day, a captain, came in. All lights were turned on.
We continued our conversation as before. The sergeant of the guards
ordered every man to his own bunk. The order was obeyed. Without warning or provocation, the guards then played a stream of water
from a garden hose over all. Some men got up from their wet beds
and protested, only to become targets for the stream. They continued their protest. . . . The guards disappeared upstairs, saying, "All
right, you'll get a damn sight worse." . . . A few moments later a
regulation power hose comandeered by military firemen headed by
the OD was brought downstairs and into position. The OD ordered
the water to be turned on and was overheard to say, "Give them
plenty of it." They did. Everything was drenched in the deluge—
straw bed sacks, blankets, wearing apparel, and personal effects.

The force of the stream tumbled Myer Bernstein to the floor.
He became hysterical and screamed as the water still played upon
him. Struggling, he half rose from the floor and was knocked pros-
trate over an adjoining lower bunk occupied by Shotkin. His wild
screaming became choking sobs. We thought he had succumbed as
they subsided.

I managed to stay in my bunk with difficulty as I received a
sideswipe from the stream. The cell was flooded. The water in the
gallery outside was well up over the ankles of the boots worn by the
firemen. The water was turned off as Bernstein's cries had become
pitiful gurgling, horribly suggestive of unconsciousness.

When the attackers withdrew we found Bernstein still conscious
but completely unnerved. We were all shivering. . . . We assisted
him to a corner bunk which was but partially wet, where he and
others sat up for the rest of the night.

Some fatigue clothes . . . which had been wrapped in raincoats
were the only things to escape soaking. With these we managed to
cover ourselves and doubled up on two more bunks which had not
received the full force of the stream.

A double cordon of guards was stationed around the cell, for no apparent reason except to maintain secrecy. But in such situations there always seems to be at least one person who has no stomach for sadism, even if he doesn't exactly sympathize with the motives of the victim. A guard walking slowly by where I stood inside the bars whispered out of the side of his mouth, "If you want to get word out, slip me a note." I managed to find a fairly dry leaf in a memo pad that had been protected by a pillow. I scribbled a note to the National Civil Liberties Bureau and dropped it where the guard could pick it up.

The next morning Bernstein had developed a severe cold and could barely speak. A medical officer who came in daily gave him some aspirin tablets. Warm clothing was proffered by our comrades in the next cell—twenty-six political conscientious objectors also—but in vain; the sergeant on duty said he had orders to allow nothing in to us. I wrote:

By night . . . our underwear and socks had partially dried. They were still damp but we put them on and bunked together as we did last night. Some of the men had removed their soaking mattresses and slept on springs covered with damp blankets.

In a few days there was a preliminary inquiry by local prison officials and the preparation of a cover-up story. When investigators came from Washington they were told that the action taken was purely disciplinary, because we had been talking and using profanity after lights were out. In the meantime, heat was restored, most of our things were dried out (with the exception of some ruined books), and we were taken back to the prison, segregated in the sixth-wing basement. We had the wing to ourselves and were not confined in cells. I wrote to Leila on May 11:

This is a great improvement over the guardhouse. There is plenty of room, fresh air, and adequate toilet facilities. Also vermin—bedbugs everywhere. . . . The religious objectors are still (in the barracks) and we are glad of that. At least they can exercise in the open

until they also are dumped back in the prison. No one ever knows
what is going to happen next.

Evan wrote that he had received my letter just in time to read
it at a dinner given to Villard of *The Nation*, who has just returned
from Europe. There were about 150 people present, representing
all shades of opinion from Jacob Schiff to Scott Nearing.

How did my letter to you ever get to *The World Tomorrow?*
Did you give it to Evan? It really was not good enough for publication.

Norman wrote me asking me to review Major Kellogg's book
The Conscientious Objector. I have been working on it for the past
few days. If it is acceptable it will probably appear in the next issue
of *The World Tomorrow*. Roderick wrote one some time ago for *The
Nation*. Do you get *The Liberator?* If not, ask Fiffi to send it to
you. . . .

Received a long letter from her the other day, also a book, *Abraham Lincoln*, by Rose Strunsky. . . . Just finished *Penguin Island*,
by Anatole France and *Candide* by Voltaire. They are both very
remarkable . . . and most timely so far as subject matter is concerned.

. . . I am terribly sorry grandmother is ill. I had no idea her
condition was so serious. I shall drop her a line tomorrow. But should
you see her before my letter arrives, tell her that she has been in
my thoughts many, many times: that I am thinking of her now and
hoping that she will be well again real soon. . . . One never stops
to think that old people are growing older, because we don't want
them to leave us. . . . Sometimes I grow frantic with the thought
that mother or dad—well, I can't write about that. I just hope and
hope and hope that I will find them still young when I return.

Among the nearly one hundred COs in the sixth-wing
basement, with diverse backgrounds from all walks of life and
many parts of the country, the creative drive of youth could
express itself only in writing, talking, and dreaming great
dreams for a future life of freedom. Roderick Seidenberg has
described how one group fought off "mental apathy":

Always we talked of the future—what we hoped to see, to experience, to feel; what we would eat, where we would go, what we

would do. Caught by the enthusiasm of Jacob Wortsman, we planned an elaborate trip in a motor boat around the Panama Canal up along the wild wooded shore of Canada to Alaska. We managed to get some chalk, and on the cement floor of the corridor we drew in full size the plans of our boat, its cabin, its engine, its decks, fore and aft, the scullery, the berths, in every detail. We were pleasantly mad.*

*Roderick Seidenberg. "I Refuse to Serve," *The American Mercury* (January 1932).

19

ONE MORNING IN JUNE 1919, most of the remaining 150 or so
COs in Leavenworth were told to pack our belongings for a
move. With some misgivings and much speculation, we quickly
gathered our few possessions and were herded toward prison
gates. We left Leavenworth in a long column, flanked by
guards, headed for the railroad station. Two days later, still
handcuffed in pairs, we arrived at Fort Douglas, at the edge
of the Wasatch Mountains overlooking Salt Lake City.

The military fort looked down upon ten acres of long wooden
barracks encircled by two seven-foot barbed-wire fences,
twenty feet apart and electrically charged. Guards patrolled
between the fences. At each corner was a tower where more
guards sat with machine guns. A grassy strip between the inside
fence and the barracks was designated a "deadline"; anyone
crossing it might be shot without challenge. This was the
internment camp for Germans and other enemy aliens. One
side of it had been cut off with another double fence and was
waiting to receive the COs in its six barracks, our new place
of captivity.

One of the buildings was equipped as a kitchen and mess
hall. But before we had anything to eat, except the hardtack
that had sustained us during the railroad trip, the commandant, with the usual retinue of captains, lieutenants, and cor-
porals, came to announce that we were all to work on roads.
We replied, courteously, but with clearness equal to his, that
we had no intention of doing anything under military orders.
We were immediately sentenced to two weeks on bread and
water, a boring repetition of the stupidity at Leavenworth.

We accepted it as nothing new and adapted to the change

in our surroundings. After all, Leavenworth was behind us. Here were mountains and green hills and good air. We could even see a bit of Great Salt Lake in the distance beyond the city. We could read and talk freely among ourselves. We could even play softball and pitch horseshoes.

How the German internees learned about our plight we never knew. Prison grapevines are necessarily a mystery. But they could see us and thought we were the palest and sickest-looking lot of men they had ever beheld. Risking their lives and sacrificing their own food, they threw cans of vegetables over the two high fences and shoved pans of baked beans on a board under them. First they threw over a note, wrapped around a stone, telling us their plan; so after dark some of us were waiting by the fence. It was a moonless night; all lights were out except those that shone along the fences from the corner towers. With everyone supposedly asleep, the guard took longer to make his rounds, stopping to chat with his counterpart at each corner.* The Germans had timed his movements, had gathered the food behind a huge cottonwood tree on their side of the fence, and as soon as he disappeared around a corner their barrage started. We pried some boards loose inside our barracks and stored our treasure between the studs.

Thus it was that after the first week on bread and water we were doing so well as to arouse suspicion, and some officers and guards suddenly appeared to make a search. They found nothing and left very much perplexed. After the second week we were able to negotiate an agreement with the army whereby we would order from the commissary and do our own cooking, provided no one would enter our compound without our permission. I was chosen by the group to make this arrangement and to organize the cooking and cleaning crews.

Things began to come through from our families: books,

---

*Julius Eichel's account of this episode says that the sentry was sympathetic and connived with the internees in their effort to feed us.

magazines, writing materials, games, and some money, with
which we bought baseballs and bats. We started to organize
all sorts of athletics. The days were filled with activity: walking, talking, reading, writing, playing games, and in the evenings staging debates on political topics.

We even got out one issue of a magazine, *Barbed Wire
Entanglements*, twenty-seven typewritten pages of prose and
poetry with a strong Socialist slant. The hand-tinted cover
drawing by Julius Greenberg showed a smiling ghostly Lenin
looking down over the Wasatch Mountains at our fenced-in
barracks and a marble monument inscribed with the names of
seventeen COs who had died in confinement.

Colonel Graham was the chief officer in charge of the Germans' compound and ours. With the exception of General Bell
at Camp Upton, he was the most gentlemanly and mild-man-
nered officer I had met. He seemed old enough to have been
retired, and I had a feeling during my conversations with him
that he was pretty bored with his job.

On one occasion he told me that they had never had a real
German spy interned there. The internees were IWWs,
Socialists, and small shopkeepers, mostly from the West Coast.
Some German sailors had been in the compound but had long
ago been repatriated. Under the wartime law, anyone could
be interned; all that was needed was a complaint and a presidential warrant. In this way many an innocent delicatessen
owner was conveniently removed and his business dissolved
or acquired by a competitor in the guise of a patriot. The
Wobblies and Socialists were mostly loggers from the North-
west who had struck for higher wages and were dealt with by
internment. From a maximum of 800, the camp still held about
195 men, who had been there two years or more without any
recourse to law or clemency.

I don't recall how they did it, but after a while some of the
internees found a way to get from their side to ours. We spent
interesting evenings listening to their stories. One man,
Everson, had been an officer in the British consulate in Shan-

tung. He gave me photographs of himself and his Chinese soldiers there and also some showing revolutionary followers of Sun Yat-sen enduring the "death of a thousand cuts" at the hands of the Manchu government.

Everson and others said that twenty of the internees had died at Fort Douglas and were buried nearby and their friends had not been allowed to mark the graves with stones. Twenty-four had been shipped East to insane asylums. Three had attempted suicide. There had been class warfare between the Wobblies and Socialists, with most other internees on their side, and a small group they called the Aristocrats, who were favored by the military authorities and acted as stool pigeons, earning all sorts of privileges. Life for most inmates had been two years of unmerited punishments, including starvation diet and solitary imprisonment, abuse and threats from the guards. Finally, a drunken guard fired three times with his shotgun into a group of men, wounding seven.

One young fellow, about twenty years old, lay in the base hospital for over six months, suffering the tortures of hell, for his whole leg was . . . a ground up mass of flesh and bone. He has now left for Germany without one cent to his name, barely able to hobble on crutches, with still running sores on his leg. . . . The punishment of the guard was a congratulation by the officer of the day and a promotion to corporal. *The Salt Lake Tribune* [reported] "A Wholesale Breakout Averted."*

I became friendly with Karl Pasche, a one-armed former soldier, who told me why he was interned. He had been in the Philippines during the Spanish-American War and later settled there, farming and prospecting for gold. He found what he thought was a rich deposit of gold in a stream in Mindanao. When he tried to get it assayed he was asked where it came from, but he refused to reveal the location. He believed that this was the reason for his immediate shipment to the United

---

* From page 11 of a carbon copy of a single-spaced typewritten report and protest by an anonymous internee, one of several that were given to me in hopes of reaching sympathetic readers outside.

States to be interned on the technicality of his German birth. When I met him he was trying to find out from Washington whether his farm in Mindanao had been confiscated and was petitioning for the proceeds of its annual crop of twelve thousand coconuts and a quantity of hemp. He received only a curt reply that no funds were available for such reimbursement.

One day our camp was honored by a visit from General Pershing, commander of the U.S. forces in World War I. He came to our compound with the fort commandant and other officers and entered the barracks that we used as a library. Many of us were reading or lying on cots, and no one moved when the post officer called "Attention!"

I was near the entrance and heard Pershing say to the commandant, "Don't these men stand at attention?"

The reply was, "If they did, they would have to be held up."

The general walked over to a table on which lay an assortment of magazines such as *The Nation, The New Republic,* Lydia Pankhurst's *Dreadnaught, The Survey,* and *The Liberator.* Picking one up and turning to the commandant, he exclaimed, "Do you mean to say that these men are permitted to read such stuff?"

The commandant answered, "You ought to see what they *write!*"

Pershing stamped out of the building, saying, "These men are dirt beneath my feet!"

It is understandable that his feelings were hurt. This was probably as great an affront to his ego as the general had ever experienced. We did not set out to hurt him, but we were not soldiers and never had stood at attention and would not make an exception for Pershing. Had he seen fit to speak to any of us, he would have received courteous attention.

When he visited the interned Germans in their section of the compound, the general recognized Paschke, standing under a cottonwood tree, as one who had saved the Pershing family during a fire at their home in Texas. Paschke was released shortly afterward, no doubt through his good offices. Before leaving, Paschke gave me a handdrawn map of the spot in Mindanao where he was certain a fortune in gold could be found. I don't know whether he himself ever got back there to look for it.

On Christmas Eve 1919, one of the Germans, a former merchant, hanged himself with a bedsheet. The war had been over for more than a year, yet these harmless men were still prisoners without trial or hearing. They were freed early in 1920 after spending nearly three years behind barbed wire.

One of the buildings in the Germans' compound had been fitted up by the YMCA as a theater, and we got permission to dismantle it and put it up on our side of the fence so that we could put on some plays. Mrs. Allen, the local representative of the National Civil Liberties Bureau and wife of a Salt Lake City industrialist, gave us some women's clothing. The garments had belonged to her daughter, who years later became the first woman judge in America. Squeezed into them I played the female part in *A Freudian Comedy*, by Susan Glaspell and George Cram Cook.

We staged this play a second time when a group of psychologists came from Washington to determine what effect prison had had on the conscientious objectors. Their visit was interpreted differently in an article in the *Salt Lake Tribune*, quoting Lieutenant Colonel R. C. Loving of the fort:

The government is inclined to believe that a large number of these men who refused to go to the aid of their country when any reasonable person could see that their actions absolutely ruined all prospects for their future, are not mentally sound.

These men subjected themselves to prison terms and a life-long disgrace for no logical reason whatever. The interned Germans were here because they were true to their country, and their confinement is without a stigma. But these cowardly individuals who disgrace the name by calling themselves Americans have no excuse, and it is up to them to prove their sanity before they are set free.

This reasoning reminded us of the comment made by Max Eastman, editor of the old *Liberator* magazine, when he heard that of the many conscientious objectors in Germany, thirty had been shot and the rest released as "harmlessly insane." It followed, he said, that the great majority who believed in war were "harmfully sane."

Whatever their mission was, the psychologists attended our performance and stayed to chat over cake and coffee, but we never did learn the result of their observations.

Our improvised theater also produced a melodrama, *The Second-Story Man*, and Shaw's antiwar satire, *Augustus Does His Bit*. Shaw was unpopular in England at the time because of his pacifism, and we heard that he had remarked that the only place his plays were being produced was an American prison camp.

One of the COs again had to face a court martial that first summer at Fort Douglas. Julius Greenberg, a soft-spoken graduate of the School of Architecture at Columbia, was charged with having "vilified and maligned" the name of President Wilson. His accuser was a major who used to come in and argue with us daily before we won the right to be undisturbed in our compound. A local lawyer, Parley P. Christianson, was retained by Greenberg's father to defend him. Christianson came to our barracks many times to see Greenberg about the trial, but also he would eat with us and fraternize; he spoke our language and was about to run for president on the Farmer-Labor party ticket. He and Ben Salmon, a CO lawyer from Denver, had met in the single-tax movement. Greenberg's trial ended with a unanimous not guilty verdict.

Waves of influenza were still sweeping over the country, and in the winter the Utah State Board of Health appealed for volunteers to help the sick with nursing and household work. Forty-three of the COs at Fort Douglas signed a letter to the board of health and to Secretary of War Baker stating our desire to volunteer, but there was no response.

On May Day, someone took a cap with a red lining, turned

it inside out, and displayed it on a broomstick atop one of the barracks. Officers at headquarters soon spotted this Socialist emblem and appeared at our gates asking for me. They demanded to know who had hoisted the red flag. I tried to explain that it was just a prank, but I would not reveal the name of the man responsible. Shortly, one of the more friendly sergeants came to the gate saying that he was sorry, but he had orders to put me in the guardhouse. I went there with him and presently was visited by Sergeant Brunt of the Quartermaster Corps, whom I knew slightly, and another sergeant called Big Jim. While Jim stood in the doorway with gun and bayonet, Brunt ordered me to clean out one of the cells. I told him I hoped he would not take it personally, but if I was to occupy a cell Uncle Sam would have to clean it. At that he pushed me into the cell, and holding me with his left hand aimed a crushing blow with his right. I ducked and received his fist on my forehead. Brunt then grabbed the wooden seat from the toilet pail and beat me with it. I remember screaming before I fell to the floor unconsicous. My cries were heard in our compound, and everyone knew I had been assaulted.

The next day I was returned to the compound with a very black eye and bruises on my head, arms, and chest. Brunt had broken three fingers of his right hand on my head. When I saw him with his arm in a sling, I greeted him in a friendly way and told him I was sorry he had hurt his hand. An investigation was held, Brunt was brought up on charges, and I was called to testify against him. I refused to make a complaint but said that if he was acting on orders he was merely doing his duty as a soldier and the one to be reprimanded was whoever gave the order. After the episode Brunt became very friendly and told me to let him know if I ever wanted anything from the Quartermaster Corps; he would see that I got it.

The Catholic chaplain at the post told me that in a talk to the Knights of Columbus in Salt Lake City he had referred to my attitude toward Brunt as one of the finest examples he had known of "turning the other cheek." For this tribute to a conscientious objector he was expelled from the Knights.

We had not tasted fresh vegetables in a long time, so in the spring of 1920 I asked Colonel Graham if we could make a garden in the "deadline" space along the barbed wire. an area several hundred feet long by ten feet wide. He seemed delighted with the idea and provided us with pipe for irrigation and several loads of manure. Some of us, including Henry Schmeider who had been a graduate student in biology at the University of Pennsylvania, Rexford Powell, and myself, spaded the whole area and planted vegetable and melon seeds sent to us by friends outside. The soil was surprisingly fertile, and by midsummer we were supplying our mess with plenty of fresh vegetables. We also planted flowers around the barracks. That summer many of the post officers asked and received our permission to come in the compound and look at our garden. By that time everyone on the post was more or less friendly to us.

We had a magpie, a native bird out there, which Henry Schmeider had found with an injured wing and nursed back to health. When Maggie could fly again she still stayed in the compound and lived on the kitchen scraps Henry and I fed her. She would follow us around, flying from rooftops to ride on our shoulders. At night her place was on the frame of our bunks, from which she would talk and tweak our toes through the blankets to arouse us at daybreak. We and others began to miss small objects such as pencils. Everyone blamed Maggie, and the blame was well deserved; but all losses could be retrieved from her cache, an old hat which Henry had hidden under the barracks.

A few of the men resented Maggie's antics and would throw stones and threaten her so finally, fearing for her life, we gave her to one of the officers at the post, advising him to confine her for a while. A couple of weeks later, when we were lined up at bugle call for the morning count, we heard Maggie's loud squawks in the sky as she came sailing in and lighted on a post, her accustomed place at the end of the lineup. She avoided capture for a while, watching us from the top of the barracks, but finally came to Henry's shoulder. When she was returned to the officer she fought and screeched, leaving us with a sense of disloyalty to an affectionate friend.

Our numbers at Fort Douglas were dwindling. All military sentences had been so reduced that some COs sentenced to fifty or twenty-five years were now being freed. We were an embarrassment, although a minor one, to the War Department, as it felt the pressure of the National Civil Liberties Union and tireless advocates of our cause such as Theodore Lunde and Norman Thomas. Magazines were publishing exposés of our treatment, and a few newspapers wondered editorially why we were still confined. Some unbelievably sentimental poems about our "martyrdom" got into print.

My mother's friend Mrs. Failing, she who had lost a son in France, got her congressman, William C. Hill, to write a long plea on my behalf to Secretary Baker, citing my Carnegie award and my work in the hospital at Fort Riley.* The mother of a soldier I had nursed there, who had written to my mother in gratitude, was enlisted in the effort.

Evan's mother wrote supportively to mine. I still have a letter she sent to me, March 1, 1920, worrying about my health and sending five dollars for me to buy eggs and milk, with a warning not to let my mother know of her concern.

In July the commandant of the post came to the compound and read us a message from Secretary Baker, stating that any of the COs who would agree to accept the commandant's orders would be discharged in two weeks. He added, "Now you men know you are a nuisance to the War Department, and if you agree to accept my orders I'll agree not to give you any." Thus the issue of accepting the status of soldier became a mere technicality. About twenty men agreed and were transferred to a barracks outside our compound until their discharge two weeks later. There were only thirty-six of us left in the compound.

*October 30, 1919, more than a year before I was released.

Ben Salmon, a Catholic and a lawyer who objected to war on both religious and political grounds, began a hunger strike. He was forcibly fed and finally transferred to a hospital for the insane, where the doctors found him rational. He maintained his hunger strike until he was released in November, three months after beginning it.

Later in the summer Colonel Graham sent for me and said, "I know that confinement is having an effect on you men, and I would like to do something about it. If you will form groups of ten or twelve men at a time, we will open the gate and you can roam the mountains. All I require is that a guard accompany the group so long as you are in the reservation and that you pick him up on your return." Colonel Graham, like General Bell, had a quality of human understanding that army life had not extinguished.

I told him I would take his proposal to the COs and report back to him. A meeting was held and agreement reached, and the next morning a small group of us set out on an all-day hike. We climbed around like goats in the Wasatch Mountains and followed the trail the Mormons had made on their trek to the Great Salt Lake. Near sunset, we picked up the guard and returned to our barracks. It was a joyful foretaste of freedom, and I felt deeply grateful to the colonel for his thoughtfulness. These walks continued whenever weather permitted, and that was nearly every day.

We anticipated a luscious feast when the melons began to ripen in our garden. But, as melons do, only two or three ripened at first. To share them with everyone at mess seemed impossible, so Henry and I gave one to an officer who had been helpful in supplying manure for the garden and finished off another with a couple of friends. This caused a revolution in the compound. The men held a meeting and decided that we had no right to give away or eat the melons without consulting the whole group. This may have been right. Anyway, I lost my job as head of kitchen operations and was replaced by one of the IWWs.

Releases continued, and finally Henry Schmeider and I were the only ones left in the compound. Officers at the fort said to us, "Why don't you men just disappear? We're waiting to go home and you are keeping us here."

At last, on the day before Thanksgiving 1920, we were officially released. A group of officers escorted us to Salt Lake City and treated us to dinner, assuring us as we ate together that in the next war they too would be conscientious objectors.

Along with my dishonorable discharge I received from the government a train ticket to New York City. But I insisted that transportation be furnished for me to Cherry Valley, and this was done. I had decided to spend the next year with my parents, who like most families of COs had suffered much, both from worry about my welfare and from expressions of scorn and hostility in their community.

20

IT WAS GOOD to be back on the home farm, feeling the love of a devoted family. But my world could never be the same as before. With the holidays approaching, my mother made plans for an old-fashioned Christmas dinner, inviting all the relatives. Aunts and uncles and cousins came, and about twenty sat around the table, but there was no festive spirit at the sumptuous meal which my mother and sister had spent hours preparing. Soon after the table was cleared the crowd left, their family duty done. I felt isolated and inhibited by the lack of any sympathy or even curiosity about what I had been through. Later, I realized that they too felt embarrassed: I had become something of a stranger, difficult to understand. This marked the end of the family reunions, which had been traditional on the Cherry Valley farm as far back as I could recall.

The relatives who did not understand me were no different from the majority of my fellow countrymen. In the village of Cherry Valley, old acquaintances would cross the street rather than confront me. When I took the milk up to the creamery each morning, the men who received and emptied the cans made a sport of throwing them back into or over the wagon with a crash that made the horses bolt. I went to the manager of the creamery and he had the harassment stopped, but there was little friendliness for me in the town where I had spent happy childhood years.

Yet the summer of hard physical labor on the farm was a pleasant one. I was exerting every effort to make the year productive, since I had disposed of all my assets before going to Camp Upton. Besides helping my father with his hay crop and small dairy, I made large plantings of buckwheat, a cash crop that would grow on newly plowed land. Evan Thomas came for a visit that summer and was very helpful with the work. He had already come to see my parents while I was still a prisoner, and they were very fond of him.

In August before the buckwheat harvest I went on a trip with my Johnstown cousin Harry Moore and his wife Edith. We toured the Adirondacks in a homemade camper and fished from Indian Lake to Alexandria Bay on the Saint Lawrence. I came home refreshed, eager to return to New York City and start a new career.

The buckwheat brought me five hundred dollars to take to the city, a good deal more than I had on my first arrival there in 1903, or again after the crash of the Whirlwind Five and Ten Cent Store. It is quite probable that I could have returned to the New York Telephone Company. Major Adler, the army psychiatrist, had told me that the company had written to the government while I was in Leavenworth testifying to my sincerity and praising my efficiency. To his surprise, I had shown no desire to see the letter. I had burned my bridges and wanted to start all over again. But where, and at what?

I answered an ad for salesmen and landed a job selling Better Brushes, in competition with the well-known Fuller Brushes. Evan Thomas, now living with his brother Norman, joined me in going from house to house in residential sections of Manhattan taking orders, which we sent in to the company. Violet Thomas, Norman's wife, volunteered to drive her car and help us deliver the brushes when they arrived. But what a disillusioning experience! Many of our customers were not at home, and more had forgotten about their commitment and couldn't or wouldn't pay for the brushes.

Next we tried selling Eureka Vacuum Cleaners from house to house, on commission. This was more successful, but Evan decided that salesmanship was not for him. He wanted to study medicine and had the prospect of a scholarship at a medical school in Dublin. I too had been attracted to medicine as a career ever since my work with Captain Henry in the flu epidemic, but I had no money for medical school.

By this time I too was living in the Thomas household. There, one day in October 1921, an agent of the Carnegie Hero Fund Commission called on me to deliver the medal that had been so long in coming. Neither the Thomases nor I liked Mr. McMurtry's patronizing manner as he expressed the hope that I would in future be a good citizen and a credit to the Carnegie Fund. I ended up telling him that I didn't want the medal and would not accept it. Someone from the commission finally made a trip to Cherry Valley to deliver it to my mother. According to my parents, this representative hinted to them that the five hundred-dollar award might be indefinitely increased if the recipient needed more help to carry out an approved purpose.

Encouraged by this possibility, I allowed myself to dream of going to medical school abroad with Evan. For several months I corresponded with Mr. Wilmot, the manager, and tried to pin him down about the availability of the award, while he at great length pointed out the difficulties facing me in my attempt to study medicine.

Meanwhile I had been promoted by the Eureka Company to a salaried job, and I began to tire of this endless dialogue about a hypothetical five hundred dollars. The commission sent another agent to see me, but I was out of town. In July 1922, Mr. Wilmot wrote a final letter full of personal questions, ending, "Will you not favor me with a prompt and full reply." Lacking his advantage of secretarial help, I never got around to doing so.

I was doing well with the Eureka Company, handling their sales to dealers. At the company's annual convention in Detroit, the vice-president, himself a dynamic salesman, urged me to take over the management of the New England district. He claimed it would earn me twenty-five thousand dollars a year.

In accepting this position I turned down one offered by the Central Hudson Gas and Electric Company to manage their appliance department at a salary of fifteen thousand dollars. Money was necessarily my prime consideration at the time. However, I arrived in Boston to find that Eureka had no organization there, and the prospect of earning the promised income was years away. I concluded that in the selling field one was forever chasing the pot of gold at the end of the rainbow.

Then I did what I should have done at first: I looked for work that utilized the studies I had pursued and the training and experience I had acquired in my years with the telephone company. The Johns Manville Company took me on and assigned me to make an appraisal of their organization and facilities in New England. While doing this I received a telegram from Edward L. Mayer, president of the company that bore his name, asking me to meet him in New York for lunch the next weekend.

I knew Edward Mayer well. He was a leading manufacturer of high-priced women's wear and was the cousin and employer of Fiffi Wurtzweiler, the talented young designer who had tripped over my feet on the Hoboken Ferry back in prewar days. I had been his guest, with Fiffi, at Sunday dinners in his Mt. Vernon home.

Lunching with Eddie Mayer at the Vanderbilt, I learned that he was building a new factory in a residential section of Woodside, in Queens. Originally the proprietor of a one-room sewing shop, he now employed 350 people and enjoyed a reputation for the elegance and style of the dresses and ensembles he produced. During the war, with French competition crippled, he had made so much money that now he was able to build a monument to himself. As he explained to the zoning authorities, this would in no way resemble a factory. Designed by Feldheimer and Wagners, architects of the Grand Central Station and other New York landmarks, it would be a three-story concrete and stucco building with leaded glass windows, revolving doors in the front entrance, and its own cafeteria for employees. The neighboring residents would have reason to be proud of it. I suspect that a considerable amount of money added weight to his assurances; anyway, the needed permit had been obtained and the building was nearly finished. Now, Eddie wanted me on his staff to take charge of it.

I completed the Johns Manville job and then, in 1926, joined the Edward L. Mayer Company with the title of personnel manager and assistant to the president. I functioned as an industrial engineer, designing the layout of equipment in the new plant, checking the construction, and approving bills. I was responsible for the maintenance of the building and machines, hiring new employees, and ordering supplies. When Eddie decided that he needed to use one-of-a-kind prints in his creations, I set up a silkscreen department to produce them.

It was an exacting business making garments that often bore thousand-dollar price tags. Our cheapest line went to Jay Thorpe at $59.50 wholesale. We also sold through Saks, Russeks, Bergdorf-Goodman, B. Altman, and other stores and created exclusive designs for individuals who could afford to pay up to $3,400 for an ensemble.

One of these special customers was the movie actress Betty Compton; her bills were sent to her admirer Jimmy Walker. However, we had difficulty collecting from the playboy mayor. When we persisted, he invited Eddie and me to have supper with him at the Central Park Casino, a rendezvous of political and society figures. With him was one of his henchmen, accompanied by Mrs. Whitehead, wife of the president of Coca-Cola. The former was a rather unsavory character, but Jimmy shone with the lighthearted charm and friendliness that had lubricated his Tammany career. After the meal, Eddie Mayer courteously asked Mrs. Whitehead to dance. When they returned to the table her escort gave her a jealous tongue-lashing that embarrassed us all. The party broke up, and at the last minute Walker's companion thrust into my hand the check that had been promised us. But the check bounced, and I had to take it to the mayor's office and hint at the possibility of a law suit. Genial as ever, he replaced it with another that proved to be negotiable.

The Mayer Company maintained a showroom at 1 East Thirty-Third Street. Its designers were sent twice a year to Paris to attend the shows that set fashion trends. Eddie ruled his business as a benevolent despot; his will was law and his artistic temperament could make stormy scenes when he was frustrated. But he gave me free rein to run the Woodside building, and his generosity to his workers ensured their devotion. Only once did we have any labor trouble, and that was not with our employees but with thugs sent by the ILGWU in an unsuccessful attempt to organize our people.

During the years of working for Eddie Meyer I was also living in his Mount Vernon home. The family consisted of his aged mother, two spinster sisters, and a Viennese cook whose dinners, and especially her strudels, were delicious beyond description. On Sundays she outdid herself when a larger company gathered around the table, usually including Fiffi and her brother and Eddie's brother Paul with his family.

I kept in touch with my own family, and as the national economy appeared more precarious during the 1920s, the farm in Cherry Valley always was my symbol of security. As soon as I was well established with the Mayer Company I paid off the mortgage on the farm. My father then sold his livestock, deeded the property to me, and retired. Thereafter I saw to it that he and my mother could spend the winters in Florida with my sister Leila and her husband John Sawyer. In the spring the four of them would return to Cherry Valley for a leisurely summer on the farm.

My salary of one hundred dollars a week could carry these expenses, but I could put aside nothing as savings. Early in the 1920s I had conceived the idea of a tree nursery as a source of supplementary income in spring and fall. I also considered the possibilities of a summer camp for children.

Pursuing the first idea, I incorporated as the Cherry Valley Nursery and ordered lining-out stock of many evergreen varieties. Before 1930 some of the trees were big enough to sell, and fifty years later they could still be recognized in the landscaping of some of the older homes in this area.

Besides using ornamental evergreens around the old farmhouse, built in 1848 and never before embellished with shrubbery, I set out a permanent reforestation in some of the former pastures, planting twenty-one thousand Norway spruce seedlings and hundreds of white spruce, balsam firs, and arbor vitae. The little trees, lost at first in grass and weeds, grew into a lofty background that changed the entire character of the place.

21

———

THE TEKAHARAWA AMERICAN INDIAN CAMP grew from a request made to me by Edwin Chinlund, vice-president of IT&T. He wanted me to take his two Chicago-bred grandsons on a camping trip in the Adirondacks. Instead, I invited them to Cherry Valley for the summer of 1931 and put them in the care of an Indian family I had met in New York. Princess Red Wing was a talented Winnebago woman whom I had seen demonstrating bead and quill work in Macy's store. The town of Red Wing, in Minnesota, was named for her. She had an older sister and a niece, Lone Deer, who was married to a Hopi, Ernest Naguayouama. These four acted as counselors to the Chinlund boys and my two nephews. They all slept in tepees on land that I leased from the Whitty family, across the road from the south fields of the Moore farm. A spring-fed stream flowed near the campsite, and the background was hemlock forest. There was pasture for ponies and for riding horses. I came up on weekends and found the boys having a wonderful time.

The following spring, I was passing through the Grand Central Station when I saw an Indian tepee on the mezzanine floor. It was part of an exhibit of the Burlington Railroad, promoting travel in the West. An Indian was in charge, wearing full, colorful costume: Max Big Man, Crow artist. I got acquainted with him and learned that he had posed for the Indian profile on the buffalo nickel. His name in the Crow tongue was Ihah-toh-heh-ed-dehsh, meaning "he who grabs the enemy's gun." A few days later we went to the Museum of Natural History together, and while we were looking around among the Indian exhibits we were surrounded by a crowd of

children who stared in awe and struggled to get close enough
to touch Big Man's costume. "Look at the *real* Indian!" they
exclaimed. The emotion in these youngsters' faces convinced
me that the idea of an Indian camp was a good one. They
awakened my own childhood memories of playing with the
Plains Indian bow and arrows that Nanny Walrad had given
me after I found them in Uncle Rance's attic.

It turned out that there were many Indians in New York
City—artists and performers, craftspeople, and structural
steelworkers on the skyscrapers. Red Wing introduced me at
the studio of the Menominee Princess Valesta, where at least
forty Indians from across the continent would gather weekly
to dance in tribal costumes. Wearing a beautiful Sioux costume that Red Wing made for me, I joined in the native dances
and met some potential camp counselors.

With a catalogue in preparation for the 1933 season, Camp
Tekaharawa received good publicity in *Redbook Magazine* and
was selected by Wanamaker's Astor Place store to be the focus
of an exhibit promoting their camping equipment. The management cleared a whole floor, created an artificial lake bor-
dered with living evergreens, put up tepees, and used my
prospective counselors to bring the scene to life. Six tribes
were represented: the Penobscot Nedabah taught archery and
fly-casting; Red Eagle, a Mohawk writer, told stories; White
Cloud, a Cheyenne, danced and played the tomtom; Wahna-
tahee, an Ojibway, along with Red Wing demonstrated bead,
quill, and feather crafts; Max Big Man and the Winnebago
Lone Deer performed an Indian marriage ceremony. I lectured on Indian Lore and sought campers for the coming summer. Additional publicity came when one of the major
broadcasting stations arranged to have Charles Wakefield
Cadman, composer of Indian songs, presented by our group
with a Seneca cornhusk mask.

Among the crowd of spectators on opening day was Kath-
erine Cloud, who brought her two daughters to Tekaharawa
and became one of the counselors. She was a niece of the

great bird artist, Louis Agassiz Fuertes. Blessed with intelligence and a fine sense of humor, she had a way with youngsters that made her invaluable. Our friendship lasted until her death in 1983.

Several camp directors showed up to see the exhibit. They congratulated me on my idea of an Indian camp but said I wouldn't make money. How right they were! But I was less interested in money than in the experiment itself. My goals for the campers were freedom, self-reliance, responsibility, tolerance, and helpfulness. I regarded the camp fee as just a contribution to help sustain the tribe. The enrollment was limited, never exceeding twenty, so we had a high ratio of counselors to children, and most of the counselors were Indians.

Our whole approach to camping was novel. Although the equipment was similar to that of some other camps, it was used in nontraditional ways. We were not interested in archery as a contest to see how many times a camper could hit the bull's-eye of a target. Archery was used to cultivate alertness, observation coupled with quick action, and correct judgment, qualities required in the hunt.

The children made their own programs, deciding the next day's activities each night at the council fire. If they planned a scouting party for hunting, the next morning would see them roaming the fields and woods looking for game, real or simulated. The woodchucks and squirrels easily evaded them, but stuffed animals had been placed in trees and on stone walls by the counselors, to be shot when seen. Each trophy was claimed by the hunter whose arrow hit it first, and much was made of the successful scout that night at the council fire, with the award of a feather, which eventually was added to a headdress.

Horses were not saddled and brought into a ring for riding, as was standard camp practice. The horses were pastured in the campgrounds and might be ridden anytime they could be caught. Of course, the children were shown how to do this by counselors equipped with sugar lumps.

If a group decided to go hiking, this was combined with nature study. The hikers learned what fruits and herbs were edible. They caught butterflies, not to impale them on pins, but to examine them closely, identify them if possible, and then let them go. This activity led into dancing, for dancing, in the Indian mode, reflected individual experience. To the beat of the tomtom later, the campers would repeat the steps and gestures they made in chasing the butterflies from flower to flower.

With the counselors' encouragement, the children built a bridge over the stream. They cut trees for beams and posts and pulled the logs into place with ropes attached to the pummels of their saddles. They learned engineering principles by trial and error. When horses could be walked over it, the bridge was considered a success.

The camp overflowed from its tepees and trading post by the swimming hole to the Moore farm across the road. My mother, then seventy, was always happy when surrounded by hungry kids. She and my sister Jane prepared the menus and supervised the cooking, and the meals were always hearty and delicious. Mother's spirit pervaded the camp, and the children, counselors, and parents all loved her.

On weekends we were inundated by visiting parents, who usually arrived in time for the Saturday evening dinner and council fire, to watch with pleased amazement their children's achievements. On Sunday they were again welcomed at meals and entertained by a rodeo that included trick riding by White Cloud and myself. White Cloud was almost as dexterous with a lariat as Will Rogers and had the same sense of humor; he was loved by everyone at the camp. The rodeo would end with a parade on horseback by all the campers in the costumes they had made or decorated with beads.

In the summer of 1933 Cherry Valley celebrated the sesquicentennial of the visit of George Washington to the village. A parade was planned, and Tekaharawa Camp was asked to head it, with costumes and with even the ponies painted and decorated with feathers. My pinto had evidently been in parades before, for without guidance he pranced from curb to curb and at the reviewing stand stood straight up before the judges. Wearing the beaded white doeskin leggins and eagle-feathered war bonnet made for me by Red Wing, I probably was not recognized by many of the spectators. The camp won the award as best entry in the parade.

Afterward as we made our way home we were followed by a Rolls Royce limousine, which refused to pass but crept along at the pace of the horses. When I dismounted at camp, the passenger in the car came up to me and introduced himself as August Busch, of the Anheuser-Busch Beer Company. He wanted to buy my horse and another of the ponies for his grandchildren. Of course, I had no idea of selling any of the horses in midseason.

Mr. Busch, however, visited us several times that summer, and we talked about the history of hop growing in the area. He invited me to his Fox Run Farm near Cooperstown and showed me around the fairyland he had created for his grandchildren, where ceramic gnomes appeared unexpectedly in the woods and along the brook.

I had to admit to myself that I too was a romantic caught up in a childhood fantasy. With the uncertainties of the mid-Depression and the demands of my job, I had to give up the camp after the 1933 season. It has been a great source of satisfaction to receive letters and visits over the years from former campers who repeat that the happiest days of their lives were spent in Cherry Valley.

22

___

As the depression deepened in the early 1930s, economists and others such as the writer Upton Sinclair were proposing plans to end it. The scheme that received most publicity for a while was Howard Scott's Technocracy, based on the idea, drawn from Veblen's *The Engineer and the Price System,* that the economy should be run by engineers, with their scientific approach, rather than by industrialists and bankers. Naturally, the establishment saw Technocracy as a threat. Few of its members had read Veblen, so they arranged a dinner at the Hotel Plaza in order to hear Scott explain his theory. Scott was an eloquent speaker, capable of meeting this challenge, but the impressive guest list, topped by J. P. Morgan, caused him to overestimate his hearers' intelligence, and he lost them in a maze of ergs and other technical terms. Their interest turned to boredom and laughter. My friend Edwin Chinlund, who was present, told me about it and said that word had gone out to the press that not a word about technocracy should be printed thenceforth. Thus a possibly useful idea was consigned to oblivion.

The Mayer Company was liquidated in 1934 as a result of the depression. It was a heartbreaking time for everyone, but the liquidation was orderly, and most of our employees owned stock in the company and were participants in a pension fund, so they were better off than most of the unemployed.

It was not only wage earners who were suffering. One of my best friends, Frank Schaffer, president of the Hugh Kelly Sugar Company, the largest American importer of sugar, was ruined by the banks, which took over his company by calling their short-term loans. This man, who had been able to borrow millions to harvest the Cuban sugar crop, was suddenly set adrift. After trying unsuccessfully to establish himself in the auto tire business, he gave up and jumped to his death from the roof of the Biltmore Hotel.

New York State responded to the unemployment crisis with a Temporary Emergency Relief Organization, headed by Harry Hopkins, who had worked at the Henry Street Settlement with Lillian Wald and Eleanor Roosevelt. Hopkins estimated that thirty thousand needleworkers were jobless in the city, and he asked Eddie Mayer to take charge of a project to put as many as possible to work. Eddie agreed to do it without pay but with me on salary as his "technical assistant." He provided free use of his two buildings in Queens, and we set up a work project making wool-filled cotton quilts, which relief organizations distributed to needy families.

In 1935 the Works Progress Administration of the federal government—the famous WPA—took over the state unemployment relief agency, expanding its program of putting people to work in the trades in which they were skilled.

I watched this effort from the beginning and saw it as the only way of hope and self-respect for millions of unemployed who had exhausted their savings, lost their homes, given up insurance policies, begged from friends and relatives, and were barely surviving on the dole. I saw the registry offices opened for WPA applications and so many people flocking in that police reserves had to be called to keep them in line. They stood hour after hour, in the bitterest weather, going without food rather than lose their places, sometimes fainting from exhaustion, in the hope of getting a job, any job.

After midnight, when the offices closed, some people stayed on the street; others came back before daylight to wait again. No one who saw those lines would listen to the cynical charge that the unemployed preferred idleness and relief to honest work.

Nor was it true, in my observation, that WPA workers

loafed on the job. I supervised young and old, whole and handicapped, black and white, with every sort of background and all shades of political loyalty, but only in rare cases of physical or mental weakness did I ever see a worker fail to do all that was expected. I recall a woman nearly eighty years old, an arrested tubercular case, who was one of my most conscientious workers. She could have stayed home on relief, indeed, was urged to do so, but would not. She had to go to one of the city hospitals for treatment but in three months was back at work. Her story was not exceptional. People who have been through the hell of joblessness and relief need no urging when the chance to work is offered.

If some of the slurs on the work program were heartless, others were mindless. The critics of the WPA, at the same time that they cried "Boondoggle!" complained bitterly because useful articles were being produced by "government competition." Often I had occasion to remind these critics that to produce goods that are not sold but given away to relief clients who could not possibly buy them did not take away a single customer from private business. On the contrary, it made the WPA worker again able to pay rent and doctor bills and to patronize the merchants. In addition, the federal projects used about a third of their funds for equipment, materials, and overhead, which helped suppliers and manufacturers, real estate owners, and utilities companies. The government through its purchases and its distribution of purchasing power to the workers revived the ailing market for private enterprise.

At the head of the WPA was General Hugh Johnson. He confirmed Harry Hopkins's appointments in the New York State work relief program, and I was given the new title of manager, which covered any manufacturing projects of the WPA in the city. Eddie Mayer retired at this time.

One of the first things General Johnson did was to distribute loyalty oath forms. I took my copy to his office and told him I was not going to sign it and proffered my resignation. He reached across the desk, crumpled the form, and threw it in the wastebasket, saying, "I know more about you than you think I do, and if you will stay on, I'll consider it a personal favor." That was in August 1935. In October I was reappointed with an increase in salary.

Besides setting up sewing shops in other parts of the city, I leased the old Segal-Cooper Department Store building on Sixth Avenue at Nineteenth Street and put in machines to employ five thousand people making underwear and outerwear for men, women, and children. This was the largest sewing plant in the world. We were cutting a million yards of material a month. Mrs. Roosevelt visited the project and was impressed by it. She asked what I thought of having an orchestra playing for the workers. I knew she was thinking of the unemployed musicians, but I was dubious about the idea. Mrs. Roosevelt, who was certainly in a position to exert pressure, graciously accepted my veto.

Other projects specialized in making sheets and pillowcases. From others, wool-filled quilts poured out by the carload; literally eleven freight cars of them were shipped to flood victims in the Ohio and Mississippi valleys early in 1937. (Although this project already was operating efficiently, its output jumped by 25 percent when the workers learned of the emergency need.)

Soon we had an increasing shortage of space for the millions of yards of material constantly arriving. I learned that there were empty buildings at the Brooklyn Navy Yard and appealed to the admiral in charge there to give us space for storage and a cutting room. He seemed to smell something offensive in the very term "relief" and looking down his nose at me said that he had no room for such a project. Sensing that the admiral's prejudices played a greater part in this decision than his lack of space, I went to Hugh Johnson and asked for a flight to Washington, which he arranged along with an appointment to see the secretary of the navy. I explained our problem to him and suggested that thousands of dollars worth of government-owned merchandise left on the harbor piers at the mercy of rats and weather, for lack of space in the navy yard, would hardly generate favorable publicity for his department. He immediately telephoned the admiral and told him to clear a building for our use by the following Monday and to cooperate in every way to facilitate the project. It was done, and navy personnel stored the shipments for us, the admiral now as helpful as he had been haughty.

In these early days of the WPA I developed a rewarding friendship with Milton Heimlich. He and his brother had a business in used sewing machines and had bought the equipment from Eddie Mayer's plant when it closed. Now he helped me find and install the vast amount of machinery needed for the WPA sewing projects. His knowledge supplemented Eddie's and my own; for example, he was able to obtain from private manufacturers many patterns that we needed for the garments we made. He was and is one of the most humanitarian businessmen I have ever known.

In 1936, a crucial election year for the Democrats, politics was thick in the air, and all the New Deal programs were assailed by malicious rumors. I was notified to appear at City Hall before a committee of investigation into alleged abuses in the WPA. When I arrived with my staff of accountants carrying all their records, I was greeted with the exclamation, "My God, have you got books?" We were asked to wait in an anteroom and never were called to testify about anything. But while we were cooling our heels and becoming exasperated, members of the committee visited some of our workrooms and asked employees why they were working so hard. They could find no basis for bringing any charge against our project.

In that same year General Johnson resigned, and Victor Ridder became administrator of the WPA. I had another increase in salary and the new title of unit manager. But I began to have difficulty in getting money for my projects. The accounting office in Washington was transferring funds to other projects. I saw growing evidence that the WPA was becoming a political football and that the whole idea of work relief for the unemployed would be discredited and eventually abandoned. In frustration and disillusionment, I finally resigned.

23

AFTER LEAVING THE WPA IN 1936, I spent a winter in Florida and a summer in Cherry Valley with my parents and sister. I also looked for employment in New York City, but I was remembering the advice I had sometimes given relief clients who came to the WPA: that if I were in their position I would start walking out of the city, and at the first farm where I could get room and board for my work, there I would stay until the economy improved.

The idea of restoring the family farm tempted me, but I would have to start from scratch, since all the stock and equipment had been sold when my father retired. By this time I did not have much of my savings left. A chance contact put me in touch with the Carnegie Hero Fund Commission again, and I inquired of them if the five hundred dollar award was still available and explained that I wanted to restock and re-equip the family farm in order to move back there and take care of my parents. The new manager, Mr. Allerdice, responded in the manner of his predecessor, with a list of questions from "1. Provided you are able to obtain the necessary equipment, etc., what prospects have you that you will be able to earn enough money and raise enough food to sustain yourself and your parents and other dependents if any?" to "9. What savings or investments have you?" I have always disliked questionnaires and felt it would be fruitless to wrestle with this one.*

---

*In 1955 another manager, Mr. Floto, wrote to me "in connection with a survey of awards that still remain unused." He sent suggestions of uses that would be accept-able to the commission and invited me to submit a proposal. At that time I was too busy to start playing this game again. But three years later yet another manager,

I shelved the idea of returning to the farm and went to work, early in 1938, for the George S. May Company, industrial engineering consultants. The company already had specialists in particular industries such as mining and steelmaking, but they took me on as an efficiency expert who could diagnose the ailments of a variety of businesses. My job was to study client companies, analyze their problems, and make recommendations. The May Company charged a flat fee for this survey, plus another fee for each week of work by its representative.

They first sent me to a small factory in New England that had successfully made insulated wire for many years but now found itself losing money. I noticed in the plant an elderly employee who was casually pouring chemicals into the rubber insulation mixture. He had become so confident of his judgment that he no longer measured these ingredients exactly. As a result, large quantities of wire were junked because of blistering of the rubber covering. When the chemicals were again combined according to formula, the trouble stopped. I also found that a poor arrangement of machines was causing lost motion. A better assembly-line process helped get the company back on a profitable basis.

My next assignment was in Winston-Salem, North Carolina, where the Bonson Company manufactured both thread and cloth in its cotton mills and had a separate plant that made air-conditioning equipment for tobacco warehouses. The business was owned by two brothers who were as different as

---

David B. Oliver, wrote a more encouraging letter: "Regulations governing approval of disbursement of award money by the Commission have recently been liberalized. Your award rightly belongs to you and we believe you should have it now." He did ask for a brief statement for their files regarding the planned use of the money. I replied suggesting that I might use it for "responding to appeals for help in antiwar activities and in defense of civil liberties and conscientious objectors; or for repairs to my home." Mr. Oliver then promptly sent me the fund's check for five hundred dollars, with a very courteous letter expressing the hope that it would be used for my second alternative, "as we like to feel that the . . . money is being used for your own personal benefit."

day and night. One, in charge of the cotton factories, was aus-
tere, puritanical, class conscious, with a pretentious home and
a likable son more interested in music than in being groomed
to succeed his father in the business. The other, a bit older,
was easygoing, democratic, a bachelor, and a mild alcoholic
who worked with and fraternized with his employees. His entire
interest was in producing the air conditioners that were his
branch of the family business. He left all financial matters to
his younger brother. There was little friendship between them.

I began the survey in the mill where raw cotton was converted into thread and yarn for chambray cloth and underwear. Immediately I felt an atmosphere of hostility on the
part of supervisors and managers, who resented my questions. The older Bonson told me laughingly at lunch that a
previous efficiency engineer had been literally chased out of
town in his underwear by the factory workers. I thanked him
for the warning and made an extra effort to be courteous and
tactful. I also suggested a meeting of all employees, at which
I told them I was not there to jeopardize their jobs but in fact
hoped with their cooperation to find ways of effecting savings
that might justify a pay increase. After that our relationship
was much more cordial.

Unfortunately, no technical deficiencies came to light. The
problem in the business grew out of the difference in point of
view between the two brothers, and that we were in no position to solve. I did suggest a possible separation of the operations into two independent companies as a way of eliminating
the tension, but as far as I know this was not done.

I was then sent down to Tampa to survey the business of
a beer and wine distributor. The company was owned and
managed by an aging Italian and his son. My examination of
the account books and the sales and shipments figures gave
rise to a suspicion that all was not well at the warehouse. At
my suggestion a detective was employed, and the son was
caught taking a truckload of beer from the warehouse at night.
The old gentleman had his son arrested and jailed.

Next I went to Dallas and joined another engineer from the May Company to survey the largest manufacturer and distributor of drygoods in the Southwest: Higgenbotham, Bailey, and Logan. But before this job was completed I was sent to New Orleans to the Wembly Tie Company. Wembly made a line of nonwrinkling, low-priced ties and a line of expensive silk ties. Their accounting system failed to separate the costs of the two lines. When this was corrected it appeared that the cost of producing the silk line was responsible for the losses being suffered by the company; so this line was dropped. I effected some further economies by rearranging machinery to eliminate waste motion.

The president of Wembly wanted me to stay on as their comptroller. Of course, my contract with the May Company prohibited taking a job with any of the clients, and I had no desire to live in New Orleans even if I could have. Still, I cannot forget to this day the good food at Antoine's and the numerous oyster bars and seafood restaurants on the shore of Lake Pontchartrain.

The May Company had repeatedly tried to have me prolong the jobs I completed, and after I refused again to go along with this unethical practice in the case of the Wembly survey, they stopped giving me any more assignments. This meant that my income stopped. After waiting a month, I turned in my resignation.

24

I WAS NOW in a position to return to Cherry Valley and start making the old farm productive while taking care of my parents. I first bought a hand-operated "Planet Junior" plow, cultivator, and planter for garden work. That was in 1939, and it is still in use forty-five years later. I repaired the old barns and filled the mows with hay for a cow and a few sheep. A small tractor, a Farmall-A, was the largest machine I ever needed. Other livestock from time to time were calves, a pig, a couple of goats, chickens, ducks, and turkeys. My parents were happy to see animals on the place again, and during the coming years of rationing we all appreciated the butter from old Gosh, the Guernsey cow.

But I planned to concentrate on small fruits and other produce. Red raspberries soon began to bring in some cash both from the berries and from the canes, which I shipped to nurseries and mail order customers. Within a few years I was in the strawberry business, supplemented by all sorts of garden produce, from asparagus in the spring to potatoes and pumpkins in the fall. Customers drove up from the Mohawk Valley towns and from Cooperstown to buy these crops and enjoy the view northward to the Adirondacks.

World War II started in 1939, a year short of the prediction Henry Schmeider and I had made when we left Fort Douglas. There was no question in my mind that this country would be involved. Pearl Harbor was only the last push on a course set by Roosevelt.

Again this time the draft law failed to provide an alternative for political or philosophical conscientious objectors. Religious objectors might be (but often were not) assigned by

their draft boards to Civilian Public Service Camps administered and financed by the so-called peace churches: the Quakers, Mennonites, and Brethren.

One such camp happened to be located in Cooperstown,
and I became acquainted there. The young Quaker in charge
invited me to speak to the men, along with newspaper col-
umnist Harry Elmer Barnes, who had a home nearby. I got
into a heated discussion with an Episcopal minister who was
present, and after that neither Barnes nor I was welcome at
the camp, which was really under the eye of the military.
However, a number of the COs continued to visit me, among
them George Kingsley, Louis Taylor, and Stanley Murphy,
all of whom later walked out of the camp and as a result suffered greatly in prison.

Evan Thomas, who was teaching and practicing medicine
in New York, took on the chairmanship of the War Resisters
League and gave himself unstintingly to assist and defend the
many conscientious objectors who did not qualify for the
church-sponsored camps or would not take refuge in them.
He would arrive for occasional weekends at the farm, weary
and full of stories of young men who were suffering under the
draft law—this time usually in federal penitentiaries rather
than military prisons.

When Congress declared war after Pearl Harbor, there
was but one dissenting voice. Jeannette Rankin of Montana,
who had voted against our entry into World War I and had
been out of office as a result, was now back in and defied
Roosevelt's wishes as she had Wilson's. I wrote and congratulated her and received a cordial note of thanks.

The government now decided to register men between
forty-five and sixty-five, in case they should be needed for any
form of national service. Norman Thomas, whose ear was close
to the ground in Washington, heard that a caution had been
expressed against the measure, that it might "stir up that hor-
nets' nest" of World War I objectors—"Moore and all that
bunch." The law was passed, and some of the old COs were

indeed stirred up. Julius Eichel, Evan Thomas, Harold Gray, Max Sandin, and myself were among the sixteen older men who made a public refusal to register. I wrote to Attorney General Francis Biddle in December 1941, but held the five-page letter until I could cool off enough to reduce it to two and mailed it in February. It said, after referring to my stand in World War I:

I am as unalterably opposed to war now as I was then, because it is my fervent belief that the resort to force, as a means of settling differences between nations, is as stupid and immoral as it is futile.

Indeed, at the very outset of present hostilities, war, as an instrument of national policy, has failed even in the matter of self-defense. It has protected neither life nor property. Instead, it has resulted in nothing but an avowed program of frightfulness to be carried on by acts of reprisal and retaliation at the sacrifice of all human rights in the name of self-defense and in a welter of blood by both sides until one side or the other succumbs to the sheer exhaustion of both men and substance. . . .

If men and women are to be denied the right to a planned existence, if, at intervals of every twenty or thirty years, their homes are to be disrupted and their children used as cannon fodder by the State, if the ethical principles and ideals with which we seek to perfect ourselves as truly Christian and civilized human beings are to be exchanged for the practices of barbarism at the command of the State, then, for me at least, life has lost all meaning and purpose.

It is not the Kaisers nor the Hitlers nor any other egomaniac who dreams of dictating human destiny, but war itself, and the supine willingness of peoples everywhere to be registered, inspected, and controlled for its purpose, which makes and supports totalitarianism in all its phases, that constitutes the real danger to America and the human race. . . .

Modern total war cannot be waged without universal military conscription and all its adjunct machinery for the regimentation, enslavement, and exploitation of whole peoples.

Registration is but the first step in the process of such . . . enslavement, and I am therefore compelled by the deepest convictions of my conscience and intelligence to refuse to comply with the law requiring such registration.

I shall await here on my farm at the above address whatever action the Government may deem necessary to take against this contemplated act of civil disobedience.

No answer was received, and on registration day, April 27, I wrote again to the attorney general, stating that as promised, I had not registered, and adding:

My parents are both old and . . . my father is a complete invalid. I mention this not as a plea for special consideration but in the hope that if the Government regards it as necessary to proceed against me . . . I may be allowed sufficient time to move my parents to relatives and also to liquidate my livestock.

It was an anxious spring on the Moore farm. I planted and cultivated without knowing who would bring in the harvest. Finally, on the last day of May 1942, a letter came from Stephen Waszkiewicz, assistant district attorney in Utica. It ordered me to report for registration at the draft board in Cooperstown not later than June 3. But, "In the event that you fail to comply with the registration it is necessary that you immediately present yourself for arrest either to the United States Marshall at Albany, N.Y., or Utica, or to the Federal Bureau of Investigation at Albany."

I phoned the CPS camp in Cooperstown and asked whether George Kingsley might accompany me to Utica, so that if I were detained there he could bring my car back to the farm and look after my parents and the livestock.

At Utica we were greeted pleasantly by the assistant district attorney, and he and I talked for two hours on the subject of war objection, with the office staff listening at desks and in doorways. At four o'clock Mr. Waszkiewicz said he was sorry but he had an appointment.

"What am I supposed to do with you?" he asked. "You know more about it than I do." I told him he was supposed to arrest me. He then called in a U.S. marshall, who said: "You are under arrest. Now you are free."

After this welcome anticlimax George and I returned home.

Probably the district attorney registered me without my signature, as was done in most of the other cases. Only Julius
Eichel had trouble. He was arrested and held for a week in
jail while his friends raised the twenty-five thousand-dollar
bail set by a prejudiced judge. He too was involuntarily registered before he was freed.

I continued, like Candide, my program of subsistence
farming, certain that there would be another war in twenty
years or so and that unless some way were found to end war,
war would end the human race.

Now, at ninety-five, I have not changed my mind. I believe
the present generation is witnessing the twilight of the nation-
state. Unless the human species arrives at a spiritual and
intellectual awareness of our interdependence and establishes
a world community using the earth's resources for the benefit
of all, we are headed for extinction.

Appendix

To be inclosed with each order into military service (Form 1028) sent to a selected man.

———

IMPORTANT NOTICE TO ALL MEN SELECTED FOR MILITARY SERVICE AND ORDERED TO REPORT TO A LOCAL BOARD FOR MILITARY DUTY.

———

The day and hour specified on the Classification List of this Local Board, and on the order and notice of induction into military service which accompanies this notice for you to report to this Local Board for military duty is the time that marks your actual obligation as a soldier of the United States.

Failure to report promptly at the hour and on the day named is a grave military offense for which you may be court-martialed. Willful failure to report with an intent to evade military service constitutes desertion from the Army of the United States, which, in time of war, is a capital offense.

Upon reporting to your Local Board, you will not need, and you should not bring with you, anything except hand baggage. You will not be permitted to take trunks or boxes with you on the train. You should take only the following articles: A pair of strong comfortable shoes to relieve your feet from your new regulation marching shoes; not to exceed four extra suits of underclothing; not to exceed six extra pairs of socks; four face and two bath towels; a comb, a brush, a toothbrush, soap, tooth powder, razor, and shaving soap. It will add to your comfort to bring one woolen blanket, preferably of dark or neutral color. This blanket should be tightly rolled, the ends of the roll should be securely bound together and the loop of the blanket thus formed slung from your left shoulder to your right hip.

You should wear rough strong clothing and a flannel shirt, preferably an olive-drab shirt of the kind issued to soldiers.

NOTE.—Local Boards may have prepared, in the form of a rubber stamp, and stamp in below or on the back hereof any special instructions such as a direction to request permission to eat and spend the last night at home, as it may desire to give.

LOCAL BOARD FOR DIVISION No. 136, CITY OF NEW YORK, STATE OF NEW YORK
2745 BROADWAY,
NEW YORK. NEW YORK

(Stamp in designation of Local Board.) 3—5116

P. M. G. O. Form 1028A

Order of Induction into Military Service of the United States.

The President of the United States,

To _Edward Walter Moore_
        (Christian name.)   (Surname.)

Order Number _1057_ Serial Number _2179_

Greeting: *Having submitted yourself to a local board composed of your neighbors for the purpose of determining the place and time in which you can best serve the United States in the present emergency, you are hereby notified that you have now been selected for immediate military service.*

You will, therefore, report to the local board named below

at _2741 Broadway_, at _9 a_ m.,
        (Place of reporting.)   (Hour of reporting.)

on the _29th_ day of _April_ , 19 _18_,
for military duty.

From and after the day and hour just named you will be a soldier in the military service of the United States.

Paul Abelson

Member of Local Board for _div 130_

Report to Local Board for _130_

2741 B'way
N.Y. City

Date ___APR 20 1918___

Form 1028. P.M.G.O. (See Sec. 157, S. S. R.)   3—6115

Form No.34. 8-5-18.5M

OFFICE OF THE EXECUTIVE OFFICER
UNITED STATES DISCIPLINARY BARRACKS
FORT LEAVENWORTH, KANSAS.

No. 15177 Result of trial.................. 11 - 11 1918

Solitary nine hours standing...... ....14.........days

Good time lost.....8.........days.........Solitary......14.......days

Your time now expires........ ....191......

T. D. MILLER

.... Executive Officer

Dishonorable Discharge from the Army of the United States

TO ALL WHOM IT MAY CONCERN:

This is to Certify, That *Howard W. Moore,*
Private Co. "A" 1st Casual Battalion,
National Army, is hereby **Dishonorably Discharged** *from
the military service of the* **United States** *by reason of the sentence of a
General Court=Martial Orders #55 Hq Camp Funston, Kan,
dated Nov. 10/18 & letter A.G. dated Nov. 11/20.*

*Said Howard W. Moore was born
in Ossining, in the State of New York
When enlisted he was 39½ years of age and by occupation a Traffic Expert*
*He had Gray eyes, Brown hair, Fair complexion, and
was 5 feet 10½ inches in height.*

*Given under my hand at Hq U.S.W.P.B. Ft Douglas Utah this
17th day of November, one thousand nine hundred and Twenty*

Bertram P Johnson
Lieut Col Infantry
Commanding.

Form No. 527, A. G. O.
Ed. Aug. 20-17—100,000.
* Insert grade and company and reg...ent or corps or department; e. g., "Corporal, Company A, 1st Infantry;" "Sergeant Quar-
termaster Corps;" "Sergeant, First Class, Medical Department."
† Insert "Regular Army," "National Army," "National Guard," "Regular Army Reserve," or "Enlisted Reserve Corps," as the
case may be.
‡ Insert number, date, and source of general court-martial order.

2—3162

ENLISTMENT RECORD.

Name: Howard W. Moore 2880108 Grade: Private

Enlisted April 29-1918, at Local Bd # 130, New York City

Serving in First enlistment period at date of discharge.

Prior service: * None

Noncommissioned officer: Never

Marksmanship, gunner qualification or rating: † Not Qualified

Horsemanship: Not Mounted

Battles, engagements, skirmishes, expeditions: None

Medals, Citations or other Decorations: None

Knowledge of any vocation: Traffic Inspector

Wounds received in service: None

Physical condition when discharged: Good

Typhoid prophylaxis completed Not Completed

Paratyphoid prophylaxis completed No record

Married or single: Single

Remarks: Sentenced to serve 5 years per G.C.M.O. 58, Hq. Camp Funston dated Nov 16/18, Unexecuted portion of sentence remitted per letter A.G. dated Nov 11/30 Conscientious Objector

Transportation furnished to New York City, N.Y.

A. J. Mac DONALD
CAPT. USA, RET'D

Capt 1 Lt. Infantry

Commanding

* Give company and regiment or corps or department, with inclusive dates of service in each enlistment.
† Give date of qualification or rating and number, date, and source of order announcing same.

3—3162

SPEECH

OF

HON. CHARLES H. DILLON

INTRODUCING EXAMPLES

OF

Brutalities, Tortures, and Deaths to Political Prisoners under Military Régime

TABULATED AT THE REQUEST OF

Hon. S. HUBERT DENT, Jr.

Chairman House Committee on Military Affairs

JANUARY, 1919

WASHINGTON
GOVERNMENT PRINTING OFFICE
1919

REMARKS

OF

HON. CHARLES H. DILLON.

Treatment Accorded Our Soldiers in Court-Martial Proceedings.

Mr. DILLON. Mr. Chairman, a number of letters have reached me relative to the treatment accorded our soldiers in court-martial proceedings and in the military prisons. I have not made any personal investigation of these alleged abuses, but information comes from so.many sources that there must be some foundation for the charges. I append a statement just received through the mail entitled "Examples of brutalities, tortures, and deaths to political prisoners under military régime":

To Congressman DENT,
  Chairman House Committee on Military Affairs, Washington.

HONORABLE SIR: At your request I beg to submit a résumé of inhuman treatment of military and political prisoners, which I respectfully recommend for your kind and immediate consideration and action, as some are already dead, others dying by inches, while all are more or less in constant jeopardy of life or health:

1. Jacob Wipf and the three Hofer brothers, religious objectors, with families, served one year in Arizona prison for failure to register. Transferred to Spanish dungeon of Alcatraz, San Francisco Bay. Stripped to underwear. "Strung up" for 36 hours. Five days without food; 1 glass of water every 24 hours. Slept on cold, damp floor in the stench of their own excrements, beaten, and otherwise manhandled. Contracted scurvy. Sent to Fort Leavenworth, from a temperate to a cold climate; put in solitary on bread and water; "strung up" nine hours per day seven days per week; slept on the bare floor with cold drafts passing over their emaciated bodies; two contracted pneumonia and died; one was sent home with the bodies. Jacob Wipf is on a hospital cot when telling this story. These men were all married and have one or more children, therefore should not have been drafted at all. (Report carried to Theo. H. Lunde, president American Industrial Co., of Chicago, by an Army officer.)

2. Clark Getts, Chicago attorney, graduate of Wisconsin University, conscientious objector, was given two periods, two weeks each, in solitary confinement on bread and water at Fort Leavenworth for smuggling to the outside world information of the cruelties practiced upon him and his confrères, after which he was put in the ward for the violently insane by Capt. Chambers; in constant jeopardy of life and mind, as the inmates are not confined in cells but mingle promiscuously. Writer's son, who with others (including officer who carried the information) vouch for Getts's mental condition, in defiance of Capt. Chambers, implores me to do something for this unfortunate man. Writer in person brought the case under the personal notice of Secretary Baker, who promised to investigate it, but whose general attitude did not impart any hope of results. The chains of the solitary are humane as compared with the physical danger and torture of a sound mind in such environments.

3. Howard Moore, conscientious objector, an efficiency expert, winner of the Carnegie medal for bravery and $500 for saving a girl from drowning; in solitary at Fort Leavenworth after much suffering at Fort Riley.

4. David Eichel, conscientious objector, statistician, formerly with prominent life-insurance company, in solitary at Fort Leavenworth. Went through 10 days' reign of terror at Camp Funston.

112619—19427

5. Francis X. Hennessy, Hyman Block, Stein, Haugan, all conscientious objectors, put in the insane ward at Fort Leavenworth, which can only be interpreted as camouflage for the benefit of inspector from Washington, being that none are insane, and that if Hennessy is possibly a little affected it is the result of the brutalities accorded him and the others at Fort Riley, where he was "strung up" and given the "water cure," and at Camp Funston, where he went through the "10-day reign of terror," under Capt. Gustave Taussig.

6. Seventh Day Adventists have been put in solitary for refusing to work on Saturday, their Sabbath.

7. Mennonites have been put in solitary because their religion forbade them to put on uniforms or prison clothes.

8. Fischer was beaten so severely that he became a raving maniac.

9. John A. Burch, No. 12358, of Wolfrun, Ohio, not a conscientious objector, enlisted July 28, 1917, and was sent to Camp Gettysburg, Pa., having failed to claim exemption though he had a wife and four children under 8. Having been refused by Capt. Hardman to see his dying mother, he took "French leave," was picked up by detectives, was refused to go home for his papers and railroad ticket which he had bought to go back to camp, was forcibly filled up on whisky, turned over to sheriff of Steubenville County, where he was kept 60 days; sent to Columbus Barracks for 30 days then to Camp Greene, Charlotte, N. C. (whither his battalion had moved); taken before a court-martial which held the entire enforced detention against him, and gave him a sentence of 10 years at Fort Leavenworth. While there his wife and two children died, and, though he offered to pay the fare of a guard to go with him, Commandant Rice refused his request for leave to see his dear ones before they were laid away.

Told by a Regular prisoner, railroaded to the detention barracks at Fort Leavenworth.

10. Peters, No. 14589, Mennonite, from Fort Oglethorpe, Ga. Lieut. Masey, when reading sentence, told him he was no longer a citizen, and therefore not entitled to hold his religious belief. Ordered to work at the point and prodding of the bayonet. Put in solitary under roof in barn, with only a small, square window for air, under a blazing August sun, on bread and water. Refusing to eat for five days, he fainted, was revived, and put back. Later taken to hospital totally demented and a wreck of a former splendid physique. Pneumonia, influenza, heart trouble, and a general breakdown. Finally discharged as mentally deficient.

Davis, No. 15582, was also a witness to this treatment.

Peters, mentioned above, saw the two following instances:

11. Detention camp, Fort Oglethorpe. Captain ordered soldiers to put C. O. waist deep in feces of latrine pit, splash him all over with the filth, sergeant in charge leaving him to be pulled out by his fellow C. O.'s.

12. Same captain, same time, ordered C. O. Schwargengraben taken by the heels and dipped to his eyes in the feces of latrine pit. Sergeant proceeded to put him "away in." Peters warned him of danger of killing by suffocation before filth could be removed from mouth and nostrils.

13. Polish drafted deserter brought to Fort Oglethorpe during August. Had yellow jaundice. No food or medical attention for two days. Provost sergeant ordered him out to work under curses and oaths. Too sick to work. Sergeant ordered him to stand up; tried, but fell back on bunk. Sergeant grabbed and beat him; too exhausted. Sergeant called prison officer, Lieut. Masey, who grabbed and shook him viciously and ordered guard with fixed bayonet to force him out. Pole, leaning against wall for support, was jabbed four times in back with bayonet, until exhausted he fainted away. Taken to guardhouse and left on bunk for two days, until chaplain, Father Shear, came to call the mail. Duncan called the reverend father's attention to Pole's condition; he was horrified; said Lieut. Masey should be court-martialed, and threatened to prefer charges. He only "bawled him out," preferring no charges.

The Pole later died in the hospital as a direct result of cruel treatment.

Duncan saw most of this, as did Davis.

14. Case of supposed spinal meningitis in this hospital. Doctor took too large culture from spine; patient now a raving maniac in barred room across hall from me, probably mentally unfit for life. Attendant who saw operation and has medical knowledge said it should have been taken in two portions.

15. Erling H. Lunde, Chicago, graduate with honors from the University of Chicago; three years engineering at Armour Institute of Technology; was re-

112619—19427

fused deferred classification on accusation of having married to evade draft. Was appointed inspector of materials on the Santa Fe, but was refused furlough and sent to camp. Application withdrawn when motive questioned. Did voluntary work at Fort Leavenworth; earned good will of Capt. Laird for establishing harmony between officers and conscientious objectors. Resented coercive measures and intolerable conditions at Fort Riley, put in solitary, court-martialed at Camp Funston, sent to Fort Leavenworth for life, commuted to 25 years in disciplinary barracks, conditions of which are so dangerous and intolerable as to cause a yearning for solitary again. Now in hospital convalescing from scarlet fever. Was declared a sincere conscientious objector by Judge Mack's commission. Author of Defense of Conscientious Objectors to war.

16. Harold Gray, son of President Gray, of the Detroit Red Cross. Took Red Cross post in England, but soon found he belonged among the conscientious objectors; returned to America and joined the others in suffering and solitary.

17. Evan Thomas, a minister, and brother of Dr. Norman Thomas, of New York; cosufferer with the above, whose sufferings in solitary were much accentuated due to his height, which compelled a stooping position when chained to the bars of the double-decked solitary cell.

18. Charles P. Larsen, artist, at Fort Leavenworth. Suffered with others the intolerable conditions at Fort Riley. Underrationed, food attacked by flies from near-by latrine used by venereally diseased soldiers. Protest punished by imprisonment in guardhouse cell in basement, dark, air foul, deprived of toilet articles, breathing sweepings, etc. Protest brought solitary confinement. Later taken to Camp Funston and was a cosufferer during 10-day reign of terror.

19. Abraham Gelerter, vegetable dealer, orthodox Jew, Camp Upton to Fort Jay, April 11. Is greatly surprised and thanks his God for having survived the terrible punishments received for merely objecting to murder. The brutal sentries beat him until he was unable to recognize himself and encouraged the other prisoners to do the same. Commandant declared that all conscientious objectors deserved to be killed. September 15 I arrived at Fort Leavenworth, and, being a vegetarian, had to go twice on hunger strike to get proper food, though far from adequate. Two periods of two weeks in solitary, handcuffed to cell nine hours per day. Compelled to bathe and shave on Saturday, my Sabbath. Dragged to the bath, knocked down, forcibly undressed, held under shower, and scrubbed with coarse soap. The brutalities of the soldiers made me scream with pain. I was taken out of the hole to the hospital November 22 for observation.

20. J. E. Haugen, sheet-metal worker, Lutheran, conscientious objector, shared the intolerable conditions at Fort Riley. Guardhouse, court-martial, transfer to Fort Leavenworth, with solitary and-accompanying cruelties.

21. The so-called "mutiny" at Fort Leavenworth: The "crusher gang," composed of physically unfit, were ordered to do twice as much work as formerly. Refusing, the "punishment gang" was sent over; but, seeing how matters stood, they also refused.

All were ordered into solitary, and Acting Warden Fletcher started after them with a bat. A prisoner, Stratton, shouted, "Don't do that," for which he was beaten into unconsciousness lasting 50 hours. When Stratton spoke, the warden drew a pistol, tried to fire at him, but cartridge failed to explode. Stratton raised a stool to protect himself, and, in fear of his life, threw it at the warden.

Floyd Ramp received a double compound fracture of the skull.

After being locked in solitary, two big brutes—Wingfield and "Mack," the former with a bat and the latter with a piece of pipe—were set to task of beating them. Ray and Axuara were beaten unmercifully, and two besides Stratton were unconscious for a long time. Many were handcuffed to doors, feet barely touching the floor. Hodges, Baskett, and Plahn were sick, and prison doctor ordered mattresses, which warden later removed. On the third day they were taken down so the prison inspector should not see them.

UNJUST AND UNFAIR COURTS-MARTIAL.

No. 12135 overdrew his bank account a couple of dollars on a $40 check, but reimbursed bank. Still, court-martial gave him six years at the disciplinary barracks.

6

No. 13055 took $4,000 from canteen, and food; admitted guilt and was sentenced to one year at disciplinary barracks. He has the money still.

No. 13054, a friend of the above, was convicted of having helped 13055 spend the money and having been his accomplice, although 13055 testified on the stand that 13054 knew nothing about the steal at all. He got one year at the disciplinary barracks.

No. ———, in sixth wing, got 25 years for being late 25 minutes on a 48-hour pass. W. McLeod (No. 14694) knows him.

A captain stole $100,000 from Q. M. fund; got six months at the disciplinary barracks and a dishonorable discharge.

A captain grafted $500,000 in an Army contract; was given a light sentence here and after one month was put in a battalion for restoration to duty.

The son of a colonel at Fort Oglethorpe, who took $10,000 from soldiers' mess fund when he was mess sergeant of his outfit; tried and found guilty by court-martial and given 10 years. Through influence of his father was reduced to six months. After spending 90 days in the guardhouse, son was set free.

No. 14112. Sentenced to 20 years for 9 days' absence without leave; another, 18 months for almost 5 months' absence without leave.

No. 14149. Train delayed by storm; got one year. Capt. Waggoner, of Fort Riley, " had· it in for him."

A lieutenant who became intoxicated at a colonel's party got out by mistake and " tore up the town." At trial the same colonel had to make an example of him and sent him to Fort Leavenworth under a heavy sentence.

Many of these young men I have met and spoken with in camp and hospital, and I pronounce them as fine and noble human material as a Government has ever exposed to abuse and destruction.

Respectfully and urgently submitted.

THEO. H. LUNDE,
President American Industrial Co.,
811 Rees Street, Chicago.

WASHINGTON, D. C., *January 13, 1919.*

———

WAR DEPARTMENT,
Washington, January 6, 1919.

MY DEAR MR. BROWN : In reply to your letter of January 3, I have to tell you that we have been informed that Clark Getts is no longer in the ward for mental cases at the disciplinary barracks at Fort Leavenworth. I hope you understand that he had been assigned there on the recommendation of the psychiatrist for observation and not as arbitrarily as your letter makes it appear. Thank you for your suggestions on general conditions·in the barracks.

Very truly, yours,

(Signed)   F. P. KEPPEL,
Third Assistant Secretary.

Mr. ALBERT PAUL BROWN,
2524 Jones Street, Omaha, Nebr.

———

2524 JONES STREET,
Omaha, Nebr., January 10, 1919.

Mr. F. P. KEPPEL,
Assistant Secretary of War, Washington, D. C.

DEAR SIR : I thank you for your kind acknowledgment of my letter of the 3d instant, and am glad to note its contents that the authorities at the United States Disciplinary Barracks, Fort Leavenworth, are able to report the remedying of the conditions surrounding Clark Getts. As to what those conditions were, I still have every confidence that I reported them correctly. The authorities had a number of C. O.'s under " observation," and I have seen the room in which they were confined while they were there several times. I know that Getts was not confined there. If all that was desired was to place him under observation, there would have been no object in placing him in a ward with insane men.

I know that Getts sent out the appeal for help, as I told you. The other conscientious objectors held under observation had nothing to complain of except lack of reading matter. Again I ask, if " observation " was all that the authori-

112619—19427

ties aimed at, why should Getts be differently treated? Personally I should feel inclined to substitute "intimidation" for "observation."

I understood at the time that it was due to the orders of the psychiatrist that Getts was confined with the insane, and it struck me then as a rather strange method of "healing the mind."

From this and other incidents it becomes evident that the authorities can cover almost any kind of treatment by a camouflaging phrase, even as Mr. Taussig now says that the conscientious objectors at Funston were given several showers a day "as a disciplinary measure" and made to sleep without beds "as a sanitary precaution"; and I do not doubt, sir, that the officials at Fort Leavenworth reported to you that Getts had been confined in the ward for mental cases as a "mental precaution." Only when the light of public opinion can reach these cases can the truth be assured. Trusting that I have helped contribute to that end, I am,

Yours, respectfully,

A. P. BROWN,
*Officer in Charge of Bureau of Designing and Drafting,
United States Engineering Corps, at Disciplinary Barracks.*

JANUARY 17, 1919.

My Chicago office just informs me that one of our returned employees, drafted and stationed at Fort Oglethorpe, confirms brutalities committed against the conscientious objectors there.

THEO H. LUNDE.

112619—19427

Conscientious Objectors

REMARKS

OF

HON. WILLIAM E. MASON

OF ILLINOIS

IN THE

HOUSE OF REPRESENTATIVES

MONDAY, MARCH 3, 1919

WASHINGTON
GOVERNMENT PRINTING OFFICE
1919

113051—19429

REMARKS
OF

HON. WILLIAM E. MASON.

Mr. MASON. Mr. Speaker, I insert here the following memorandum in refutation of the charge that conscientious objectors have been treated with leniency, furnished me by the National Civil Liberty Bureau, of 41 Union Square, New York.

The matter referred to is as follows:

The charge has been made that conscientious objectors in this country have been treated with undue leniency. What are the facts? Actually there are authentic, undenied statements of cases on record where conscientious objectors have been beaten, prodded with bayonets, immersed in filthy latrines, held for periods of from 15 to 45 minutes under cold shower baths, fed only bread and water, and placed for long periods in solitary confinement.

At the United States Disciplinary Barracks at Alcatraz Island, Cal., four religious objectors—three Hofer brothers and Jacob Wipf—were placed in a perfectly dark dungeon where water seeped in from the sea, their outer clothing being removed, and where they were fed only small amounts of bread and water. At the end of the fifth day they were removed by the recommendation of the medical examiner and placed in isolation. Later they were transferred to Fort Leavenworth, where they were at once placed in solitary confinement. Two of the Hofer brothers died of pneumonia within 10 days of their arrival at Fort Leavenworth. The body of one of these men was sent home dressed in the military uniform of the United States Army, although he had gone to prison because of his refusal to wear this uniform.

At Camp Funston a group of conscientious objectors for six weeks were put through a course of the roughest sort of hazing and brutality. They were not allowed to communicate with anyone during this time, and were subjected to physical coercion—struck with whips and dragged about with ropes, etc. (see Exhibit A, annexed hereto). Other undenied stories of brutalities have come from Camp Sherman, Camp Meade, Camp Wadsworth, Fort Jay, Fort Riley, and numerous other cantonments (see Exhibit B, annexed hereto).

Finally, over 500 objectors were sent to the military prison at Fort Leavenworth, with sentences ranging from 5 to 40 years. Here some of the objectors who refused to fall in line with the military discipline were kept for over nine weeks in solitary confinement, during most of which time they were manacled, standing to the bars of their cells nine hours a day, every alternate two weeks being spent on a diet of bread and water (see Exhibit B. annexed hereto). This was done with the express authorization of the War Department, as was tacitly admitted in Secretary Baker's order of December 6, abolishing menacing.

Yet, in spite of these facts, charges are brought that the War Department discriminated in favor of conscientious objectors. The explanation of this is to be found in the policy adopted by the War Department. It is true that the War Department did issue a confidential order providing for conscientious objectors, thereby giving color to the charges of special leniency. But in practice this policy worked out both to the disadvantage of the Army and the unnecessary and brutal coercion of objectors. It was the policy which sought ultimately to deal with con-

3

scientious objectors as a problem of military discipline. The officers in charge of these men found themselves forced to treat as soldiers men who were determined at all costs not to accept that status. The inevitable result of this policy was the coercion of objectors. Any other result under the circumstances would have meant that both officers and objectors were more than human.

In the case of objectors who were finally court-martialed the War Department has insisted upon treating these men as individual recalcitrant soldiers. This has resulted in the fact that to-day many of them have been released on one pretext or another, while others, actually no more radical in their protests against military service, are still in prison.

A further result of the War Department's policy has been that all objectors released from military prison have practically been forced to accept back pay as a condition of their discharge. This has served to discredit men who while in camp refused to sign the pay roll and so had back pay credited to them. According to a recent statement of the War Department, however, over $5,000 of the pay thus given to objectors has been returned direct to the Department.

Conscientious objectors have been sentenced by courts-martial to prison terms of exceeding severity. The War Department has announced its policy of reviewing each individual case with a view to possible clemency. This policy seems another mistake, because all of these men are imprisoned for the reason that their consciences upon one ground or another forbade their becoming a part of the military organization. Their cases all have the common basis of conscience and all have shown their sincerity by endurance of severe punishment. If one should be freed, all should be freed. If any are to serve out their sentences, all should. Their prison terms are the unhappy by-product of a military system essentially inconsistent with American democratic ideals, and which was created for the purpose of serving the country in a particular crisis. The crisis is now over and their release becomes now not a matter of clemency in individual cases but a matter of ordinary democratic justice.

Exhibit A.

REPORT OF TREATMENT OF CONSCIENTIOUS OBJECTORS AT THE CAMP FUNSTON GUARDHOUSE.

THURSDAY, *September 5, 1918.*

Seven conscientious objectors arrived at the military police guardhouse from the guardhouse at Riley.

SATURDAY, *September 7.*

We were ordered to fold our arms and stand at attention by the officer of the day, Capt. Buckley. Failing to comply with this order, he proceeded to abuse and insult us, referring to those of Jewish birth as "damn kikes," etc. He then had our beds and blankets taken from us and ordered that we be given raw rations—pork and beans—which we were to cook in the latrine, if we wanted to eat. He suggested to the prisoners that they beat us up. We had no supper and slept on the bare floor in our clothes.

SUNDAY, *September 8.*

Very little sleep was had because of the extreme chilliness of the night.

No other provisions having been made for the preparation of food, we ate nothing on this day.

We again slept on the bare floor without blankets.

MONDAY, *September 9.*

Food conditions remained the same until supper when we were informed that a kitchen for preparing our food would be furnished us if we would do our own cooking. We were able to prepare supper. Upon returning from this meal we were informed that henceforth we would be given bread and water only. Upon this fare we continued until September 15.

SATURDAY, *September 14.*

Col. Barnes, the provost marshal, called at the guardhouse. He ordered us to stand at attention, and when we refused to comply he proceeded to kick the legs of the men. Kaplan had his legs and angles bruised as a result. Upon leaving he hinted to the prisoners that he would be tempted to pardon them if they would beat us up.

4

MONDAY, *September 16.*

We were again placed upon bread and water diet. This continued until the following Sunday, September 22, on which day we had regularly prepared meals, so that between September 7 and 22 we had only two days of regular rations.

—

MONDAY, *September 23.*

We were ordered to stand at attention by the incoming officer of the day and upon refusal we were told that we would be taken out every two hours during the night. This procedure was inaugurated that very night when we were awakened at these periodic intervals, taken out and kept out a while and sent back to bed.

—

THURSDAY, *September 26.*

While walking about in the courtyard the men were kicked and shoved about for not obeying an order to walk in prescribed military fashion— Kaplan and Breger being the particular targets.

In the afternoon Larsen was brutally assaulted, being choked, his head banged against the wall, and dragged around the room, by the sergeant of the guards for refusing to clean quarters other than our own.

—

FRIDAY, *September 27.*

Again, while exercising, the men were grossly maltreated. The bayonet was applied to all of us—Larsen receiving a scar. Kaplan and Breger were beaten with the butt end of the rifle. All were kicked and shoved about.

Eight conscientious objectors came here from Fort Riley guardhouse. After supper we were ordered outside where we formed in double rank. The sergeant of the guards issued some military commands to us. When we did not obey promptly he shoved us about violently. We then began marching around the building. Orders were given to "double time." Bayonets were pressed against the bodies of Larsen, Silver, and others to obtain compliance, but no one ran. The guards now insisted that we walk in strick military posture and cuffs, kicks, and blows were rained upon those who failed to do so. Eichel refused to submit to this abuse and informed the guard that since in his opinion exercise was optional with conscientious objectors he would march no more under such brutal impositions. A guard seized him by the neck and forced him around the building, heaping blows and kicks upon him at the same time. When he was finally released the back of his head was covered with bumps and he was sore all over.

At about 9 that evening we were again ordered out and again put through the same ordeal. This time Steiner ceased walking. He was seized by the ears and dragged around the building. Another guard after a while seized him by the throat and choked him so forcibly that he sank breathless to the ground. Steiner reported his treatment to the officer of the day, a second lieutenant, who refused to give his name and who insisted that he was carrying out orders.

We were informed that we would be called out every two hours. At 11 p. m. we were awakened and ordered out. We refused. It was debated whether or not to forcibly drag us out. They finally decided to leave us alone. However, none could sleep, for the thought that we might be roused any moment kept preying upon our minds.

—

SATURDAY, *September 28.*

At 8.30 p. m. the sergeant of the guards ordered us out. Expecting a repetition of yesterday's affair, especially so since the sergeant was a veritable brute, we refused. Kaplan, half undressed, was the first to rouse his venom. He was lifted bodily off his bed and thrown headlong through the door. He was dragged back again, lifted off his feet and thrown against the bedstead so forcibly that his skull might have been smashed. He was then ordered to put on his shoes. He refused. The sergeant seized him and put him out barefooted. The other men were similarly handled. When we were finally lined up outside, the sergeant following us out—and never did man gloat so over his accomplishment—he remarked that he was carrying out the major's orders, meaning Maj. Taussig, the military police officer. After marching around a while we were permitted to return to quarters. Threats of subsequent and periodic repetition of this treatment again had the effect of keeping us awake and expectant all night.

The instructions that conscientious objectors are to be permitted to exercise is being utilized as a means to impose hardships upon us. We are kept outdoors in all sorts of weather, from six to eight hours each

5

day, and the guards are instructed to see to it that we keep moving continually. This is a source of constant irritation and friction between us and the guards, for some of us find it physically impossible to keep walking all day.

Our corresponding privilege has been restricted to one letter a week. The letter must be written upon one side of one small sheet. Its contents are subjected to careful censorship.

A general and thorough raid was made upon our quarters for books, magazines, and any other reading matter.

All prisoners were ordered to take a cold shower.

FRIDAY, *October 4.*

Orders were issued that conscientious objectors are to be given but one helping of food and "d—— little at that." Not even an extra piece of bread is allowed us. We are kept hungry from meal to meal.

—

SATURDAY, *October 5.*

We were ordered to take a cold shower. Da Rosa, feeling that cold showers are detrimental to him, and having taken a bath but one-half hour previous to the issuing of the above order, refused to undress. The corporal of the guards thrust him under the spray with his clothes on. Da Rosa returned to the guard room, wearing his dripping clothes. The corporal ordered him to undress and take a thorough shower. When Da Rosa again refused, the corporal tore his clothes from his body and at the same time delivered upon him some telling and effective blows. He was then placed under the cold shower.

We were compelled to take a cold shower once in the morning and once in the afternoon. A guard stood watch and checked each man.

—

SUNDAY, *October 6.*

In the afternoon, Sandin collapsed while taking his second cold shower of the day. We explained to the doctor who called, the nature of the treatment we had been receiving lately. We also informed him that we were being underfed.

The captain, who was "officer of the day" ordered that we be deprived of supper because we did not stand at "attention" at roll-call.

At midnight we were suddenly and unexpectedly roused by the sergeant of the guards and ordered to take a cold shower. It was obvious that this was an unreasonable and vicious imposition and most of us refused to get up. We were then violently dragged into the shower-room and held underneath the spray, night clothes and all, until thoroughly exhausted. Kaplan, Breger, Block, Powell, Franklin, Eichel, Downey, Steiner, and Da Rosa were so treated. The "officer of the day" was present and directed the proceedings.

—

MONDAY, *October 7.*

Breenberg, Block, Bernstein, and others have gone on sick report this morning, suffering from colds. Block and Bernstein were given asperin tablets to make them perspire. Though the day was rainy and damp, all hands were ordered out for exercise. We were kept outside in the drizzle, until ordered to come in for a cold shower. Even those who had taken asperin tablets were not excused from the prescribed bath.

Breger, Monsky, Ott, Silver, Da Rosa, Block, and Eichel have already declared an absolute hunger-strike as a vehement protest against this treatment.

Another cold shower was administered to us in the afternoon. At 8 p. m. the "officer of the day," a captain, and the sergeant of the guards ordered all to undress in the squadron and prepare for a cold shower, the third that day. We were marched to the latrine in a body. The captain himself brought forth scrubbrushes, used ordinarily for cleaning toilet seats and brooms used for sweeping, and ordered that we scrub each other with them. Franklin refused to use the filthy brush. He was seized and roughly thrown to the cement floor, dragged back and forth and viciously belabored until thoroughly exhausted. He was then placed under the cold spray and left there until he collapsed. Eichel and Shotkiu helped him back to his bed. When he recovered he became hysterical.

The captain wished to know what had happened. Eichel explained that Franklin was suffering from myocarditis and the constant and frequent impositions of cold showers had in all probabilities aggravated this ailment. Eichel then requested the captain to permit him to see the post commander. This the captain refused to do, although he told

6

Eichel that he was carrying out the instructions of the post commander in treating us so.

—

TUESDAY, *October 8.*

Franklin, Sandin, and Hennessey have joined the hunger strike as protest against our inhuman treatment.

At about 8 p. m. the order was issued to prepare for a cold shower. Monsky informed the captain, who directed proceedings that he would not undress. The captain ordered a guard to undress and keep him under the shower twice as long. The sergeant of the guards timed everyone. Monsky was kept under the spray an unusually long time. He finally heard the captain say, " If he suffers, keep him there ; but if he isn't suffering let him go."

Franklin, because of his collapse the previous evening, was given an extra. dose and again collapsed. Eichel again requested to be permitted to see the post commander and again was refused.

Quite a few of the men, thoroughly chilled by the shower, had gone to bed to warm up. "Attention" was suddenly called and those in bed were dumped by the guards and dragged to their feet. Half naked the guards proceeded to place them in military posture. Towels, socks, and ropes were utilized to tie their hands in proper position. Then the captain addressed us. " How many of you will now become sensible objectors and go out to do some work this afternoon?" Receiving no favorable response he said tersely : "All right, another cold shower at 10.30 a. m."

We were then ordered to dress and go out for exercise. Quite a few refusing to do this were rudely dressed and dragged outside.

Promptly at 10.30 o'clock we were ordered in for our cold shower. Monsky, Block, Breger, Franklin, and Eichel, feeling that this was unquestionably punishment for their refusal to work, refused to undress. They were taken to the shower room in their clothes. There Eichel was again ordered to undress. When he refused, a corporal slapped his face vehemently and dragged him back to the squad room. There the order was repeated, and when Eichel maintained his attitude the corporal belabored him viciously with slaps across the face and blows upon the head. He was taken back to the shower room, and he as well as the others who had refused to undress were placed and kept underneath the spray in their clothes.

Hennessey had undressed for the shower and had stepped underneath. No one was paying any particular attention to him. Suddenly he emitted a wild shriek, began tottering and swinging aimlessly. If some one had not grabbed him instantly, he might have dashed his head against the cement. He was carried to his bed, all the time maintaining his wild cries. Presently his struggles subsided and he remained in a state of coma for almost an hour. No doctor was sent for. Ott now asked permission to see the post commander, and was given the expected response.

Those who had taken the shower in their clothes undressed and went to bed. At about 2 p. m. the order came to get out for exercise. The wet clothes were put on the men and they were thrust outside. We were walking around when the corporal informed us that the major (Taussig) had ordered that we walk more rapidly. Franklin attracted the guards' attention first. He was rushed violently against the wire fence, thrown to the ground, and his head banged against the rocks. Monsky next received the brunt of attention. The corporal and guard pommeled, shoved, and abused him. A group gathered to watch the spectacle. Amongst the latter were some friends of the active guard. To please them, he seized Monsky from behind and ran him around the inclosure. Then, acting upon the suggestion of one of the spectators, he deliberately strove to step upon Monsky's bare feet. The latter succeeded for a while in thwarting him, but the inevitable happened and Monsky sank to the ground in agony. His ankle had been sprained.

This cowardly act completely unnerved Breger. " Hurray ! Hurray for our brave American !" he yelled, and clapped his hands vehemently in applause. He was stopped, but he no longer was master of himself. He stopped, took off his shoes and exclaimed, " Here, do the same to me and show your bravery !" He walked on a while and suddenly let forth an uncanny yell and fell to the ground. He struggled painfully, all the time maintaining his gruesome cries. His struggles ceased finally and amid jeers of " He's all right " he was raised to his feet. Monsky in the meanwhile had been dragged all over the ground, his clothes torn from his body, and was practically unconscious.

The " officer of the day " now came upon the scene. He ordered those who would not walk to be placed in solitary confinement on

113051—19429

7

bread and water. Breger and Monsky were the first to be punished. Eichel discontinued walking. He was dragged around a while and then placed in solitary confinement on bread and water. Steiner now refused to walk, and he, too, was placed in solitary. Silver next attracted the guard's attention. The doctor had come, and Silver informed him that since he had not eaten for two days his physical condition would not permit his exercising, and hence he would walk no more. He was ordered back into the ring by the "officer of the day," and when he refused a guard seized him and threw him to the ground. He then lifted him by the legs, to the intense delight of the spectators, and banged his head against the ground. This act was repeated a number of times. Then Silver, thoroughly shaken up, was placed on the restricted bread-and-water diet.

Breger, in the squad room, again gave vent to those wild paroxysms. His cries and intense internal struggles continued intermittently for over an hour.

—

WEDNESDAY, *October 9*.

Steiner joined the hunger strikers because he had been placed on bread and water.

Eichel was undressed and given a cold shower.

Col. Barnes, the provost marshal, called while some of the objectors were taking their enforced exercise. He ordered them to stand at "attention." When they refused, he beat them vigorously with his heavy riding crop. Shotkin was badly hurt, the colonel breaking his crop over the former's ankles. He deprecated the ruining of his stick and implied that the only reason he did not brain Shotkin was that he wasn't worth the trouble. He then addressed the men before him. "You have declared a famine strike on me. Well, the Third Assistant Secretary of War, your friend, knows it and has instructed that I permit you to starve to death."

Shotkin, limping, returned to quarters. A guard straightway ordered him outside. Shotkin insisted that he could not walk and demanded medical attention. Though the doctor was in the room at the time, no treatment was given him. On the contrary, though suffering intense pain, he was dragged outside and two guards pushed him around the inclosure.

Steiner was dragged from his solitary cell and ordered to walk. Failing to obey, a guard seized him by his fingers and dragged him around. Steiner suffered intense pain, for the slightest resistance on his part meant the pulling of his finger out of joint.

After supper two slices of bread were given to those who were presumably on bread and water, despite the fact that every one of them was on hunger strike. The sergeant informed them, "Not a d—d drop of water do you get until this bread is consumed."

—

THURSDAY, *October 10*.

Ott and Da Rosa, both materially weakened by their hunger strike, were forcibly dressed and put on exercise in the afternoon.

Ott was shoved around a while and then left unmolested.

Da Rosa was pushed about, then thrown to the wet ground, punched, kicked, and spat at by the guards. He was raised to his feet and dragged around some more. Presently he was dropped and one guard seized him by the hair and rubbed his face in and banged his head on the ground. His cheek and forehead were bruised, leaving two ugly skin wounds.

Then four guards carried him to the shower room, stripped him of what little clothes remained on his person, placed him on the cold cement floor in an exhausted condition, and turned the cold spray upon him. The soldiers then scrubbed him viciously with filthy brushes and brooms. One guard tickled his feet. He was finally brought back to the squad room in a semiconscious state.

Downey, Brandin, Bernstein, and Kaplan, feeling they could not conscientiously continue eating while their fellow conscientious objectors were being so brutalized, joined in with the hunger strikers.

—

FRIDAY, *October 11*.

Brandin, because of extreme weakness, was unable to walk. A guard pricked him with a bayonet, and then the sergeant of the guards himself pushed him around.

—

SATURDAY, *October 12*.

In the afternoon all the men, regardless of their physical condition, were ordered to dress and go out for fresh air. Those who refused were

113051—19429

206 ————

8

forcibly dressed and thrust outside. The men, because of their weakened state, sprawled all over the ground, while groups of spectators watched the miserable and sorry sight. At various times during the afternoon Block, Breger, and Silver collapsed from total exhaustion.

After supper the men were taken out of the solitary cells and returned to the regular squad room.

MONDAY, October 14.

Maj. Taussig, accompanied by another major, who introduced himself as our investigator, came into the room in the morning. The latter gazed sneeringly and insolently about the room and without much ado dismissed most of the men from his mind as "Russian foreigners." His questioning was confined for the most part in ascertaining the birth and nativity of the men and establishing them as "Pro-Germans and members of Von Ludendorf's third division." He finally asked, with studied irony, whether any man was in danger of losing his reason or even his life. His final remark was, "There isn't a single American in the crowd."

Our writing tablets and what little money was in our possession were taken from us. A special guard was placed over us.

TUESDAY, October 15.

Silver was examined by the doctor, and it was apparent that his condition was very poor. He was hardly able to get out of bed. In the afternoon he was taken out of our squad room and placed in a solitary cell.

THURSDAY, October 17.

The men felt that the hunger strike had accomplished its purpose, in that brutalities had been discontinued for the past few days, and decided to eat supper. Bread and milk was given us to break our fast.

FRIDAY, October 18.

Black coffee and bread was sent us for breakfast. Such food at this time most of us felt was actual poison for our systems. Hence, with one or two exceptions, we declined to eat this repast. No other food was furnished us.

SATURDAY, October 19.

Immediately after breakfast Eichel was viciously and suddenly struck two stinging blows in the mouth for failing, through no fault of his, to properly "cover off" for count.

Later, Ott and Eichel were ordered to clean the latrine by the sergeant of the guards, and when they refused the former slapped, punched, and shoved them violently against the wall and other projections.

MONDAY, October 21.

The major who made the perfunctory investigation Monday, October 14, returned and began calling each man to explain the mistreatments he had experienced and witnessed.

We wish it known that during this tense period we were held absolutely incommunicado. Packages containing food and delicacies, sent us from home at a great expense of time, money, and sentiment, were viciously and wantonly destroyed and their contents dumped in the garbage cans, though we had at no time been told that we could not receive such packages.

The above is only a brief summary of the atrocities perpetrated upon us. The situation can never be described with sufficient vividness and intensity to impart to the authorities a real impression of the mental and physical anguish suffered by us. Most of the mistreatments took place outside, with large groups watching the sorry and revolting spectacle of defenseless men being most brutally punched, shoved, and abused.

While we do not wish to impugn the motives of the investigator we have reason to believe, because of his own statements and his obviously antagonistic attitude, that the report of his investigation would be prejudiced and not strictly in accordance with the fullest testimony of the men. We therefore feel justified in submitting this report, which we are willing to affirm under oath, merely as a confirmation to his report.

The men reached the guard house at Funston on the following dates, and went through the above experiences from the day of their arrival:

113051—19429

9

September 5.—Bernstein, Breger, Greenberg, Kaplan, Henessey, Øar-
sen, and Powell.
September 27.—Downey, Eichel, Franklin, Ott, Sandin, Shotkin, Sil-
ver, and Steiner.
September 30.—Block, Da Rosa, and Monsky.
October 8.—Brandin.
A copy of this report has been given to the investigator.
We, the undersigned, consider the above a fair and accurate account
of our treatment at the military police guard house of Camp Funston,
Kans.

> Morris Franklin. Thomas Shotkin, Herman Kaplan, Lester
> G. Ott, Joseph Brandin, Ulysses Da Rosa, Mayer Bern-
> stein, Henry Monsky, Max Sandin, Emanuel Silver,
> Benjamin Breger, Rexford Powell, David Eichel, Julius
> R. Greenberg, Chas. P. Larsen, Francis Steiner, Francis
> X. Henessey, and John Downey.

EXHIBIT B.

POLITICAL PRISONERS IN FEDERAL MILITARY PRISONS—MEN, STRIKING
IN PROTEST AGAINST THE TREATMENT OF FELLOW PRISONERS, ARE
MANCLED IN SOLITARY CONFINEMENT IN DARK UNDERGROUND CELLS ON
A DIET OF BREAD AND WATER—IT IS ONLY A QUESTION OF HOW MANY
DAYS THEY CAN LAST BEFORE PHYSICAL OR MENTAL COLLAPSE PUTS
AN END TO THIS PHASE OF THEIR SUFFERING.

The National Civil Liberties Bureau has come into possession of information regarding conditions in the military prisons of the United
States which it believes it would not be justified in withholding from
the public. These prisons, called "disciplinary barracks," are located
at Fort Jay, Governors Island, N. Y.; Fort Leavenwortu, Kans.; and
Alcatraz Island, San Francisco Bay. Concerning the last-named prison
we have at present no information. The other two are fairly well run
as prisons go, with the exception of the form of punishment for recalcitrant prisoners, which consists of solitary confinement in dark cells,
manacling, and a diet of broad and water. The conditions are described in the following documents. Primarily this protest has nothing
to do with the offence for which the prisoners were sentenced. The
first point is that torture inflicted upon any prisoner for any reason is
as stupid as it is wicked and abhorrent to the American spirit. The
second point is the justice of a distinction between political and criminal offenders.

I. STATEMENT OF CONDITIONS AT FORT JAY ON AUGUST 20, AS REPORTED BY
DR. JUDAH L. MAGNES AND MR. JOHN S. CODMAN.

AUGUST 27, 1918.

Mr. John S. Codman, of Boston, and I went to Governors Island on
the 3.15 boat and returned on the 6.30 boat.
Maj. Ward received us very courteously, and gave us every opportunity to interview the three conscientious objectors, and to examine
the conditions under which they are now imprisoned.
He took us to the cells where Sterenstein and Eichel are in solitary
confinement. These cells are on the top floor of the prison. Maj. Ward
informed us that most solitary confinement cells are in the cellars of
prisons. He gave Mr. Codman later the dimensions of these cells.
They are small and all but completely dark. Light and air come in
from a very small opening on the top, and through a small iron grating
(in the door). Maj. Ward informed us that in many solitary confinement cells there is only the opening at the top. The door of Sterenstein's cell was opened first. We found him with his wrists shackled
to the iron bars of the small opening in the door. He was in his
underwear and in bare feet. There was no pail in his cell. The only
thing in the cell was a blanket. When Eichel's cell was opened we
found him shackled in the same way to the bars of the grating in the
door. He was in his underclothes and had on one stocking. There
was a pail in his cell.
Maj. Ward explained to us that they were sentenced to solitary confinement for refusing to work and obey prison instructions. (Such refusal to work will be found throughout these documents to be one of
the chief sources of difficulty between the conscientious objector and
the military. To the average reader it may seem difficult to understand
and quite indefensible. The objectors' position may be clarified by the
following explanation: (1) In certain cases the objectors felt that
the work assigned to them amounted to the noncombatant service which
they had refused in the first place because it relieved other men to do
the very work in the Army to which they were conscientiously opposed.

Other objectors considered that the mere acceptance of work under
military orders was a recognition of the whole principle of conscription
which they are convinced must be everywhere condemned before the
world can ever become safe for real democracy. (2) At Fort Leavenworth all but a few of the objectors had consented to work, but a number finally ceased working, not so much because they were opposed to
the work itself, but because such a stand was the only effective way by
which to register their protest against the brutal treatment of fellow
prisoners in solitary confinement. Rather than acquiesce in such wrong
they would share their suffering.) They were shackled to the bars of
the grating from 7.30 a. m. to 11.30 a. m. and then from 12.30 p. m.
to 4.30 p. m.—the theory being that this is equivalent to an eight-hour
working day. They are given two slices of bread three times a day
and a pitcher of water three times a day. They are given no water
with which to wash. If they wish to wash they must use some of their
drinking water. They are not permitted a tooth brush. They are
taken on Saturday night and given a shower bath.

"After 14 days of such confinement the prisoners are released into
the prison yard for 14 days. They are given raw food, an ax for
chopping wood, cooking utensils, and shelter at night. Otherwise they
are regarded as men on a desert island, bound to shift for themselves.
If after these 14 days of desert island life, they are still unwilling to
yield their conscientious convictions, they are placed in solitary confinement again for another 14 days. This can go on indefinitely for
the term of 20 or 30 years to which these men have been sentenced
or until they are broken, either physically or mentally.

"We were then shown into the chaplain's office by the major, who
said that we might interview each of the three prisoners separately,
provided that we would give them nothing nor in any other way break
the prison rules. We told him that we were particularly anxious to
question the men as to the attitude of the board of review toward them.

"Robinson was the first prisoner admitted. He was not in solitary
confinement, having served his 14 days. He was now undergoing the
desert-island treatment, and had been for a few days. He had a
healthy color and clear eye. He answered all of our questions simply
and in a straightforward and in almost an objective way. We told
him, as we did the others, that we were members of the National Civil
Liberties Bureau, and that Mr. Baldwin had reported on their status
from time to time; that we were interested in the general problem
of conscientious objectors and that we had come to ask them particularly as to the attitude of the board of review. Robinson said that
the board of review had interviewed him for only a few minutes, perhaps two or three, and that after that interview had declared him to
be insincere. They regarded him as insincere because, so he thought,
when they asked him if he would shed blood in self-defense he answered that he did not know what he would do under such circumstances. He said that he had not received any official notice as to
what his sentence was, but that he had been informed through newspaper reports that he had been first sentenced for life and that then
his sentence had been reduced to 20 years. He was a conscientious
objector from every point of view—from the religious, the humanitarian, the political, the antimilitarist. He was of a farmer's family.
He had been farming himself, and was for that reason better able
physically, so he said, to endure the solitary confinement than the
other men, who came from the city. He did not know how long it
would be possible for him to stand the solitary confinement, but there
was no doubt in his mind that, after the expiration of his 14 days of
desert-island treatment, he could stand another 14 days of solitary
confinement. Although most anxious to hear from his family, he
could not hear from them because he had refused to sign the necessary
papers. He regarded these papers as military documents and refused
to sign them for that reason. He had no complaint to make as to the
food that was being given to him during the desert-island treatment.
His general complaint about the solitary confinement cell, and this
was the general complaint of the others as well, was that it was
almost impossible to sleep at night because the cells were full of
vermin—bedbugs and another brown bug being particularly numerous—
so numerous, in fact, that, after sleeping fits they had to be brushed
in large quantities from their limbs. When we told the major afterwards of this he was quite indignant and said that he did not believe
the cells were full of vermin ; that he was sure they were lying, but
that he would make a note of it, anyway. (I may as well remark
here that the major in conversation afterwards did not seem to be as
well posted as he might be on conditions in a prison to which he is
supposed to be giving his complete time and attention.

11

"The next prisoner admitted was Sterenstein. He came into the room blinking because of the light, after the darkness of his cell. He had been permitted to put on his prison garb. We were very grateful that because of our visit both he and Eichel were given a few minutes' respite from their shackles. Sterenstein had quite a heavy growth of beard. (The prisoners in solitary confinement not being permitted, of course, to shave.) He seemed to be physically the weakest of the three. He informed us that he had been sentenced to 30 years for refusing inoculation and refusing to work. Neither he nor Eichel had been adjudged as insincere by Judge Mack's board. It was his opinion that he and Eichel were being kept at Fort Jay because it was necessary for the authorities to subject a few men to severe punishment as an example to others. Other men who held precisely the same views and who had refused to obey certain orders had been transferred to Fort Leavenworth. He said that as a Socialist and humanitarian it was not possible for him to do anything to further the war; that he realized his life did not belong to him at a time when thousands of men were losing their lives, and that he was ready to be shot if only in that way he might give testimony to the faith that was in him. When he and Eichel came to Fort Jay they were undecided as to whether or not they would work on the stone pile. They worked on the stone pile for one day and then came to the conclusion that it was wrong to do this, because they would then be relieving some other men for military work. They thereupon refused to do other prison work and were placed in solitary confinement for this. Maj. Ward later cited their one day's work as conclusive evidence of their insincerity. Sterenstein complained of the petty annoyances to which the objectors were being treated by some of the guards. He was ready to serve his complete sentence without flinching; but did not think that they should be subjected to severer treatment than their sentence called for. He said that guards had beaten up at least two men to his knowledge, one of them in a cell, and that Maj. Ward himself had declared that one man would have to be beaten up, inasmuch as that was the only way to deal with him. Maj. Ward declared afterwards that as far as he knew no man had been beaten up at the prison for a whole year. Sterenstein said that at certain times of the day some rays of light came into his cell so that it was possible for him to read surreptitiously. He pulled out a tattered copy of the New Testament from his stocking, saying that he had been able to conceal this. He complained of the trouble the vermin gave at night. He thought also that if he might be permitted, when shackled, to stand in his shoes it would be easier for him, because he had flat feet. He had a handkerchief during the 14 days, inasmuch as there was one in his clothes. No handkerchief had been offered him by the authorities. When asked if he objected to our repeating some of his remarks, he said that he was entirely willing to suffer any reprisal that might be meted out if only the cause of the conscientious objector might thus be helped.

"Eichel appeared to be stronger physically than Sterenstein and just as steadfast in his determination to hold out as long as he could. His attitude was practically the same as that of Sterenstein. There was no discrepancy between the statements of any of the three prisoners. Eichel was particularly anxious to have his family know that he was still at Fort Jay. They had not been permitted to hear from their families."

As a result of our complaint to the War Department, based upon this and other reports, the conscientious objectors in question were transferred to Fort Leavenworth, where the cells are said to be more sanitary; but the use of these cells at Fort Jay for the punishment of recalcitrant prisoners still continues to this day.

II. STATEMENTS AS TO CONDITIONS AT THE DISCIPLINARY BARRACKS, FORT LEAVENWORTH, KANS.

This is the chief military prison in the United States. At this time it contains approximately 3,000 prisoners, of whom about 300 are conscientious objectors. Most of these latter are under sentences ranging from 10 to 30 years. Whatever the particular charges on which they were court-martialed, they are imprisoned for one reason only, and that is their steadfast refusal on religious or other conscientious grounds to accept any form of conscript service under military authority.

The documents which follow come from prisoners whose names we can not publicly disclose, but who are known to us to be trustworthy:

1. Bulletin on conditions within the prison as they were about November 6. [We know the author of this bulletin and can vouch for his character and accuracy.—Ed.]

"Evan W. Thomas finally refused to continue work * * *, and the following day he was put in solitary confinement.

113051—19429

12

" His final statement was that in going to the ' hole ' he was protesting against the entire prison system, as well as the fact that conscientious objectors are not distinguished from ordinary criminals and against the mistreatment of individual conscientious objectors.

" He believes that officials here are acting according to instructions from authorities in Washington.

" He plans to remain in ' solitary ' until he collapses physically if conditions are not changed.

" Nine conscientious objectors, serving long sentences at the United States Disciplinary Barracks for refusal to submit to military conscription, are in solitary confinement in the institution because they have declined to engage in prison labor. * * *

" Five of these men have been brutally beaten and manhandled since they arrived.

" These nine men are handcuffed and chained by their wrists to the bars of the door for nine hours a day in darkened cells. The solitary cells here are in the sub-basement of the prison. Prisoners in such confinement are rationed on bread and water. Most of these executive sentences are for 14 days, but some of the objectors have been in solitary 30, 40, or even, in one case, 50 days. * * *

" Following is a list of the nine conscientious objectors enduring solitary punishment :

" Thomas Reed (colored), religious, arrived from Fort Jay, N. Y., on September 13, in solitary since September 15.

" Hyman Bloch, religious, from Camp Funston, September 20, in solitary since November 4.

" Jacob Wurtzman, socialist, from Fort Riley, November 4.

" Henry Monsky, socialist, from Camp Funston, November 4.

" Abraham Gelerter, orthodox Jew, from Fort Jay, September 13.

" Jake Conovaloff, religious, Camp Funston, October 20.

" Fred Uren, religious, Camp Funston, October 20.

" Morris Shuben, religious, Camp Funston, November 2.

"Andre Shuben, religious, Camp Funston, October 28.

" Prisoners, including at least two conscientious objectors, witnessed the brutal treatment given Dan Yoder and S. Herschberger, both from Camp Sherman, Ohio, November 1, and their accounts are substantially as follows :

" These men are members of the Ammish Mennonite sect, one of the religious rules of which forbids the wearing of clothes fastened by buttons. Upon their arrival they refused to don the uniform of military offenders. They were taken to the clothing storeroom and undressed forcibly by sentries, and were put into prison clothes.

" Sergt. Morris, foreman of the clothing storeroom, then took the two prisoners to the bathroom. There they again refused to cooperate. Again they were disrobed roughly. They were led under the cold showers and held there for between 10 and 15 minutes.

" Herschberger took the coarse ' laundry ' soap that was forced upon him and washed himself. Yoder was led, or almost dragged, by the hair, shivering and crying noisily. Sergt. Morris, who was holding him, still by the hair, then ordered all the warm water to be turned off. Yoder refused to wash himself. The sergeant took a large cake of soap and a heavy fiber brush and began to scrub him, rubbed the soap up and down over his face and roughly applied the scrubbing brush to his body.

" They refused to put on the uniform. Herschberger dried himself and was dressed by other prisoners and sentries. Yoder, in the hands of the sergeant, was knocked down onto the cold cement floor. Without being dried, he was forced into the uniform. During this process his head was held between the knees of Sergt. Morris. When his underclothes were on, the sergeant lifted him up by the ears. This treatment has caused these two men to submit to prison labor against their beliefs.

" Instances can be multiplied. Geleiter, when he refused to drill, was beaten by sentries before he was put into solitary. Even there he was deprived of his phylactery, a religious article, indispensable to him. Uren and A. Shuben were beaten in the executive office. Corpl. Harry Hunter inflicted the bodily punishment in these last cases. His actions were unauthorized, and in consequence he has been suspended as yard corporal.

" But that is the only show of justice that the authorities of the institution have given in respect to these outrages. The incidents of Yoder and Herschberger were reported by two prisoners to Capt. Harry Mitchell, adjutant, and by him to Capt. L. A. Humason, intelligence officer. Nothing further has been done. It is not known whether reports of these affairs were allowed to reach officials in Washington

13

or whether proper punishment is to be meted out to the soldiers who committed these brutalities. * * *

"Thomas has stated briefly how most of the political conscientious objectors regard this situation. When he submitted his letter to Col. Sedgewick Rice, the commandant, he was read an order from Washington stating that conscientious objectors who have been sentenced shall be treated as the ordinary criminal soldier."

2. Extract from letter written November 7:

"You will wonder at my sanity if I tell you that I am trying to pick a vegetarian existence out of the limited rations in the mess hall. There are several of us now. * * * One is Rose, from New York, who passes on all the books sent to prisoners; another is Sylva, just arrived from Funston and still weak from the effects of his hunger strike; another is a robust athlete from Denver; and the other four are Israelites from Benton Harbor who tremble lest by eating a morsel of animal fat they will violate the exhortations of Holy Writ. The table has contributed so many to the ' hole ' that some begin to fear it is enchanted. Block, from Riley, has just gone down for refusal to work; Geleiter, from Fort Jay, has been in solitary for weeks, and several Russians have gone after him.

" In the ' hole,' a dungeon in the subbasement, the men are fed only bread and water, and are handcuffed to their cell doors for nine or more hours a day. During the first week they stand with their hands crossed at their breasts; during the second they hang by their wrists. [We presume, with their feet on the floor.—Ed.]

"The ' screws ' [sentries] are brutal. I have gone down with food from the mess hall several times to observe them. The air reeks with curses and foul drule. I have not heard these fellows suggest anything nearer a human reaction than a bestial laugh at some lewd tale. It follows that these men handle the prisoners with little gentleness. Geleiter has been beaten periodically. I saw him dragged by the collar, choking, across the rough floor of the corridors and the barber shop into the bath. One sentry knocked him down upon the cement floor, another undressed him with such brutality that he screamed with pain, and three of them forced him into the shower and scrubbed him with coarse soap.

" The Russians from Riley came out of confinement yesterday wan and staggering. They have gone to work. Both are religious objectors. Some of the Russians now in confinement have gone through the worst experiences in jail which the worst of the Tzars had to offer. They say that there they were permitted to cook their own food and were let alone. They swear that their life there was easy in comparison to this.

" Fellows who came from Camp Sherman last week declined to don the prison garb. (From other sources we learn that this was because of religious scruples against wearing buttons.) Two of them persisted. They were beaten into submission and the clothes were forced on them. For a time one of them wore his bundle around his neck, refusing to touch it; but he, too, was forcibly dressed. It is said that a captain witnessed the original beating and that he turned his back and walked off without interceding. The sentries to whom he left the job dragged the boys to the bathroom and treated them to Geleiter's experience, scrubbing the flesh of one with the ubiquitous galvanic soap and a coarse scrubbing brush. The water was so cold that the rest of us spent scarcely three minutes under it and retreated. Yet these C. O.'s were held under it for nearly 15 minutes. Corporal ——— is being tried for beating up two Russians—Holy Jumpers from Texas— for their refusal to salute and work. He administered one of his pummelings in the office of the executive officer, who himself had to stop the struggle. But he is being tried because his specific act was not authorized. The ' hole ' treatment is known by everyone in all its details and is accepted by the authorities. * * * "

3. Letters of November 14 and 15 on the situation to date.

Box 60, FORT LEAVENWORTH, November 14.

MY DEAR ———: Francis Hennessy has asked me to send you this message, for just now he can not write.

The group of boys from Fort Riley and Camp Funston came to Leavenworth more than a week ago. Most of them began working in and about the prison, but practically all have refused to work longer and are now doing penance in the " holes." The " hole " is our jail, you know—a black, cold place in the subbasement. The men hang there chained by their wrists to their cell doors for nine hours a day. They sleep on the cold cement floor between foul blankets and are given bread and water, if they will eat at all. They can not speak, and of

course they can neither read nor write. [That is, they are not allowed, being chained in the dark.—Ed.]

There is brutality enough, too. Some of the men have been beaten
periodically. I saw one man dragged by his collar across the rough
corridor floor, screaming and choking, to the bath. He was knocked
about on the floor for failing to undress, and was then stripped roughly
and thrust under a cold bath. * * * He has since gone to the
hospital.

Several Russians—Holy Jumpers from Arizona—have been hunger
striking in the hole. Two of them were beaten so bestially that even
the authorities were shocked, and the sentry is to be court-martialed.
The sentry is being tried, however, only because he exceeded his authority. The other beatings and tortures are matters of general
knowledge and are accepted by the authorities as justifiable. These
Russians were so weak at the end of six days that two of them had to
be sent to the hospital—veritable ghosts. * * * They are ready
to die in this dungeon. Their courage, so firm and beautiful, shames
the others of us.

Evan Thomas, Howard Moore (on Nov. 8, 1918, the Carnegie Hero
Fund Commission awarded Howard Moore a hero medal and $500 for
the gallant rescue of Miss Hanney off Bell Island, Conn. When the
award was made, he was prisoner at Fort Leavenworth for conscience
sake. Other of his comrades are no less brave). Rose (of Philadelphia),
Hennessy, and about 20 others are now in the pit. They are protesting
against the brutalities and tortures, compulsory work, compulsory chapel
on Sunday, and against the imprisonment itself. The local officers are
relentless in punishing this breach of discipline, and promise one man
a court-martial, I am told, as a lesson to the rest of us. Little more
could be expected of them. But from Washington we hope that some
recognition of the condition may be drawn. We hope, of course, that
the administration will act as liberally as it has so often spoken and
that it will recognize the right to be free-minded, religiously and politically. We feel that if the Government is not committed by deed to the
principle, the sacrifice we have been making has accomplished nothing
except, perhaps, to create a splendid social propagandist material.

We wish that some one could visit us and see with his own eyes the
results of the repressive policies which these military persons call
justice. * * *

We have all come to love Francis in the few days that he has been
here. He is a lad of the quietest courage. He has not the slightest
hesitancy about stepping into this dungeon. He wants you to be assured that he will come through happily.

Very truly, yours,

(Signed) ——— ———.

NOVEMBER 16.

This is a supplement to the letter I sent concerning Francis Hennessy.
The boys in the dungeon are hunger striking now, demanding their
release. They are being forcibly fed in the usual manner. I can not
learn whether Francis is among them, but he said when he left me that
he intended going the limit. He was getting on quite happily on bread
and water yesterday morning.

Rose, of Philadelphia, who struck for 25 days in Camp Meade, was
taken from the wing yesterday and ordered to begin breaking rock. He
refused and was forced to stand all day, the cold wind cutting his
flesh, eating nothing. He went to his cell in the evening shuddering
with chills and burning with fever. To-day he is out in the yard again,
professing health and liberty. He is to be court-martialed, he is told,
and given a long term of years in the Federal penitentiary.

Others will be joining the hunger strike day by day. None will die,
for the officers do not want the responsibility of making explanations
to enraged parents and friends, and the public generally; but they will
all have a sober time of it. As long as I am at liberty myself, I shall
be happy to tell you of the condition of Hennessy and of the others.

Very truly,

(Signed) ——— ———.

4. Digest of a report by an investigator sent to Fort Leavenworth by
the National Civil Liberties Bureau:

NOVEMBER 18, 1918.

The investigator states that at the time of his visit there were in
confinement at Fort Leavenworth 280 conscientious objectors, and that
several had died of the recent epidemic of influenza. The assistant
commander refused absolutely to allow him to copy the names of any
of these men, nor would he state what treatment was given to objectors
who refused to do work assigned to them. The investigator adds that

113051—19429

15

from his observations " they would not be accorded very much consideration as human beings," that they are " very thinly clad," " are constantly under the eye of an armed man," and that " hundreds of armed guards of the rough-house type are with the men at all times."

5. Documents illustrating the reason why some of the men quit work in protest against the punishment of certain of their comrades.

(a) Letter of prisoner No. 14822 to The Adjutant General, Washington, D. C.:

UNITED STATES DISCIPLINARY BARRACKS,
Fort Leavenworth, November 5, 1918.

From : General Prisoner Evan W. Thomas, Serial No. 14822, United States Disciplinary Barracks, Fort Leavenworth, Kans.
To : The Adjutant General, Washington, D. C.
Subject : Treatment of conscientious objectors.

SIR : In a letter written by you dated August 18, 1918, to David E. Eichel at Fort Riley, Kans., you declared that it is not the policy of the Government to coerce the conscience of individual objectors, but that, on the other hand, great and liberal concessions have been made to conscientious objectors. I know that the same impression has been given by the Government to many other individuals through letters as well as through the public statements of officials.

Yet the fact remains that in accordance with the regulations a number of the many conscientious objectors now confined in the disciplinary barracks here are in solitary confinement, chained to the bars of their cells nine hours a day for conscience' sake. I have been witness of the mental anguish through which some of the men have gone because they could not work in this institution, no matter what the consequences might be. I myself have on repeated occasions before coming here declared to Army officers that I would not work in the disciplinary barracks if the consciences of others were coerced or if the work was the same as noncombatant service in the Army.

Nevertheless, since my arrival here, on October 20, I have been working. It is not my desire, even if it were possible, to interfere with the discipline of this institution, nor do I believe that that is the intention of the objectors now in solitary confinement. But the fact remains that in spite of the many liberal statements made by the Government the conscientious objector is being treated exactly as the recalcitrant or criminal soldier.

In view of the explicit promises made by the Government, can not some provision be made to relieve the situation here?

Respectfully, yours,

(Signed)   EVAN W. THOMAS.

(b) Memorandum sent to mother of prisoner No. 14822 in reply to her questions with regard to her son :

NOVEMBER 13, 1918.

MEMORANDUM FOR COMMANDANT.

Circumstances under which No. 14822 came into the office and the reasons for going into solitary confinement rather than work.

1. I was in need of two reliable copyists in the office and was entering the office of the executive officer to apply for these men and remarked my needs to Capt. Leard, who was also entering the office of the executive officer. He pointed out No. 14822 and said, " There is the very man you want. He is a graduate of Princeton and has had two years at Oxford, and he is now going to the executive officer to decline to work and to take his medicine for conscience' sake and what he supposes to be his duty."

I asked the executive officer about this man and told him that such a man was at least entitled to an interview, and asked him to send 14822 to my office.

I talked to this prisoner, No. 14822, for 30 minutes trying to convince him that he was really arraying himself on the side of disorder as against the law of his country and order, however his case of injustice and inconsistency might appear to him. The interview closed with my giving him the permission of coming into the office the next day, and suggested that he would save himself further trouble by being useful to us and his country.

He came into the office the next day and said he had concluded to work for me and I put him to work with the purchasing department. Two days later, we found that it was necessary to put another man on the records of our registered stock. I called for 14822 and told him that I had concluded to give him this work, as it was the most accurate work in its requirements in the office. He informed me that he was on the point of asking for an interview to tell me that he had made a mistake in not going to the executive officer and refusing to work in the first

16

place, but feeling as he did about it, he felt that to save himself the ordinary punishment of his refusal was an act of cowardice, and that he was really diverted from his refusal to work by fear. He had thus concluded to take his medicine. I said to him, " You have fully determined on this course—there is no further use of conversation or argument?" and he said, " No, sir."
I directed him to report to the executive officer.

(Signed)   SAMUEL A. SMOKE.
Major, United States Army, Retired.

In connection with these documents it may perhaps be added that almost all of these objectors came to Fort Leavenworth after months of segregation or imprisonment in guardhouses, where many of them suffered severely from the brutality of guards and petty officers.

We are not issuing these documents to argue the question of conscientious objection. It is plainly evident, however, that the charge of physical cowardice so often leveled against the conscientious objector is false in the case of the men who are confined in Leavenworth. Without exception, they could have avoided their heavy sentences merely by accepting noncombatant service. Many, in an effort to protest against the treatment of fellow prisoners, have gone so far as to choose deliberately a course which led inevitably to the horrors of the " hole." Misguided perhaps, fanatics perhaps, but not cowards!

The treatment administered to these men can not conceivably be the only or the best course open to the State. They are capable of the quixotic generosity of a sympathetic strike in prison, they are eager to serve high causes outside prison walls ; the State seems to confess its weakness and perplexity in finding no alternative to the brutal method of crushing them in mind or body.

The facts which we have cited raise two issue :

(1) The use of torture in military prisons to enforce obedience. This is as unnecessary as it is barbarous. Conscientious objectors may be rendering a real social service in calling attention to the use of solitary confinement, such as we have described, to which ordinary military offenders have been subjected for years.

(2) Political prisoners, of whom conscientious objectors are one group, should be distinguished from ordinary offenders against the criminal law. Such is the almost universal practice in Europe. In Great Britain the so-called " absolutists " objectors were never confined in military prisons and no sentences exceeded two years. This policy was carried out in the heat of the war. Our own Government has repeatedly declared its intention not to coerce the conscience of any recognized objector. yet by confining these men in military prisons, it raises the question of coercion in an acute form. From the standpoint of the well-being of the State, as truly as of the ancient American liberties of conscience and free speech, what possible good end is served by the indefinite confinement of political prisoners who are eager to render useful service outside prison walls? The situation is urgent. This torture can have but one end—the utter breaking of the men in body. mind, or spirit.

No solution of this problem short of complete pardon will satisfy the generosity or sense of fair play of the American people. But in the meantime it is our particular purpose to urge (a) the immediate release of men now chained in solitary confinement and the permanent abolition of this and similar obsolete forms of discipline in military prisons: (b) the recognition of the status of conscientious objectors as political prisoners.

113051—19429

BAKER RELEASES LAST OF 600 WAR DRAFT OBJECTORS

Thirty Three of Most Fractious, Just Freed, Claimed Attention of Entire Country.

(Special to The World.)

WASHINGTON, Nov. 24.—The last of the conscientious objectors has been set free, and the prisons of the United States, long after those of the other parties to the great war, are empty of men who refused to take part in the conflict.

Secretary of War Baker made this action known in response to a query from The World regarding a report that all the C. O.'s were to be released, save one—this one to be held so that it could not be said amnesty had been granted this class. Mr. Baker's reply was:

"The cases of the thirty-three conscientious objectors who remained in custody have been reviewed finally by the Secretary of War, on the recommendation of the Adjutant General's Office, and the remainder of their sentences remitted and the men discharged.

"Each one has been considered on its merits, the principle of commutation being to remit so much sentence as exceeded the peace-time penalty for the charged. The major part of these men have been in confinement for more than two years and those just discharged were the men who refused to do any sort of work while in confinement."

Many Cases Became Famous.

Six well known objectors had been ordered released before Secretary Baker took up the final review which cleared the records of the last of the 600-odd names of the men who refused during the draft to accept furloughs for farm work, to be assigned to non-combatant duty or to yield to military authority of any kind.

Howard W. Moore of Cherry Valley, N. Y., was the chief of these six. Moore already was in prison in 1912 when the Carnegie Hero Fund Commission granted him a gold medal and $500 for saving the life of a girl at Sound Beach, Conn., two years before. He was typical of the "absolutists" and while he was at Leavenworth Disciplinary Barracks was credited with having "scored more infractions of the rules than any other man ever confined there." This was because he resolutely refused to obey any order given him by a man in military uniform.

A second of the six was W. Oral James of St. Louis, who was released from the War Prison Barracks at Fort Douglas, Salt Lake City, on Tuesday. James is legally the ward of Roger Baldwin, who himself served a sentence in the Essex County Peni-

(Continued on Fourth Page.)

BAKER RELEASES DRAFT OBJECTORS

(Continued From First Page.)

tentiary for refusal to register, and is now a director of the American Civil Liberties Union of New York. Two others were Peter Masukas and Harry Schmieder, whose term would have expired Dec. 10. Morris Franklin and Rexford Powell, both Socialists, went free at the expiration of the two-year terms to which their twenty-five and fifteen year sentences respectively had been reduced.

Refused Food for Three Months.

One freed under the blanket action of the Secretary of War is Benjamin J. Salmon, who attracted attention not only because he was a Roman Catholic—a faith which produced but one other conscientious objector—but because he was on a hunger strike for more than three months. The only food he has taken since July was forced down his throat.

Salmon finally was sent from Fort Douglas to St. Elizabeth's Hospital for the Insane at Washington. Alienists pronounced him mentally sound more than a month ago and recently he was transferred to the Walter Reed General Hospital. Of Salmon's case the Secretary said to-day:

"Salmon was the last case considered and disposed of, by reason of the fact, among others, that legal proceedings instituted by him in the civil courts delayed consideration."

Others released include, Philip B. Grosser, a Socialist, who was the one C. O. remaining at Alcatraz Island, San Francisco; Lester C. Ott, the last at Fort Leavenworth, and George Yaeger, the last in the Federal Penitentiary at Leavenworth. Yaeger, a young Kansas farmer, is said by his friends to have been in an isolation cell for the past seventeen months, following a charge that he led a "mutiny" in the prison dining room.

Objectors Mostly Socialists.

Ott's case has attracted much attention because he was a member of the Home Guard at Hamilton, O., when he was drafted. He refused to submit to discipline, explaining the apparent conflict of attitude on the ground that his employment depended on his joining the Home Guard and without employment he could not support his mother. In the report received by The World that one man would be held in confinement by the authorities it was said that Ott would be this man.

The other men released were:

Socialists—Joseph A. Berman, Mayer Bernstein, William Breidert, Fred Briehl, Harry M. Clare, Samuel Gutler, Jacob Haugen, Fred Jerger, Julius Katz, Knud Lassen, N. La Cassele, Frank Minnik, Frank Mozer, Eric R. Platen, Emanuel Silver, Francis Steiner and S. Sternstein.

I. W. W.—H. E. Bermeister, Alfred Buzzi, Robert C. Cage, Lewis J. Gergotz, William C. Sandberg.

Religious—John E. Downey, E. H. Daniels, Fred R. Davis, James Livingston.

No Organization—W. M. Doty, Jacob W. Rose, F. X. Hennessey.

Bibliography

THIS IS a partial list of American sources on conscientious objection in World War I. Starred entries contain references to Howard Moore.

MAGAZINE ARTICLES

American Civil Liberties Union. "The Conscientious Objectors Set Free." *The Nation*, December 8, 1920. Describes and criticizes treatment of conscientious objectors.

"Forgotten 'Conscientious Objectors.' " Editorial. *The Literary Digest*, November 1, 1919. Quotes extensively from William C. Allen's report on a visit to the U.S. disciplinary barracks at Alcatraz, describing and criticizing the treatment of conscientious objectors there.

A Political. "How Political Prisoners Are Tortured at Leavenworth." *Pearson's Magazine*, July 1920. An emotional account of the treatment of IWWs and other leftist conscientious objectors.

Sayre, John Nevin. "American War Prisoners. *The Socialist Review*, January 1920.

*Seidenberg, Roderick. "I Refuse to Serve." *American Mercury*, January 1932. A lively and perceptive firsthand account of the Leavenworth experience.

*Thomas, Evan. "Disciplinary Barracks." *The Survey*, February 1, 1919. Thoughtfully describes his own and others' experiences at Leavenworth, with references to events at Camp Upton and Fort Riley.

*Thomas, Norman. "For Their Principles: The Present Status of the Conscientious Objectors." *The Survey*, October 9, 1920. Reports the current status of imprisoned conscientious objectors and appraises government policy toward them.

"The Torturing of Conscientious Objectors." *Pearson's Magazine*, February 1919.

"Uncle Sam, Jailor." *The Survey*, September 6, 1919.

BOOKS

Boyle, Beth Ellen, ed. *Words of Conscience: Religious Statements on Conscientious Objection.* 10th ed. Washington, D.C.: National Interreligious Service Board for Conscientious Objectors, 1983. See pages 21–23 for mention of World War I conscientious objectors.

*Eichel, Julius. *The Judge Said "20 Years": The Story of a Conscientious Objector in World War I.* New York: War Resisters League, 1981.

*Gray, Harold S. *Character "Bad."* Edited by Kenneth Irving Brown. New York: Harper and Brothers, 1934; reprint ed. New York: Garland, 1971.

*Hennacy, Ammon. *The Book of Ammon.* Privately printed, 1965. Chapter 2 reports this writer's experience in prison in World War I.

*Meyer, Ernest L. *Hey! Yellowbacks: The War Diary of a Conscientious Objector.* New York: John Day, 1930.

Sibley, Mulford Q., and Jacob, Philip E. *Conscription and Conscience.* Ithaca: Cornell University Press, 1952. See pages 10–16 for a summary of the U.S. experience with conscientious objectors in World War I.

*Thomas, Norman. *The Conscientious Objector in America.* New York: B. W. Huebsch, 1923.

Thomas, Norman. *Is Conscience a Crime?* New York: Vanguard, 1927.

Index